The Look of Things

THE LOOK OF THINGS

Essays by John Berger

Edited and with an Introduction
by Nikos Stangos

A RICHARD SEAVER BOOK
The Viking Press / *New York*

Published in England under the title *Selected Essays and Articles:
The Look of Things*

Essays Copyright © 1959, 1960, 1962, 1963, 1965, 1966, 1968, 1969,
1970, 1971 by John Berger

Introduction Copyright © 1971 by Nikos Stangos

A Richard Seaver Book/The Viking Press

Published in 1974 by The Viking Press, Inc.
625 Madison Avenue, New York, N.Y. 10022

Library of Congress Cataloging in Publication Data
Berger, John.
    The look of things; essays.
    "A Richard Seaver book."
    Reprint of the 1972 ed. published by Penguin, Harmondsworth, in
series: Pelican books.
    I. Title.
AC8.B4737   1974   082   74-12428
ISBN 0-670-43987-8

Printed in U.S.A.

(Page 251 constitutes an extension of this copyright page.)

A

Contents

Contents

Acknowledgements

The essays on 'Drawing' and 'The Life and Death of an Artist' (here reprinted under the title 'Jack Yeats') are from *Permanent Red* by John Berger, copyright © John Berger, 1960, 1962, published in England by Methuen, 1960, and in the U.S.A., under the title *Toward Reality*, by Alfred A. Knopf, 1962. (Reprinted by permission of Alfred A. Knopf Inc.) 'The Moment of Cubism', 'The Changing View of Man in the Portrait' and 'Image of Imperialism' (here reprinted under the title ' "Che" Guevara') are from *The Moment of Cubism and Other Essays* by John Berger, copyright © John Berger, 1969, published in England by Weidenfeld & Nicolson and in the U.S.A. by Pantheon Books, 1969. (Reprinted by permission of Pantheon Books, a division of Random House, Inc.)

Versions of the following essays and articles, sometimes under different titles, appeared in *New Society*: 'Victor Serge' (1968), 'Alexander Herzen' (1968), 'Walter Benjamin' (1970), 'Painting a Landscape' (1966), 'Understanding a Photograph' (1968), 'The Political Uses of Photo-Montage' (1969), 'Revolutionary Undoing' (1969), 'Past Seen from a Possible Future' (1970), 'Czechoslovakia Alone' (1968 and 1969), 'The Nature of Mass Demonstrations' (1968); and the following in the *New Statesman*: 'Through the Bars' (1959), 'Le Corbusier' (1965), 'Romantic Notebooks' (1959), 'A Belief in Uniforms' (1959), 'Thicker than Water' (1960). A different version of the essay 'Fernand Léger' was first published

Acknowledgements

in *Marxism Today* (1963). The essay 'Past Seen from a Possible Future' was also published as an introduction to *Encyclopedia of Themes and Subjects in Painting*, Thames & Hudson, 1971.

Introduction

A woman being bundled into a taxi by two men; a lion and a lioness in their cage at a zoo; the imprint of a hand near Le Corbusier's modular man; the photograph of Guevara's corpse in a stable, surrounded by a colonel, a U.S. intelligence agent, a number of Bolivian soldiers and journalists; Watteau's doomed world of aristocratic elegance; Léger's substantial world; the interaction between empty space and filled space, between structure and movement, between the seer and the thing seen, in Cubist painting; the equation of art: the artist, the world, the means of figuration; a gallery attendant standing at a tall window, gazing down at the animated figures in a courtyard with a fountain, weeping willows, benches, statues, old people and women with children; the loneliness of Czechoslovakia; a demonstration in the Corso Venezia on 6 May 1898.

These are some of the subjects and images in this collection of John Berger's essays and articles. They seem unrelated and they were not meant by Berger to be brought together under one title. One may of course read each individual piece and admire it in itself; and yet they are most importantly parts of a whole. It is the purpose of this collection to demonstrate, in a somewhat kaleidoscopic way, a deep unity in Berger's writings, a vision, a consistent and coherent ideological preoccupation and development of certain general ideas which is more far-reaching than any of the individual pieces of which it is made up. With this in mind, the articles and essays in this collection are accordingly arranged in groups to give this book a certain dynamic structure which I hope will underline and illuminate Berger's ideas.

Some of these essays are contained in the two collections of essays previously published, *Permanent Red* and *The Moment of Cubism*. Many have appeared in weekly magazines, in the *New Statesman* and in *New Society*. Some are published in this volume for the first time.

Anyone acquainted with Berger's writing will know that most of it, in whatever form, is about art; this collection contains, quite deliberately, several pieces that are not. The general themes that run through his writings are far more important than mere abstract aesthetic considerations or, especially, art-critical quibbles. And yet, although not all of his writing is about art, there must be some reason why so much of it is.

Art, to Berger, is the most complex and rich human creative activity. The art object, whatever it is, sums up the spiritual and physical nature of man. At the same time, the work of art is by its very nature an existential event of unique dialectical unity. Berger's interest is not art-historical or analytical, but an interest in what, to him, is the most profound existential creative situation that man is capable of reaching.

Art, as an existential, creative, human activity or situation, has many aspects; it can be seen from several sides. First, there is the artist himself, his life. Not only his life as an artist, but his life as a human being that eats, sleeps, makes love, is a member of society and also works. His work is making art. Secondly, there are the works of art themselves, their physical presence, their materiality, the materials they use, the techniques employed in making them becoming an inherent part of them, their existence among us, as part of our everyday life, their existence as ordinary objects. Thirdly, the work of art is a concrete manifestation of what we call man's spirit. It is man's language that embodies his beliefs, principles, hopes and fears. Finally, the work of art has moral, social, political and epistemological implications. To Berger, all these are inherent aspects of art, inseparable one from the other, uniquely fused together in each and every work of art. The equation becomes infinitely more complex when another prime factor is taken into consideration: the viewer.

The artist, the work of art (the object) and the viewer should, in their totality, dictate any consideration about art. It is, in fact, the merging of these factors that makes art possible. Berger, with a totally consistent singlemindedness, refuses in all his writing about art to separate these components, or even to discuss momentarily any of them independently. Art is, to him, of unique interest precisely because it is constituted of these elements simultaneously and each element can only be discussed in terms of the others. To concentrate exclusively on any one of these components would be a betrayal not only of art but of man as a totality. It's not only the critic of art who is required to keep all these points of view in mind, however: the artist himself must also integrate in his vision all these elements. To say, like the artist in Wallace Stevens's poem, *The Man with the Blue Guitar*,

> I sing a hero's head, large eye
> And bearded bronze, but not a man,
>
> Although I patch him as I can
> And reach through him almost to man

is to fail.

Berger longs for the restoration of unity in man, in society and in the work of art as a dynamic phenomenon that evolves in three stages: before it is made, while it is made and when it is perceived. As he says in *The Moment of Cubism*, the work of art that succeeds is the work which, like a piece of music that is just beginning, makes one aware of the silence that precedes it, and of the possibilities it opens up and generates while the moment lasts, uniting the past, the present and the future. However, unless the hope, the expectation generated by the moment is fulfilled, the work fails.

It is this total integration that he requires of man, of a work of art, of our way of seeing it and judging it that makes Berger impatient with mere analysis. He has no interest in and no time for the merely analytical art historian or art critic. And this is why Berger cannot be properly called an art critic, and his writings on art are not 'art criticism', at least, not according to the current, specialist use of these words. Berger pushes beyond, towards a total, integrated interpretation that passes over the mere analytical details.

His implicit, and sometimes explicit, anti-analytical attitude is of special interest today, in this age of professional fragmentation and an analytical approach applied indiscriminately to the humanities as well as to the natural sciences. One is conditioned into accepting as 'serious' art criticism only what is analytical, specialist and, therefore, fragmented. This kind of positivist analytical attitude is the result of misapplied scientific and technological thinking and methods that have trapped one into believing not only that all intellectual activity ought to be of this nature, but that man himself can only make sense if fragmented in this way. At times one feels almost as if Berger is fighting a losing battle: we believe, most of us, that the kind of integration he requires, amounting to a metaphysical attitude, is no more than an inability to think clearly or 'objectively'.

Contrary to positivist analysis, the dialectical, Marxist approach aims at synthesis: the restoration of the totality of human nature and experience. What Berger's position implies is that pseudo-scientific thinking is not only limiting when applied to art or to human activity or behaviour, it is basically anti-human. One main reason why it is anti-human is that it restricts man's nature, because it curtails his freedom of choice by arbitrarily limiting its spectrum and thus limiting or entirely removing the crucial notion of freedom in an existential situation. And this is the key to Berger's writing. Berger sees this existential situation in a dialectical, Marxist way. Analysis opposes integration and, therefore, the richness of possible alternatives in a dialectical, situational context. Freedom is the exercise of choice between alternatives that coexist in a dialectical way, in a totally integrated way, in any particular situation. Analysis fragments this integration and therefore denies freedom, it shatters and violates the work of art which is a dialectical unity.

Berger further suggests that the main criterion for judging

the degree of success or failure of a work of art – or of any human situation – is the extent to which the work in question is characterized by a dialectical complex of elements in tension, providing the greatest possible number of alternatives. In other words, the degree of freedom, in this sense, presented by a work or an action determines its success or its failure.

A logical consequence of this notion of freedom is Berger's view about property, and specifically property as it relates to works of art. In several of these essays and articles, he expresses his intense dislike and disapproval of property. To him, property is the negation of freedom. The prevailing western attitude to art as property is the total negation of art, since property is the negation of freedom in that owning something, or the desire to own or possess something, is the wish to enslave it, reduce it from a living, dialectical complex of alternatives to a dead object. The 'image of imperialism' is the photograph of Guevara's corpse, a human existence reduced to an object that has become the property of the forces responsible for his death. The photograph of Guevara's corpse is an image of the negation of freedom.

Freedom, to Berger, is specific to a situation, it is a creative/productive potential contained in the situation, whether this is a work of art, a daily act, a political event, or the life of a person. To release this potential is to succeed; to deny, ignore or be frightened of it is to fail. Property, on the other hand, is the denial of this potential in that it reduces the situation, the work of art, the life of a human being, into a single, non-dialectical, non-ambivalent entity, the sole meaning of which rests in its possession. Thus, the woman who is bundled into a taxi against her will, Guevara's assassination, the moment of Cubism, the invasion of Czechoslovakia, a demonstration, are all concrete images of the success or failure to release the potential of freedom contained in each one of these situations.

NIKOS STANGOS
London, Spring 1970

Behind Bars

On the Edge of a
Foreign City

1   It was called the Café de la Renaissance. It was on the big lorry route, near the level-crossing by the railway station. Inside it was not really like a bar at all. Indeed there wasn't a bar. It was just a small front parlour which was called a café. The bottles – only about half a dozen anyway – were kept in a kind of corner medicine cupboard. Three men and a woman were sitting at one of the tables playing cards – belote. The eldest of the men got up to welcome us. He had the face of a fanatic – a Jansenist face: the face of a man who had recognized the vanity of the world and its ways. He showed us to another marble-topped table and wiped it. The whole place was filthy – unswept and untouched for weeks, except at the end where the card-players were and where there was a door into the kitchen. There was a certain homeliness there: where we were – four yards away – was like an outhouse, full of the last tenants' junk. On the table next to ours was an open and tattered black umbrella. A bicycle leant against the table. On the wall behind were pinned some postcards and snapshots of a Mediterranean beach. All of them had gone potato yellow. Behind us was a large wooden cupboard: butterflies were pinned to the door of it. The wings of the butterflies were frayed and torn, so that in places you could see through them, as you could see through the umbrella.

We ordered some red wine and got out our bread and sausage to eat. Having brought us the wine, the proprietor with the

Jansenist face hurried back to his game. We watched them play. The players consisted of the proprietor, another old man who looked like a brother, a young man and a young woman. They were playing with considerable concentration : their eyes fixed on their cards, occasionally a hand banging a card on the table – with the authority of the hammer that strikes the bell of a public clock. But they were not playing aggressively, with personal ill-feeling. Nor were they drinking. After a while, the brother got up and a woman came in from the kitchen, wiping her hands on her apron, and sat down to take his place. Two young children followed her and started to jump about by the door on to the street. The conversation of the card players was only about the cards. They were playing for chips, not directly for money. As we watched them, we had the sensation more and more strongly that it was like watching the backs of four people bent over the parapet of a bridge and gazing at a river, a boat, a shoal of fish which we could not see. We could in fact see their faces, but they revealed nothing, except their degree of concentration. It was their cards we couldn't see.

An older woman came out of the kitchen and smiled at the players approvingly. When she noticed us, she came over and wished us a good appetite. Then she said : 'It's a good thing to eat sometimes, it's like a recall to order.' She went back and stood for a moment looking down at the cards in the hands of the proprietor. Again she nodded approvingly – as though from the parapet she had seen a golden barque pass by.

On the wall behind the players was a local bus timetable. It was the newest and brightest thing in the room. But there was no clock and when later I asked the proprietor the time he had to go out and ask in another café two doors down the street.

The four went on playing. Each could see what nobody else in the world could see – his own cards. The world didn't care. But the three other players did; they recognized the importance of every particular that with this deal had befallen him. Such interest and such concern amounted to a kind of dependence; each to some degree ruled the others, up to the moment when the hand was finished and the victor declared and at that moment the victor's victory was also terminated. Thus they established an equity juster than any existing in the world. And thus too they were able to accept the most extreme demands of the cards as a proof of the purity of their actions and intentions. The code to which they submitted, like the code of anarchists, was violent, absolute and closer to their own understanding and longing than any existing in the everyday world. Each card played on the table helped to undermine the authority of this world. It was a conspiracy that we were watching. And one that we might easily have joined.

2   Outside the cathedral of St Jean many cars and two buses are parked: men are in their shirtsleeves. It is Sunday morning when the croissants have more butter in them.

Inside it is crowded. All the chairs are taken and the aisles are full of people standing. It is unusual to see a church so full in this country. But as we make our way forward, towards the priests, the explanation becomes clear. In the centre of the church, surrounded and hidden on three sides by the rest of the congregation and on the fourth side facing the carpeted steps leading up to the high altar, is a square of a hundred girls in white. The white of their long dresses, the white of their gloves and the white of their veils is spotless and uncrumpled. At home a hundred irons must still be warm.

The girls are between eleven and thirteen years old. Against the white their faces look nut-brown. They are caught between the questions and responses which they exchange with the priest and the gaze of their parents and guardians who are in the front ranks of the surrounding congregation and who watch their every move. Caught like this, they seem very still: and, having forgone their freedom of independent movement, very peaceful.

It is somewhat like watching children who are asleep. To the eye of the watcher they acquire a false innocence. In fact if one watches carefully enough, one can distinguish between various degrees of experience. Some are only pretending to sleep and in their white shoes wriggle their toes until they can say what they are dying to say to their companions. Out of the corner of their eyes they have observed the remarkable behaviour of the widow who is watching her niece and constantly smoothes down her own black dress over her old hips with thin hands – thirty times a minute.

Some are so aware of what they are wearing, so aware of the white which draws the eyes of all who surround them, that they have begun to dream of getting married.

A few feel impure before the shining purity of the recipient of their vows, and on the faces of these there is a kind of beatitude – as there is in the sight of a white sail so far away that the hull of the ship is invisible.

There is one girl who is a little taller than most of the others and among the nearest to us. She has an aquiline nose and large, dark eyes. Her veil is so crisp that it looks like a linen napkin. Her family are perhaps richer than those of the others. She is proud and self-possessed – as though, if she were sleeping, she would sleep in exactly the position she had decided upon. For her the religious experience which she is now undergoing is part of her private plan for her own development. It is no seduction. It is a long-arranged engagement. But none the less intense. All that will be done unto her will be done in the way that she selects. Always provided that no disaster occurs so that her wishes and decisions become incidental, her life no more than a movement which catches a sniper's eye.

By the west door the man who sells tracts sits behind his table and reads a newspaper.

The girls as they answer sound like doves.

Some of their mothers, pressed right forward to the front rank round the square of girls, have to restrain themselves from putting out a hand and touching their daughters. Their excuse for doing this would be the smoothing of a dress, the straightening of a cuff. But their desire to do so comes from the need to share their memories. They want at this moment to touch their daughters not because their daughters might need their support, but because they want their daughters to know that twenty years ago they too were confirmed in white dresses.

The men stand further back: as though the degree of proximity were inversely related to the degree of scepticism. They watch a ceremony. One or two consult their watches. All are dwarfed by the vast height of the piers. After the ceremony they will go to cafés and restaurants to celebrate. This evening some will play bowls. For many scepticism is mixed with calculation. If their daughters' being received into the church offers in one way or another the possibility of their children being better protected, then indeed they are glad that at last it has come to this – their confirmation. Caution fills their souls.

3   There were three youngish Italians behind the bar, all wearing white shirts – no jackets for it was hot – and black ties. The boss was called Angelo. Outside in the street you could hear the music of half a dozen different juke boxes. Men, mostly middle-class, were strolling down the street, coming from their shops or offices on their way home. The girls were coming downstairs to begin work and take up their places by the bars. In the shop windows between the cafés were cheap but raffish men's clothes – jeans, leather belts, plastic jackets, cowboy hats. There were also one or two food-shops with sausages in their windows – sausages and gherkins and smoked fish. It was all food which was sharp enough to taste even after a lot of drinks or many cigars. And the skins of all these foods were wrinkled.

She sat on a stool by the bar. She was fat, but still pretty in a bursting kind of way. Her face was wide with thick lips. With her was a middle-aged Pakistani businessman in an expensive suit. One of his hands was wedged between her knees. He was drinking too much, and she was trying to dissuade him lest he become incapable. Otherwise they talked of food and of whether beef was better than chicken.

Local clients dropped into the bar, but she steadfastly refused to recognize them and remained apparently absorbed in the man from Karachi. Occasionally she glanced quickly round the bar to keep account. The man from Karachi was wearing a large gold ring, and was beginning to tell her about his children.

Suddenly – and to the clear annoyance of Angelo – a young, very thin man strolled in from the street. He wore white trousers and a leather belt, buckled at the back. He put a hand on her bare, round shoulder. She looked up surprised, and then smiled a message at him. She introduced him to the man from Karachi as her brother. The man from Karachi moved away and offered her brother the stool between them. He accepted, pulling the stool back a little so that the other two could still sit within touching distance of each other. Then he picked up a magazine and began flicking through its pages. From the point of view of the man from Karachi, the young man's face was hidden by the magazine: all he could see were his hands holding the paper, and his stick-like legs between him and the girl.

The man from Karachi observed that surely her brother was married because he wore a ring. She might have let this pass, but couldn't. She explained, no, he wasn't married but he wore the ring because he was a great lover boy. He didn't look up from his magazine. The Pakistani ordered another whisky and poured it into his beer. You must eat, she said. And she also said he had the nicest face she had ever seen. All he could eat, he replied, was chicken, but they didn't serve chicken here. They could send out for it and get it specially, she said. No, he said, he did not want it got specially. Then when her hand once more came to rest on his, he gripped it, and looked at the round stockings over her thighs.

Then you must have some dry beef, she said. What is that?

he asked. It is very, very nice, she said. Her brother put down his magazine and nodded. She asked Angelo to bring a portion of Viande des Grisons.

When it arrived the young man stood up. Please, he said and stepped to the bar. She told her man from Karachi that her brother wanted to prepare the meat for him. The young man picked up the slice of lemon on the edge of the plate and squeezed drops of lemon juice on the paper-thin slices of reddish-brown meat. Then he took the pepper mill – a tall wooden one as large as a thermos flask – and bending over it, as though using all the power of his slender shoulders and thin arms, as though summoning every ounce of energy for the task, he ground the pepper over the slices of meat for the older man.

4   An hour's drive from the centre is a mountain. It is 1,800 metres high. In the hollows are small patches of frozen snow, over which children slide and toboggan on rubber mats – this even in June.

None of the ascents is steep or dangerous. If they take their time, quite elderly couples can walk to the summit.

Today is Sunday and there must be 3,000 people on this mountain.

The road stops a few hundred metres from the top. On the grass – springy as only grass that is several months of the year under snow can be – the cars and a bus are parked. In the evening when they are all gone, the hill looks like any other. There are no kiosks or litter-bins. Only the grass that owes its special nature to the snow.

At the summit there are a few rocks. Otherwise the sides are all grass, and among the grass are mountain flowers: gentian, arnica, mountain anemones – and thousands of jonquils.

It is possible to scramble up the mountain from any direction, but there is a path which takes the easiest route. Along this path there is a constant traffic of couples, fathers carrying babies, grandparents, schoolchildren. Many of them are barefoot. From below, the procession, ascending and descending, looks a little like a medieval vision of some exchange with heaven. The more so because most of those coming down are carrying armfuls of jonquils, white-gold in colour.

From the summit one can see the ranges extending to the horizon. The rock joins with the sky and their common blue discounts every difference.

Towards the south one can also see the plain, intensely cultivated, the colour of greengages. Such a view is archetypal. It is the antithesis of a view of the grave.

Across the plain moves the shadow of one white cloud. Where the shadow is, the green is the green of laurel leaves.

The crowd, which is made up of hundreds of dispersed groups, is easy and at home. It is as if the mountain were their common ancestor.

5 Today there was a woman being bundled into a taxi: but she refused to bend her back, so she wouldn't fit inside the door. There were two men struggling with her. Quite respectable middle-aged men steeling themselves in righteousness against the doubting eyes of the crowd that had gathered. Then the woman began to shout. I couldn't understand a word. But she shouted in such a way that it was obvious she believed that across the street, somewhere near where I was standing, there was somebody who understood what she was suffering and the reasonableness of her simple wish not to be bundled into the car and taken somewhere else. After several minutes' struggling the two men gave up: she wouldn't fit through the door. So they took her back, still shouting, and her knees bent as they

dragged her along – she was only a woman of about forty-five – to the chemist's shop where they had originally been. Inside the shop she still fought, and one of the men had to stand with his back against the glass door to prevent her running out and away. It appeared that the chemist was trying to help them calm her. The taxi-driver waited, the door of his taxi still open. Because one of the men was leaning with his back against the door, no customer could enter the shop. I watched through the window. There were the drugs and the medicines on the shelves. There was the woman with her will, that would have done what she wanted done and would prevent what she did not want. And between the shelves and the woman there were the men, hesitating.

Through the Bars

All kinds of types end up in the zoo. There's even a jackdaw there who used to ride regularly on the shoulder of a motor-cycling friend of mine. When the lights were against him, he'd stop, and the bird would fly on. Finally the landlady's complaints (the same friend also kept a fox in his room) led to the bird's being given to a London park. And from there – because he stole so many handkerchiefs, trinkets and hats – he was transferred to the zoo. The zoo is a penitentiary, a theatre, an almshouse, a laboratory, a conference room, a microcosm.

The agouti comes from South America. In its natural surroundings it's a night animal, staying under cover most of the day. The one here in London is female and about the size of a large hare, only she is round and cumbersome. Her hind legs are larger than her front ones, which, like a squirrel, she uses to hold the food she nibbles and to handle whatever she finds and does not fear. In fact she fears almost everything.

She has an extraordinarily cowed look, as if she were constantly trying to make herself as scarce as possible. Perhaps this is partly because she appears to have no tail, although actually she does have one, no larger than a small pink teat. She is hopelessly vulnerable. Her only defence is her bouncing gallop. Her teeth are only for nuts and fruit. Her claws are feeble. Even her rather coarse brownish hair is sparse. Indeed, with her round-bottomed body, her drooping shoulders and her withdrawn face retreating from one shock after another, she looks

like a middle-aged woman whose house has caught fire in the
night, and who has been forced into the street with only a
blanket pulled round her.

When she sits on her haunches to suckle her offspring, who
push their round heads between her front paws, when she herself is eating with the nervous, acquisitive little bites of all
rodents (count the pennies and the pounds'll take care of themselves – that's how they eat), or when she is licking her young,
breathing in their smell, cleaning them and recognizing the
familiar, all the time her warning system is picking up and
deciphering signs of foreign approach and danger. She breathes
in rumours with the air. Full of natural illusions, her young
scurry back to her for safety. Yet she can do no more than
scurry them and herself away. A life of dread. But she is no
more aware of that than a petit-bourgeois shopkeeper brought
up in a Wesleyan chapel.

How different another kind of timidity! The tree-shrew is
from Malaya. He is only about six inches long with a narrow,
pointed, inquisitive face and sharp pink front paws. In the back
wall of his cage are three round holes, not much larger than
pennies, which open into a dark box behind. Most hours of the
day and night he stays there in the dark. If, however, you wait
long enough, you will at last see a long face with unblinking
eyes peering through one of the holes. It is a tight fit, the hole
no bigger than a collar for his neck. Face out – and then face
back into the dark where it is safe. But wait longer. He is per-
sistent, this one, and his method is one of trial and success.

He has noticed your finger between the bars and he intends to
investigate it. Glance away and you may miss him; he'll be out
into the cage and then back into one of his holes and all you'll
glimpse is his bushy tail as he disappears head first. But fix your
eyes on him and you'll see him dare perhaps three inches of his
open cage before he bolts back. He has tested three inches.
They are safe: nothing pursued him. Next time he tests five
inches. Then back again: head first: tail in: head out. Then
seven inches. And so on, till he's reached your finger. He touches
it with his nose and shows his teeth which are no larger than

the points of wooden tooth-picks. He bolts back. And ventures out again. If you move your finger slightly he will now snarl and snap at it before retreating. His snarl is unexpected: a brief spitting sound like the crackle of one flame flickering in a single gust of wind. A six-inch rodent dragon breathing fire!

After several attempts to bite your finger off – and you will find it quite difficult not to pull your finger away for his teeth are as sharp as his eyes and his persistence – he will try to pull it through the bars with his front paws. These are a whitish pink like his muzzle and gums. After each sustained grasp and tug he bolts back to one of his holes. If you make a noise now, the whole process may begin again. If you are still, he grasps and tugs, flies back, re-emerges, grasps and tugs – until you give up.

And this, they say, is one of the most timid animals in the whole zoo. They are wrong. He is careful – like a wise man on thin ice. He is furtive – like any good sniper. And he is incorruptible. Not to be diverted from his purpose. Romantics could learn from him.

*

A lion and a young lioness. The lion is on a low bench in the darkest corner, half asleep. She lies on a high platform, a kind of rostrum in the middle of their cage. Her tail swings like a loose rope from a boat in a harbour where there's a slight swell. Her paws are relaxed and heavy and look overlarge – like hands with boxing gloves on. Her eyes are drowsy, flickering. But every other minute a noise alerts them. Suddenly one of the noises becomes urgent. I can hear nothing. But for her something has changed; the possible has become probable. She sits up. Everything is now battened down. The tail is still. The ears stand up to gather as much as they can, like two people trying to peer over the heads of a crowd. The eyes are undistractable. She is looking into the distance as expectantly as lovers look into one another's eyes – except that the signs she is seeking will be given involuntarily by whatever has alerted her. Wind, sound, shadow have become extensions of her sensory system, as tools for men are extensions of their hands.

She lands on the ground and awaits further events: events which, by the nature of a zoo, can never occur. The lion watches her in such a way that it is impossible not to conclude that he is more knowing. She still waits. It is a full half minute before she relaxes. Relaxed, she looks smaller. She ambles over to the far corner of the cage and there, squatting like a bitch, she piddles.

The lion continues to watch her but now, after she has done, he begins to move. He walks slowly over to the puddle and takes a lick of it. Then, as if still holding the taste on his tongue, he straightens himself up, and raising his head to the sky, bares his teeth. His head is enormous, far wider than any section of her body. He licks again, and again raises his enormous head and draws back the flesh of his mouth. It is a threatening grimace but it is directed against no one. It is a kind of physical swearing. He continues to lick and after each lick he swears at the sky – as a man may grind his teeth in the street as he suddenly remembers touching a breast.

The lioness is now lying on the bench. He goes over to her directly. And there rubs his face against hers. She is indifferent. But he persists, rubbing especially the hard plane between his eyes against her soft ears. Their heads are almost the same colour, but the shape of hers is self-contained, pear-shaped, whilst his is like a cauliflower that has gone to seed.

*

Apart from the monkeys whose show has also never closed, and the elephants who work as hard as tax-collectors, all day long receiving and docketing cake, leaves and paper bags, apart from these, the tortoise is among the most popular of the animals. Why? Is it because a tortoise can never take us by surprise? Or is it because it looks so much like a stone and yet is alive, alive enough, with luck, to outlive any of us? Most animals are partial images in a mirror for us. The tortoise, we think, is our anti-thesis. We look upon them as we look upon history in the abstract. And of course it's equally a mistake. They do not carry the world on their backs. We do.

Portraits

The Changing View of Man
in the Portrait

It seems to me unlikely that any important portraits will ever be painted again. Portraits, that is to say, in the sense of portraiture as we now understand it. I can imagine multi-medium memento-sets devoted to the character of particular individuals. But these will have nothing to do with the works now in the National Portrait Gallery.

I see no reason to lament the passing of the portrait – the talent once involved in portrait painting can be used in some other way to serve a more urgent, modern function. It is, however, worth while inquiring why the painted portrait has become outdated; it may help us to understand more clearly our historical situation.

The beginning of the decline of the painted portrait coincided roughly speaking with the rise of photography, and so the earliest answer to our question – which was already being asked towards the end of the nineteenth century – was that the photographer had taken the place of the portrait painter. Photography was more accurate, quicker and far cheaper; it offered the opportunity of portraiture to the whole of society: previously such an opportunity had been the privilege of a very small élite.

To counter the clear logic of this argument, painters and their patrons invented a number of mysterious, metaphysical qualities with which to prove that what the painted portrait offered was incomparable. Only a man, not a machine (the camera), could interpret the soul of a sitter. An artist dealt with the sitter's destiny : the camera with mere light and shade. An artist judged : a photographer recorded. Etcetera, etcetera.

All this was doubly untrue. First, it denies the interpretative role of the photographer, which is considerable. Secondly, it claims for painted portraits a psychological insight which ninety-nine per cent of them totally lack. If one is considering portraiture as a genre, it is no good thinking of a few extraordinary pictures but rather of the endless portraits of the local nobility and dignitaries in countless provincial museums and town halls. Even the average Renaissance portrait – although suggesting considerable presence – has very little psychological content. We are surprised by ancient Roman or Egyptian portraits, not because of their *insight*, but because they show us very vividly how little the human face has changed. It is a myth that the portrait painter was a revealer of souls. Is there a qualitative difference between the way Velazquez painted a face and the way he painted a bottom? The comparatively few portraits that reveal true psychological insight (certain Raphaels, Rembrandts, Davids, Goyas) suggest personal, obsessional interests on the part of the artist which simply cannot be accommodated within the *professional* role of the portrait painter. Such pictures have the same kind of intensity as self-portraits. They are in fact works of self-discovery.

Ask yourself the following hypothetical question. Suppose that there is somebody in the second half of the nineteenth century in whom you are interested but of whose face you have never seen a picture. Would you rather find a painting or a photograph of this person? And the question itself posed like that is already highly favourable to painting, since the logical question should be : would you rather find a painting or a whole album of photographs?

Until the invention of photography, the painted (or sculptural) portrait was the only means of recording and presenting the likeness of a person. Photography took over this role from painting and at the same time raised our standards for judging how much an informative likeness should include.

This is not to say that photographs are *in all ways* superior to painted portraits. They are more informative, more psychologically revealing, and in general more accurate. But they are less tensely unified. Unity in a work of art is achieved as a result of the limitations of the medium. Every element has to be transformed in order to have its proper place within these limitations. In photography the transformation is to a considerable extent mechanical. In a painting each transformation is largely the result of a conscious decision by the artist. Thus the unity of a painting is permeated by a far higher degree of intention. The total effect of a painting (as distinct from its truthfulness) is less arbitrary than that of a photograph; its construction is more intensely socialized because it is dependent on a greater number of human decisions. A photographic portrait may be more revealing and more accurate about the likeness and character of the sitter; but it is likely to be less persuasive, less (in the very strict sense of the word) conclusive. For example, if the portraitist's intention is to flatter or idealize, he will be able to do so far more convincingly with a painting than with a photograph.

From this fact we gain an insight into the actual function of portrait painting in its heyday : a function we tend to ignore if we concentrate on the small number of exceptional 'unprofessional' portraits by Raphael, Rembrandt, David, Goya, etc. The function of portrait painting was to underwrite and idealize a chosen social role of the sitter. It was not to present him as 'an individual' but, rather, as an individual monarch, bishop, landowner, merchant and so on. Each role had its accepted qualities and its acceptable limit of discrepancy. (A monarch or a pope could be far more idiosyncratic than a mere gentleman or courtier.) The role was emphasized by pose, gesture, clothes and background. The fact that neither the sitter nor the successful professional painter was much involved with the painting of these parts is not to be entirely explained as a matter of saving time : they were thought of and were meant to be read as the accepted attributes of a given social stereotype.

The hack painters never went much beyond the stereotype; the good professionals (Memlinck, Cranach, Titian, Rubens, Van Dyck, Velazquez, Hals, Philippe de Champaigne) painted individual men, but they were nevertheless men whose character and facial expressions were seen and judged in the exclusive light of an ordained social role. The portrait must fit like a hand-made pair of shoes, but the type of shoe was never in question.

The satisfaction of having one's portrait painted was the satisfaction of being personally recognized and *confirmed in one's position* : it had nothing to do with the modern lonely desire to to be recognized 'for what one really is'.

If one were going to mark the moment when the decline of portraiture became inevitable by citing the work of a particular artist, I would choose the two or three extraordinary portraits of lunatics by Géricault, painted in the first period of romantic disillusion and defiance which followed the defeat of Napoleon and the shoddy triumph of the French bourgeoisie. The paintings were neither morally anecdotal nor symbolic : they were straight portraits, traditionally painted. Yet their sitters had no social role and were presumed to be incapable of fulfilling any. In other pictures Géricault painted severed human heads and limbs as found in the dissecting theatre. His outlook was bitterly critical : to choose to paint dispossessed lunatics was a comment on men of property and power; but it was also an assertion that the essential spirit of man was independent of the role into which society forced him. Géricault found society so negative that, although sane himself, he found the isolation of the mad more meaningful than the social honour accorded to the successful. He was the first and, in a sense, the last profoundly anti-social portraitist. The term contains an impossible contradiction.

After Géricault, professional portraiture degenerated into servile and crass personal flattery, cynically undertaken. It was no longer possible to believe in the value of the social roles chosen or allotted. Sincere artists painted a number of 'intimate' portraits of their friends or models (Corot, Courbet, Degas, Cézanne, Van Gogh), but in these the social role of the sitter is reduced to *that of being painted*. The implied social value is either that of personal friendship (proximity) or that of being seen in such a way (being 'treated') by an original artist. In either case the sitter, somewhat like an arranged still life, becomes subservient to the painter. Finally it is not his personality or his role which impress us but the artist's vision.

Toulouse-Lautrec was the one important latter-day exception to this general tendency. He painted a number of portraits of tarts and cabaret personalities. As we survey them, they survey us. A social reciprocity is established through the painter's mediation. We are presented neither with a disguise – as with official portraiture – nor with mere creatures of the artist's vision. His portraits are the only late nineteenth-century ones which are persuasive and conclusive in the sense that we have defined. They are the only painted portraits in whose social evidence we can believe. They suggest not the artist's studio, but 'the world of Toulouse-Lautrec': that is to say a specific and complex social milieu. Why was Lautrec such an exception? Because in his own eccentric manner he believed in the social roles of his sitters. He painted the cabaret performers because he admired their performances: he painted the tarts because he recognized the usefulness of their trade.

Increasingly for over a century fewer and fewer people in capitalist society have been able to believe in the social value of the social roles offered. This is the second answer to our original question about the decline of the painted portrait.

The second answer suggests, however, that given a more confident and coherent society, portrait painting might revive. And this seems unlikely. To understand why, we must consider the third answer.

The measures, the scale-change of modern life, have changed the nature of individual identity. Confronted with another person today, we are aware, through this person, of forces operating in directions which were unimaginable before the turn of the century, and which have only become clear relatively recently. It is hard to define this change briefly. An analogy may help.

We hear a lot about the crisis of the modern novel. What this involves, fundamentally, is a change in the mode of narration. It is scarcely any longer possible to tell a straight story sequentially unfolding in time. And this is because we are too aware of what is continually traversing the story-line laterally. That is to say, instead of being aware of a point as an infinitely small part of a straight line, we are aware of it as an infinitely small part of an infinite number of lines, as the centre of a star of lines. Such awareness is the result of our constantly having to take into account the simultaneity and extension of events and possibilities.

There are many reasons why this should be so: the range of modern means of communication: the scale of modern power: the degree of personal political responsibility that must be accepted for events all over the world: the fact that the world has become indivisible: the unevenness of economic development within that world: the scale of the exploitation. All these play a part. Prophesy now involves a geographical rather than historical projection; it is space, not time, that hides consequences from us. To prophesy today it is only necessary to know men as they are throughout the whole world in all their inequality. Any contemporary narrative which ignores the urgency of this dimension is incomplete and acquires the oversimplified character of a fable.

Something similar but less direct applies to the painted portrait. We can no longer accept that the identity of a man can be adequately established by preserving and fixing what he looks like from a single viewpoint in one place. (One might argue that the same limitation applies to the still photograph, but as we have seen, we are not led to expect a photograph to be as conclusive as a painting.) Our terms of recognition have changed since the heyday of portrait painting. We may still rely on 'likeness' to identify a person, but no longer to explain or place him. To concentrate upon 'likeness' is to isolate falsely. It is to assume that the outermost surface *contains* the man or object : whereas we are highly conscious of the fact that nothing can contain itself.

There are a few Cubist portraits of about 1911 in which Picasso and Braque were obviously conscious of the same fact, but in these 'portraits' it is impossible to identify the sitter and so they cease to be what we call portraits.

It seems that the demands of a modern vision are incompatible with the singularity of viewpoint which is the prerequisite for a static painted 'likeness'. The incompatibility is connected with a more general crisis concerning the meaning of individuality. Individuality can no longer be contained within the terms of manifest personality traits. In a world of transition and revolution individuality has become a problem of historical and social relations, such as cannot be revealed by the mere characterizations of an already established social stereotype. Every mode of individuality now relates to the whole world.

'Che' Guevara

October 1967   On Tuesday, 10 October 1967, a photograph was transmitted to the world to prove that Guevara had been killed the previous Sunday in a clash between two companies of the Bolivian army and a guerrilla force on the north side of the Rio Grande river near a jungle village called Higueras. (Later this village received the promised reward for the capture of Guevara.) The photograph of the corpse was taken in a stable in the small town of Vallegrande. The body was placed on a stretcher and the stretcher was placed on top of a cement trough.

During the preceding two years 'Che' Guevara had become legendary. Nobody knew for certain where he was. There was no incontestable evidence of anyone having seen him. But his presence was constantly assumed and invoked. At the head of his last statement – sent from a guerrilla base 'somewhere in the world' to the Tricontinental Solidarity Organization in Havana – he quoted a line from the nineteenth-century revolutionary poet José Martí: 'Now is the time of the furnaces, and only light should be seen.' It was as though in his own declared light Guevara had become invisible and ubiquitous.

Now he is dead. The chances of his survival were in inverse ratio to the force of the legend. The legend had to be nailed. 'If,' said the *New York Times*, 'Ernesto Che Guevara was really killed in Bolivia, as now seems probable, a myth as well as a man has been laid to rest.'

42

We do not know the circumstances of his death. One can gain some idea of the mentality of those into whose hands he fell by their treatment of his body after his death. First they hid it. Then they displayed it. Then they buried it in an anonymous grave in an unknown place. Then they disinterred it. Then they burnt it. But before burning it, they cut off the fingers for later identification. This might suggest that they had serious doubts whether it was really Guevara whom they had killed. Equally it can suggest that they had no doubts but feared the corpse. I tend to believe the latter.

The purpose of the radio photograph of 10 October was to put an end to a legend. Yet on many who saw it its effect may have been very different. What is its meaning? What, precisely and unmysteriously, does this photograph mean now? I can but cautiously analyse it as regards myself.

There is a resemblance between the photograph and Rembrandt's painting of *The Anatomy Lesson of Professor Tulp*. The immaculately dressed Bolivian colonel with a handkerchief to his nose has taken the professor's place. The two figures on his left stare at the cadaver with the same intense but impersonal interest as the two nearest doctors on the professor's left. It is true that there are more figures in the Rembrandt – as there were certainly more men, unphotographed, in the stable at Vallegrande. But the placing of the corpse in relation to the figures above it, and in the corpse the sense of global stillness – these are very similar.

Nor should this be surprising, for the function of the two pictures is similar: both are concerned with showing a corpse being formally and objectively examined. More than that, both are concerned with *making an example of the dead*: one for the advancement of medicine, the other as a political warning. Thousands of photographs are taken of the dead and the massacred. But the occasions are seldom formal ones of demonstration. Doctor Tulp is demonstrating the ligaments of the arm, and what he says applies to the normal arm of every man. The colonel with the handkerchief is demonstrating the final fate – as decreed by 'divine providence' – of a notorious guerrilla leader, and what he says is meant to apply to every guerrillero on the continent.

I was also reminded of another image: Mantegna's painting of the dead Christ, now in the Brera at Milan. The body is seen from the same height, but from the feet instead of from the side. The hands are in identical positions, the fingers curving in the same gesture. The drapery over the lower part of the body is creased and formed in the same manner as the blood-sodden, unbuttoned, olive-green trousers on Guevara. The head is raised at the same angle. The mouth is slack of expression in the same way. Christ's eyes have been shut, for there are two mourners beside him. Guevara's eyes are open, for there are no mourners: only the colonel with the handkerchief, a U.S. intelligence agent, a number of Bolivian soldiers and the journalists. Once again, the similarity need not surprise. There are not so many ways of laying out the criminal dead.

Yet this time the similarity was more than gestural or functional. The emotions with which I came upon that photograph on the front page of the evening paper were very close to what, with the help of historical imagination, I had previously assumed the reaction of a contemporary believer might have been to Mantegna's painting. The power of a photograph is comparatively short-lived. When I look at the photograph now, I can only reconstruct my first incoherent emotions. Guevara was no Christ. If I see the Mantegna again in Milan, I shall see in it the body of Guevara. But this is only because in certain rare cases the tragedy of a man's death completes and exemplifies the meaning of his whole life. I am acutely aware of that about Guevara, and certain painters were once aware of it about Christ. That is the degree of emotional correspondence.

The mistake of many commentators on Guevara's death has been to suppose that he represented only military skill or a certain revolutionary strategy. Thus they talk of a setback or a defeat. I am in no position to assess the loss which Guevara's death may mean to the revolutionary movement of South America. But it is certain that Guevara represented and will represent more than the details of his plans. He represented a decision, a conclusion.

Guevara found the condition of the world as it is intolerable. It had only recently become so. Previously, the conditions under which two thirds of the people of the world lived were approximately the same as now. The degree of exploitation and enslavement was as great. The suffering involved was as intense and as widespread. The waste was as colossal. But it was not intolerable because the full measure of the truth about these conditions was unknown – even by those who suffered it. Truths are not constantly evident in the circumstances to which they refer. They are born – sometimes late. This truth was born with the struggles and wars of national liberation. In the light of the new-born truth, the significance of imperialism changed. Its demands were seen to be different. Previously it had demanded cheap raw materials, exploited labour and a controlled world market. Today it demands a mankind that counts for nothing.

Guevara envisaged his own death in the revolutionary fight against this imperialism.

Wherever death may surprise us, let it be welcome, provided that this, our battle-cry, may have reached some receptive ear and another hand may be extended to wield our weapons and other men be ready to intone the funeral dirge with the staccato chant of the machine-gun and new battle-cries of war and victory.[1]

His envisaged death offered him the measure of how intolerable his life would be if he accepted the intolerable condition of the world as it is. His envisaged death offered him the measure of the necessity of changing the world. It was by the licence granted by his envisaged death that he was able to live with the necessary pride that becomes a man.

At the news of Guevara's death, I heard someone say: 'He was the world symbol of the possibilities of one man.' Why is this true? Because he recognized what was intolerable for man and acted accordingly.

The measure by which Guevara had lived suddenly became

---

1. 'Vietnam Must Not Stand Alone', *New Left Review*, London, No. 43, 1967.

a unit which filled the world and obliterated his life. His envisaged death became actual. The photograph is about this
actuality. The possibilities have gone. Instead there is blood, the
smell of formol, the untended wounds on the unwashed body,
flies, the shambling trousers: the small private details of the
body rendered in dying as public and impersonal and broken as
a razed city.

Guevara died surrounded by his enemies. What they did to
him while he was alive was probably consistent with that they
did to him after he was dead. In his extremity he had nothing to
support him but his own previous decisions. Thus the cycle was
closed. It would be the vulgarest impertinence to claim any
knowledge of his experience during that instant or that eternity.
His lifeless body, as seen in the photograph, is the only report
we have. But we are entitled to deduce the logic of what happens when the cycle closes. Truth flows in the reverse direction. His envisaged death is no more the measure of the necessity for changing the intolerable condition of the world. Aware
now of his actual death, he finds in his life the measure of his
justification, and the world-as-his-experience becomes tolerable
to him.

The foreseeing of this final logic is part of what enables a
man or a people to fight against overwhelming odds. It is part
of the secret of the moral factor which counts as three to one
against weapon power.

The photograph shows an instant: that instant at which
Guevara's body, artificially preserved, has become a mere object
of demonstration. In this lies its initial horror. But what is it
intended to demonstrate? Such horror? No. It is to demonstrate,
at the instant of horror, the identity of Guevara and, allegedly,
the absurdity of revolution. Yet by virtue of this very purpose,
the instant is transcended. The life of Guevara and the idea or
fact of revolution immediately invoke processes which preceded
that instant and which continue now. Hypothetically, the only
way in which the purpose of those who arranged for and
authorized the photograph could have been achieved would have
been to preserve artificially at that instant the whole state of

the world as it was: to stop life. Only in such a way could the content of Guevara's living example have been denied. As it is, either the photograph means nothing because the spectator has no inkling of what is involved, or else its meaning denies or qualifies its demonstration.

I have compared it with two paintings because paintings, before the invention of photography, are the only visual evidence we have of how people saw what they saw. But in its effect it is profoundly different from a painting. A painting, or a successful one at least, comes to terms with the processes invoked by its subject matter. It even suggests an attitude towards those processes. We can regard a painting as almost complete in itself.

In face of this photograph we must either dismiss it or complete its meaning for ourselves. It is an image which, as much as any mute image ever can, calls for decision.

December 1967   Prompted by another recent newspaper photograph, I continue to consider the death of 'Che' Guevara.

Until the end of the eighteenth century, for a man to envisage his death as the possibly direct consequence of his choice of a certain course of action is the measure of his *loyalty* as a servant. This is true whatever the social station or privilege of the man. Inserted between himself and his own meaning there is always a power to which his only possible relationship is one of service or servitude. The power may be considered abstractly as Fate. More usually it is personified in God, King or the Master.

Thus the choice which the man makes (the choice whose foreseen consequence may be his own death) is curiously incomplete. It is a choice submitted to a superior power for acknowledgement. The man himself can only judge *sub judice*: finally it is he who will be judged. In exchange for this limited responsibility he receives benefits. The benefits can range from a master's recognition of his courage to eternal bliss in heaven. But in all cases the ultimate decision and the ultimate benefit are located as exterior to his own self and life. Consequently death, which would seem to be so definitive an *end*, is for him a *means*, a treatment to which he submits for the sake of some aftermath. Death is like the eye of a needle through which he is threaded. Such is the mode of his heroism.

The French Revolution changed the nature of heroism. (Let it be clear that I do not refer to specific courages: the endurance of pain or torture, the will to attack under fire, the speed and lightness of movement and decision in battle, the spontaneity of mutual aid under danger – these courages must be largely defined by physical experience and have perhaps changed very little. I refer only to the choice which may precede these other courages.) The French Revolution brings the King to judgement and condemns him.

Saint-Just, aged twenty-five, in his first speech to the Convention argues that monarchy is crime, because the king usurps the sovereignty of the people.

It is impossible to reign innocently: the madness of it is too clear. Every king is a rebel and a usurper.[2]

It is true that Saint-Just serves – in his own mind – the General Will of the people, but he has freely chosen to do so because he believes that the People, if allowed to be true to their own nature, embody Reason and that their Republic represents Virtue.

In the world there are three kinds of infamy with which Republican virtue can reach no compromise: the first are kings: the second is the serving of kings: the third is the laying down of arms whilst there still exists anywhere a master and a slave.[3]

It is now less likely that a man envisages his own death as the measure of his loyalty as a servant to a master. His envisaged death is likely to be the measure of his love of Freedom: a proof of the principle of his own liberty.

-----

2. Saint-Just, *Discours et Rapports*, Editions Sociales, Paris, 1957, p. 66 (translation by the author).

3. ibid., p. 90.

Twenty months after his first speech Saint-Just spends the night preceding his own execution writing at his desk. He makes no active attempt to save himself. He has already written:

Circumstances are only difficult for those who draw back from the grave.... I despise the dust of which I am composed, the dust which is speaking to you: any one can pursue and put an end to this dust. But I defy anybody to snatch from me what I have given myself, an independent life in the sky of the centuries.[4]

'What I have given myself.' The ultimate decision is now located within the self. But not categorically and entirely; there is a certain ambiguity. God no longer exists, but Rousseau's Supreme Being is there to confuse the issue by way of a metaphor. The metaphor allows one to believe that the self will share in the historical judgement of one's own life. 'An independent life in the sky' of historical judgement. There is still the ghost of a pre-existent order.

Even when Saint-Just is declaring the opposite – in his defiant last speech of defence for Robespierre and himself – the ambiguity remains:

Fame is an empty noise. Let us put our ears to the centuries that have gone: we no longer hear anything; those who, at another time, shall walk among our urns, shall hear no more. The good – that is what we must pursue, whatever the price, preferring the title of a dead hero to that of a living coward.[5]

But in life, as opposed to the theatre, the dead hero never hears himself so called. The political stage of a revolution often has a theatrical, because exemplary, tendency. The world watches to learn.

Tyrants everywhere looked upon us because we were judging one of theirs; today when, by a happier destiny, you are deliberating on the liberty of the world, the people of the earth who are the truly great of the earth will, in their turn, watch you.[6]

---

4. ibid.
5. ibid.
6. ibid. Saint-Just to the Convention, on the Constitution.

Yet, notwithstanding the truth of this, there is, philosophically, a sense in which Saint-Just dies triumphantly trapped within his 'stage' role. (To say this in no way detracts from his courage.)

Since the French Revolution, the bourgeois age. Amongst those few who envisage their own death (and not their own fortunes) as the direct consequence of their principled decisions, such marginal ambiguity disappears.

The confrontation between the living man and the world as he finds it becomes total. There is nothing exterior to it, not even a principle. A man's envisaged death is the measure of his refusal to accept what confronts him. There is nothing beyond that refusal.

The Russian anarchist Voinarovsky, who was killed throwing a bomb at Admiral Dubassov, wrote:

> Without a single muscle on my face twitching, without saying a word, I shall climb on the scaffold – and this will not be an act of violence perpetrated on myself, it will be the perfectly natural result of all that I have lived through.[7]

He envisages his own death on the scaffold – and a number of Russian terrorists at that time died exactly as he describes – as though it were the peaceful death of an old man. Why is he able to do this? Psychological explanations are not enough. It is because he finds the world of Russia, which is comprehensive enough to seem like the whole world, intolerable. Not intolerable to him personally, as a suicide finds the world, but intolerable *per se*. His foreseen death 'will be the perfectly natural result' of all that he has lived through in his attempt to change the world, because the foreseeing of anything less would have meant that he found the 'intolerable' tolerable.

In many ways the situation (but not the political theory) of the Russian anarchists at the turn of the century prefigures the contemporary situation. A small difference lies in 'the world of Russia' *seeming* like the whole world. There was, strictly speak-

---

7. Quoted in Albert Camus, *The Rebel*, Penguin Books, 1962, p. 140.

ing, an alternative beyond the borders of Russia. Thus, in order to destroy this alternative and make Russia a world unto itself, many of the anarchists were drawn towards a somewhat mystical patriotism. Today there is no alternative. The world is a single unit, and it has become intolerable.

Was it ever more tolerable? you may ask. Was there ever less suffering, less injustice, less exploitation? There can be no such audits. It is necessary to recognize that the intolerability of the world is, in a certain sense, an historical achievement. The world was not intolerable so long as God existed, so long as there was the ghost of a pre-existent order, so long as large tracts of the world were unknown, so long as one believed in the distinction between the spiritual and the material (it is there that many people still find their justification in finding the world tolerable), so long as one believed in the natural inequality of man.

The second newspaper photograph shows a South Vietnamese peasant being interrogated by an American soldier. Shoved against her temple is the muzzle of a gun, and, behind it, a hand grasps her hair. The gun, pressed against her, puckers the prematurely old and loose skin of her face.

In wars there have always been massacres. Interrogation under threat or torture has been practised for centuries. Yet the meaning to be found – even via a photograph – in this woman's life (and by now her probable death) is new.

It will include every personal particular, visible or imaginable: the way her hair is parted, her bruised cheek, her slightly swollen lower lip, her name and all the different significations it has acquired according to who is addressing her, memories of her own childhood, the individual quality of her hatred of her interrogator, the gifts she was born with, every detail of the circumstances under which she has so far escaped death, the intonation she gives to the name of each person she loves, the diagnosis of whatever medical weaknessess she may have and their social and economic causes, everything that she opposes in her subtle mind to the muzzle of the gun jammed against her temple. But it will also include global truths: no violence

51

has been so intense, so widespread or has continued for so long as that inflicted by the imperialist countries upon the majority of the world: the war in Vietnam is being waged to destroy the example of a united people who resisted this violence and proclaimed their independence: the fact that the Vietnamese are proving themselves invincible against the greatest imperialist power on earth is a proof of the extraordinary resources of a nation of thirty-two million: elsewhere in the world the resources (such resources include not only materials and labour but the possibilities of each life lived) of our 2,000 millions are being squandered and abused.

It is said that exploitation must end in the world. It is known that exploitation increases, extends, prospers and becomes ever more ruthless in defence of its right to exploit.

Let us be clear: it is not the war in Vietnam that is intolerable: Vietnam confirms the intolerability of the present condition of the world. This condition is such that the example of the Vietnamese people offers hope.

Guevara recognized this and acted accordingly. The world is not intolerable until the possibility of transforming it exists but is denied. The social forces historically capable of bringing about the transformation are – at least in general terms – defined. Guevara chose to identify himself with these forces. In doing so he was not submitting to so-called 'laws' of history but to the historical nature of his own existence.

His envisaged death is no longer the measure of a servant's loyalty, nor the inevitable end of an heroic tragedy. The eye of death's needle has been closed – there is nothing to thread through it, not even a future (unknown) historical judgement. Provided that he makes no transcendental appeal and provided that he acts out of the maximum possible consciousness of what is knowable to him, his envisaged death has become the measure of the parity which can now exist between the self and the world: it is the measure of his total commitment and his total independence.

It is reasonable to suppose that after a man such as Guevara has made his decision, there are moments when he is aware of this freedom which is qualitatively different from any freedom previously experienced.

This should be remembered as well as the pain, the sacrifice and the prodigious effort involved. In a letter to his parents when he left Cuba, Guevara wrote:

Now a will-power that I have polished with an artist's attention will support my feeble legs and tired-out lungs. I will make it.[8]

---

8. E. 'Che' Guevara, *Le Socialisme et l'homme*, Maspero, Paris, 1967, p. 113 (translation by the author).

Jack Yeats

He is an old, very tall, thin man. His face is that of an old, tall, upright man; no literary image should be used to describe the face of this life-long image maker. And when I told him, thinking of how many tinkers, and horse traders, and wanderers he had painted, that Léger had said that the artist was in the same class as the *clochard*, because in their common desire for the danger of maximum freedom they backed the same horse, the only difference being that the artist won and the *clochard* lost – when I told him this, he smiled, sharing his own experiences with himself, and added like an old man, and exactly like an old man and nothing else – except that he was attentive enough to nod at the speed with which I was drinking his Irish whisky – he added, 'Yes, but some of the best people are losers. I've known some terrible brilliant men – all brilliance on the outside, and all morality inside, as a second line of defence.'

How he hates morality, this octogenarian. For him morality is a foreign imposition brought on the point of the bayonet. A romantic conception? But this man is one of the last living romantics – not because he is still alive, but because he lives his philosophy. On the periphery of the twentieth century, he has challenged Thoreau's nineteenth-century remark, 'It is now noble to profess because it was once noble to live.' He has not played with light effects so that the critics, goggling, search for the right word, earn their money by their hard struggle, and eventually spell out the label Romanticism; he is a romantic who has always walked out into the darkness, so that when he meets his travellers there is no need to portray them in fancy dress, for they already wear all that he has imagined in his own previous dark solitary journey. When a man advances into a cave, the dark winds round his throat and trails behind him like a scarf. When a girl stands on the shore, look how the sea becomes her – in both palpitating senses of that word *become*. When soldiers are seen striking camp for the *second* time, all movements are automatic and even the dawn is tarnished, because 'supposing you know you must die at dawn and you prepare yourself, and supposing you are reprieved and then have to face another dawn with the same knowledge – that is hard indeed'.

No one has ever been allowed to watch him paint. Before his wife died he used to take a white pipe-cleaner – 'like a sheep's leg' – and bend it into a circle and put it on the knob of his studio door to warn her that he was at work. A question of professional secrets? No, a question of his being desperately – and to us rational materialists, almost incomprehensibly – anxious that he might not be able to rediscover his own secrets. 'And Carlyle,' he laughs, 'thought ninety-nine per cent of genius was taking pains. I am sure now his poor wife had something to say about that. A painting is an event. And that's what that old Gamp Fry – do you still read him? – a grey-minded man and a timid painter, too – that's what he never understood. You can plan events, but if they go according to your plan they are not events.'

I disagreed with him about art being amoral and said that I thought the artist had a moral obligation: namely, to identify himself to the full with his subject.

His reply was to fill up my glass, refocus his eyes and tell me about his subjects. He sang 'The boy I love is in the gallery' with Marie Lloyd, he showed me with his long, thin hands the secrets of the grabbing, conjuring tricks plied at the horse fairs, he fought old fights in the ring, he brought in a horse suspiciously offered for sale in the middle of the night, and examined it with a lantern, he kept a late rendezvous in the East India

Docks, and then coming back to my point he said: 'Maybe. But too many moral people expect you to be respectful to your subjects. And how can you be that if you identify yourself with them? And then these same people come along and ask you, "How long did it take you to do that painting?" and if you say months, they think it's worth a lot. That's morality for you.'

Referring to Jack Yeats's paintings, Samuel Beckett wrote, 'He grows Watteauer and Watteauer.' That is a perceptive stimulating remark. The differences are obvious: the folds in the silk have become tears in rough cloth: the artificial gestures of the *fête* in the enclosed garden have become the so similar but *naturally* exaggerated gestures with which travellers greet each other on a deserted open plain. The nervousness of the technique has become magnified, as though one square centimetre of Watteau were painted to the scale of a square foot: Yeats is coarser – and gayer. But their subjects – transience, mortality – are the same, and, although Watteau's vision was melancholically ironic and Yeats's, just because it is coarser, is heroic – death for him is the condition for human consciousness and therefore for freedom – there has been no artist between these two who has specifically dealt with the same subject so poignantly and unsentimentally.

Thus Yeats's theme is universal. That is not to say that his works would fit easily into the modern cosmopolitan museum. They would not, for the works which are prefabricated for that museum are by artists who prefer to 'profess' rather than live. And it is because Yeats realizes that this profession of being all things to all men means the denial of living art, that he has always refused to allow his work to be reproduced in colour and bound in sumptuous volumes. The fact that he has consequently lost international recognition means less to him than the fact that each painting is an event – a single event. And when publishers have promised him the most accurate and faithful reproductions, he has replied: 'The better they are the worse they are.'

Like all artists who achieve a degree of universality, Yeats is closely bound with the local and particular. Cézanne seems formalized until one has seen Provence through his eye. Yeats seems too 'mobile', over-spontaneous, until one has watched the west coast of Ireland. And watched is the word, for the landscape there is a fast series of events, not a view – an unchanging structure. The land is as passive as a bog can be. The sky is all action. I am told that the sky is similar in California, and perhaps along any ocean coast facing west. But in Ireland the sky is a dancer, tender and wild alternately, and then furious, ripping her clothes and parading her golden body to get just one glimmer of response from the peat. And she gets it. For in the ruts and bog puddles and along the wet shoulders of a tarpaulin the water flashes back, seeming by contrast with its surroundings even brighter than her. And it is this wild dancing and wilder response that Yeats has painted. This is how the green lying on a distant hill is pulled, by the sheer movement of a foreground head turning, into that head's eyes, whilst the miles between the head and the hill remain. This is how a red streak in the sky becomes the gauntlet of a rider and the belly of his horse below.

Not that Yeats has ever been a literal landscape painter. He transforms everything within his imagination. And if I had to give a single reason why I believe he is a great painter I would cite the consistency of this power of his to transform. Like Giorgione or Delacroix, he can cast his spell even over the foreground of his pictures. Most modern romantics because they do not live their philosophy can never bring their romantic vision nearer than the middle distance: the foreground simply remains a frame. Yeats – and in this he is unlike his brother – has never stepped out of his vision. He has continued to embrace mortality in the face of every moral warning. But he has been able to do this because his vision has its roots in his country: visually in the Irish landscape: poetically in Irish folklore: and ideologically in the fact that Ireland has only up to now been able to fight English imperialism with the image of the independent individual Rebel.

*

Jack Yeats is now dead. For those who are at all aware of an artist as a man his paintings change after his death. Whilst he is alive all his works, even those that are declared finished, are seen to some extent as works in progress; as you look at them you relate them to an imagination that still exists and is still working; his works then chart a progress. After his death they become final and definitive; they no longer chart his progress, they gather together to form his destination. In Dublin I wanted to ask Yeats about his paintings. Today similar questions do not even come to mind. The living artist is either more or less open to intervention, persuasion, influence, questioning, which is why his work can have an urgency for us which is different in kind from anything we can get from works of the past. From them we can only learn. There is thus a logic in the fact that only when an artist is dead can he be fully recognized as a master. While he is alive he can, of course, be recognized as great, as a source of understanding and inspiration, but this is different, for our relationship with him then cannot be purely a pupil–teacher one: we are also related to him by a hundred and one other mutual responsibilities because both he and we are alive. Yeats has now become a master.

Very many of Yeats's last pictures are implicitly, but not explicitly, concerned with death. *Sleep Sound:* two figures lie on a moor, the sky above them heavy as the breathing of those who might keep their wake. *The Hours of Sleep:* a man nods in a mountain field of gentians and behind him is a monolithic, immovable, dead block of stone. *The Nights Are Closing In:* two figures talk against a sky being torn to tatters. *Tir-na-n-Og:* which means the country where neither age nor death exists and where the Irish peasant believes 'you will get happiness for a penny'.

How is it then, the reader may ask, that I, a Marxist, can find so much truth and splendour in the art of an arch-romantic such as Yeats? Professor George Thomson has already answered this question by quoting the painter's brother:

> Sing on: somewhere at some new moon,
> We'll learn that sleeping is not death,
> Hearing the whole earth change its tune.

What, in other words, we have in common with the genuine romantic is a sense of the future, an awareness of the possibility of a world other than the one we know. (I say *genuine* romantic to distinguish men like Yeats or Géricault, who lived their romanticism, from those who merely use romantic poses.) Strange as it may sound, no European country had until recently a greater sense of the future than Ireland. This was partly because no bourgeoisie had destroyed its popular art, which was an art of longing, and partly because its colonial status bred rebels. Even the fairies, the ghosts, the banshees, the famous songs, the notorious and magnificent edifices of words that could be built in a few moments out of nothing, were partly expressions of an Irish conviction that there was something beyond the facts of that poverty which quite simply halved their population in the second half of the nineteenth century. Even today (in 1958) the I.R.A. flickers with something of the same spirit. Ireland has not yet reached that critical point where she can only defend her way of life : she is still striving, staggering, suffering and dreaming towards one. And however much the keep-art-pure-sirs may hate it, it is impossible to appreciate Yeats fully without understanding something of this.

It is this which explains how Yeats was a modern painter – he had no nostalgia for the art styles of the past – and yet was apparently quite uninfluenced by Cubism and abstract art. It is also this which explains why his work, which is expressionist in character, is nevertheless quite free from the sense of personal desperation found in mid-European Expressionism. (In this Yeats resembles the Indonesian painter, Affandi, and it may well be that this kind of romantic but outward-facing expressionism is the natural style of art for previously exploited nations fighting for independence – modern classicism requires an industrial society.) Yeats's romantic view of life brought him closer to his subjects – his horsemen, actors, lovers, talkers, beggars – instead of separating him from them. His paintings, as opposed to the landscapes they include, do not convey loneliness; on the contrary, they appear to be made out of the stuff of legends that have been as much handled and commonly slept in as the blankets on the inn's bed for travellers. Further, it is Yeats's Irish background which explains why his direct influence on younger European painters would be a dangerous one, leading to theatrical mannerism.

What his background cannot directly explain is Yeats's pictorial genius as a painter: his sense of colour, like a Venetian's, but derived from rags and a lean shimmering world, instead of from velvets and mellow feasts: his draughtsmanship, nervous, spontaneous – sometimes achieved, I suspect, by painting with the very nozzle of the tube of pigment, occasionally becoming incoherent, but at its best describing forms breaking against the surface of the mist, the dusk, the sunlight, like fishes breaking the surface of water as they leap across it: his sense of pictorial unity, so that for all the shreds of colour and the shimmer and the speed, his canvases as a whole are permanently calm.

Both Yeats's pictorial genius and his spirit can be epitomized by a small canvas called *The First Away*. It represents simply a man's head and shoulders against the sky. The way in which the smooth milky surface of the sky and the curdled paint describing the man's features are held together in unity is a miracle of tonal and colour adjustment, as refined as any passage in Braque. As for the content: the man's eyes in his pale shriven face are closed in rapture. Is it he or is it the horse who is first away? And away to where?

To where:

> Delight makes all of the one mind,
> The riders upon the galloping horses
> The crowd that closes in behind.

Now that he is dead, Yeats has become a master: he teaches us to hope.

Peter Peri

I knew about Peter Peri from 1947 onwards. At that time he
lived in Hampstead and I used to pass his garden where he displayed his sculptures. I was an art student just out of the Army.
The sculptures impressed me not so much because of their
quality – at that time many other things interested me more
than art – but because of their strangeness. They were foreign
looking. I remember arguing with my friends about them. They
said they were crude and coarse. I defended them because I
sensed that they were the work of somebody totally different
from us.

Later, between about 1952 and 1958, I came to know Peter
Peri quite well and became more interested in his work. But it
was always the man who interested me most. By then he had
moved from Hampstead and was living in considerable poverty
in the old Camden Studios in Camden Town. There are certain
aspects of London that I will always associate with him: the
soot-black trunks of bare trees in winter, black railings set in
concrete, the sky like grey stone, empty streets at dusk with
the front doors of mean houses giving straight on to them, a
sour grittiness in one's throat and then the cold of his studio and
the smallness of his supply of coffee with which nevertheless
he was extremely generous. Many of his sculptures were about
the same aspects of the city. Thus even inside his studio there
was little sense of refuge. The rough bed in the corner was not
unlike a street bench – except that it had books on a rough shelf

above it. His hands were ingrained with dirt as though he worked day and night in the streets. Only the stove gave off a little warmth, and on top of it, keeping warm, the tiny copper coffee saucepan.

Sometimes I suggested to him that we went to a restaurant for a meal. He nearly always refused. This was partly pride – he was proud to the point of arrogance – and partly perhaps it was good sense : he was used to his extremely meagre diet of soup made from vegetables and black bread, and he did not want to disorient himself by eating better. He knew that he had to continue to lead a foreign life.

His face. At the same time lugubrious and passionate. Broad, low forehead, enormous nose, thick lips, beard and moustache like an extra article of clothing to keep him warm, insistent eyes. The texture of his skin was coarse and the coarseness was made more evident by never being very clean. It was the face whose features and implied experience one can find in any ghetto – Jewish or otherwise.

The arrogance and the insistence of his eyes often appealed to women. He carried with him in his face a passport to an alternative world. In this world, which physically he had been forced to abandon but which metaphysically he carried with him – as though a microcosm of it was stuffed into a sack on his back – he was virile, wise and masterful.

I often saw him at public political meetings. Sometimes, when I myself was a speaker, I would recognize him in the blur of faces by his black beret. He would ask questions, make interjections, mutter to himself – occasionally walk out. On occasions he and my friends would meet later in the evening and go on discussing the issues at stake. What he had to say or what he could explain was always incomplete. This was not so much a question of language (when he was excited he spoke in an almost incomprehensible English), as a question of his own estimate of us, his audience. He considered that our experience was inadequate. We had not been in Budapest at the time of the Soviet Revolution. We had not seen how Bela Kun had been – perhaps unnecessarily – defeated. We had not been in Berlin in 1920. We did not understand how the possibility of a revolution in Germany had been betrayed. We had not witnessed the creeping advance and then the terrifying triumph of Nazism. We did not even know what it was like for an artist to have to abandon the work of the first thirty years of his life. Perhaps some of us might have been able to imagine all this, but in this field Peri did not believe in imagination. And so he always stopped before he had completed saying what he meant, long before he had disclosed the whole of the microcosm that he carried in his sack.

I asked him many questions. But now I have the feeling that I never asked him enough. Or at least that I never asked him the right questions. Anyway I am not in a position to describe the major historical events which conditioned his life. Furthermore I know nobody in London who is. Perhaps in Budapest there is still a witness left: but most are dead, and of the dead most were killed. I can only speak of my incomplete impression of him. Yet though factually incomplete, this impression is a remarkably total one.

Peter Peri was an exile. Arrogantly, obstinately, sometimes cunningly, he preserved this role. Had he been offered recognition as an artist or as a man of integrity or as a militant antifascist, it is possible that he would have changed. But he was not. Even an artist like Kokoschka, with all his continental reputation and personal following among important people, was ignored and slighted when he arrived in England as a refugee. Peri had far fewer advantages. He arrived with only the distant reputation of being a Constructivist, a militant communist and a penniless Jew. By the time I knew him, he was no longer either of the first two, but had become an eternal exile – because only in this way could he keep faith with what he had learned and with those who had taught him.

Something of the meaning of being such an exile I tried to put into my novel *A Painter of Our Time*.[1] The hero of this

---

1. John Berger, *A Painter of Our Time*, Secker & Warburg, 1958; Penguin Books, 1965.

novel is a Hungarian of exactly the same generation as Peri. In some respects the character resembles Peri closely. We discussed the novel together at length. He was enthusiastic about the idea of my writing it. What he thought of the finished article I do not know. He probably thought it inadequate. Even if he had thought otherwise, I think it would have been impossible for him to tell me. By that time the habit of suffering inaccessibility, like the habit of eating meagre vegetable soup, had become too strong.

I should perhaps add that the character of James Lavin in this novel is in no sense a *portrait* of Peri. Certain aspects of Lavin derived from another Hungarian émigré, Frederick Antal, the art historian who, more than any other man, taught me how to write about art. Yet other aspects were purely imaginary. What Lavin and Peri share is the depth of their experience of exile.

Peri's work is very uneven. His obstinacy constructed a barrier against criticism, even against comment, and so in certain ways he failed to develop as an artist. He was a bad judge of his own work. He was capable of producing works of the utmost crudity and banality. But he was also capable of producing works vibrant with an idea of humanity. It does not seem to me to be important to catalogue which are which. The viewer should decide this for himself. The best of his works express what he believed in. This might seem to be a small achievement but in fact it is a rare one. Most works which are produced are either cynical or hypocritical – or so diffuse as to be meaningless.

Peter Peri. His presence is very strong in my mind as I write these words. A man I never knew well enough. A man, if the truth be told, who was always a little suspicious of me. I did my best to help and encourage him, but this did not allay his suspicions. I had not passed the tests which he and his true friends had had to pass in Budapest and Berlin. I was a relatively privileged being in a relatively privileged country. I upheld some of the political opinions which he had abandoned, but I upheld them without ever having to face a fraction of the consequences which he and his friends had experienced and suffered. It was not that he distrusted me: it was simply that he reserved the right to doubt. It was an unspoken doubt that I could only read in his knowing, almost closed eyes. Perhaps he was right. Yet if I had to face the kind of tests Peter Peri faced, his example would, I think, be a help to me. The effect of his example may have made his doubts a little less necessary.

Peri suffered considerably. Much of this suffering was the direct consequence of his own attitude and actions. What befell him was not entirely arbitrary. He was seldom a passive victim. Some would say that he suffered unnecessarily – because he could have avoided much of his suffering. But Peri lived according to the laws of his own necessity. He believed that to have sound reasons for despising himself would be the worst that could befall him. This belief, which was not an illusion, was the measure of his nobility.

Zadkine

Last night a man who was looking for a flat and asking me about rents told me that Zadkine was dead.

One day when I was particularly depressed Zadkine took us out to dinner to cheer me up. When we were sitting at the table and after we had ordered, he took my arm and said: 'Remember when a man falls over a cliff, he almost certainly smiles before he hits the ground, because that's what his own demon tells him to do.'
I hope it was true for him.

I did not know him very well but I remember him vividly.

A small man with white hair, bright piercing eyes, wearing baggy grey flannel trousers. The first striking thing about him is how he keeps himself clean. Maybe a strange phrase to use – as though he were a cat or a squirrel. Yet the odd thing is that after a while in his company, you begin to realize that, in one way or another, many men don't keep themselves clean. He is a fastidious man; it is this which explains the unusual brightness of his eyes, the way that his crowded studio, full of figure-heads, looks somehow like the scrubbed deck of a ship, the fact that under and around the stove there are no ashes or coal-dust, his clean cuffs above his craftsman's hands. But it also explains some of his invisible characteristics: his certainty, the modest manner in which he is happy to live, the care with which he talks of his own 'destiny', the way that he talks of a tree as though it had a biography as distinct and significant as his own.

He talks almost continuously. His stories are about places, friends, adventures, the life he has lived: never, as with the pure egotist, about *his own opinion of himself*. When he talks, he watches what he is telling as though it were all there in front of his hands, as though it were a fire he was warming himself at.

Some of the stories he has told many times. The story of the first time he was in London, when he was about seventeen. His father had sent him to Sunderland to learn English and in the hope that he would give up the idea of wanting to be an artist. From Sunderland he made his own way to London and arrived there without job or money. At last he was taken on in a wood-carving studio for church furniture.

'Somewhere in an English church there is a lectern, with an eagle holding the bible on the back of its outspread wings. One of those wings I carved. It is a Zadkine – unsigned. The man next to me in the workshop was a real English artisan – such as I'd never met before. He always had a pint of ale on his bench when he was working. And to work he wore glasses – perched on the end of his nose. One day this man said to me: "The trouble with you is that you're too small. No one will ever believe that you can do the job. Why don't you carve a rose to show them?" "What shall I carve it out of?" I asked. He rummaged under his bench and produced a block of apple wood – a lovely piece of wood, old and brown. And so from this I carved a rose with all its petals and several leaves. I carved it so finely that when you shook it, the petals moved. And the old man was right. As soon as the rush job was over, I had to leave that workshop. When I went to others, they looked at me sceptically. I was too young, too small and my English was very approximate. But then I would take the rose out of my pocket, and the rose proved eloquent. I'd get the job.'

We are standing by an early wood-carving of a nude in his studio.

'Sometimes I look at something I've made and I know it is good. Then I touch wood, or rather I touch my right hand.' As he says this, Zadkine touches the back of his small right hand, as though he were touching something infinitely fragile – an autumn leaf for example.

'I used to think that when I died and was buried all my wood carvings would be burnt with me. That was when they called me "the negro sculptor". But now all these carvings are in museums. And when I die, I shall go with some little terracottas in my pocket and a few bronzes strung on my belt – like a pedlar.'

Drinking a white wine of which he is very proud and which he brings to Paris from the country, sitting in a small bedroom off the studio, he reminisces.

'When I was about eight years old, I was at my uncle's in the country. My uncle was a barge-builder. They used to saw whole trees from top to bottom to make planks – saw them by hand. One man at the top end of the saw was high up and looked like an angel. But it was the man at the bottom who interested me. He got covered from head to foot in sawdust. New, resinous sawdust so that he smelt from head to foot of wood – and the sawdust collected even in his eyebrows. At my uncle's I used to go for walks by myself down by the river. One day I saw a young man towing a barge. On the barge was a young woman. They were shouting at each other in anger. Suddenly I heard the man use the word CUNT. You know how for children the very sound of certain forbidden words can become frightening? I was frightened like that. I remembered hearing the word once before – though God knows where I had learnt that it was forbidden – I was going along the passage between the kitchen and the dining-room and as I passed a door I saw a young man from the village with one of our maids on his knee, his hand was unbuttoning her and he used the same word.

'I started to run away from the river and the shouting couple by the barge towards the forest. Suddenly, as I ran, I slipped and I found myself face down on the earth.

'And it was there after I had fallen flat on my face as I ran away from the river, that my demon first laid his finger on my sleeve. And so, instead of running on, I found myself saying – I will go back to see why I slipped. I went back and I found that I had slipped on some clay. And again for the second time my demon laid a finger on my sleeve. I bent down and I scooped up a handful of the clay. Then I walked to a fallen tree trunk, sat down on it and began to model a figure, the first in my life. I had forgotten my fear. The little figure was of a man. Later – at my father's house – I discovered that there was also clay in our back garden.'

It is about ten o'clock on a November morning seven years ago. The light in the studio is matter of fact. I have only called to collect or deliver something. It is a time for working rather than talking. Yet he insists that I sit down for a moment.

'I am very much occupied with time,' he says, 'you are young but you will feel it one day. Some days I see a little black spot high up in the corner of the studio and I wonder whether I will have the time to do all that I still have to do – to correct all my sculptures which are not finished. You see that figure there. It is all right up to the head. But the head needs doing again. All the time I am looking at them. In the end, if you're a sculptor, there's very little room left for yourself – your works crowd you out.'

Zadkine's masterpiece remains his monument to the razed and reborn city of Rotterdam. This is how he wrote about it:

It is striving to embrace the inhuman pain inflicted on a city which had no other desire but to live by the grace of God and to grow naturally like a forest. . . . It was also intended as a lesson to future generations.

Le Corbusier

It was on market day in the nearest town that I saw the headlines announcing the death of Le Corbusier. There were no buildings bearing the evidence of his life's work in that dusty, provincial and exclusively commercial French town (fruit and vegetables), yet it seemed to bear witness to his death. Perhaps only because the town was an extension of my own heart. But the intimations in my heart could not have been unique; there were others, reading the local newspaper at the café tables, who had also glimpsed with the help of Corbusier the ideal of a town built to the measure of man.

Le Corbusier is dead. A good death, my companions said, a good way to die: quickly in the sea whilst swimming at the age of seventy-eight. His death seems a diminution of the possibilities open to even the smallest village. Whilst he lived, there seemed always to be a hope that the village might be transformed for the better. Paradoxically this hope arose out of the maximum improbability. Le Corbusier, who was the most practical, democratic and visionary architect of our time, was seldom given the opportunity to build in Europe. The few buildings he put up were all prototypes for series which were never constructed. He was the alternative to architecture as it exists. The alternative still remains, of course. But it seems less pressing. His insistence is dead.

We made three journeys to pay our own modest last respects. First we went to look again at the Unité d'Habitation at Marseilles. How is it wearing? they ask. It wears like a good example that hasn't been followed. But the kids still bathe in their pool on the roof, safely, grubbily, between the panorama of the sea and of the mountains, in a setting which, until this century, could only have been imagined as an extravagant one for cherubs in a Baroque ceiling painting. The big lifts for the prams and bicycles work smoothly. The vegetables in the shopping street on the third floor are cheap as those in the city.

The most important thing about the whole building is so simple that it can easily be taken for granted – which is what Corbusier intended. If you wish, you can condescend towards this building for, despite its size and originality, it suggests nothing which is larger than you – no glory, no prestige, no demagogy and no property-morality. It offers no excuses for living in such a way as to be less than yourself. And this, although it began as a question of spirit, was in practice only possible as a question of proportion.

The next day we went to the eleventh-century Cistercian abbey at Le Thoronet. I have the idea that Corbusier once wrote about it, and anybody who really wants to understand his theory of functionalism – a theory which has been so misunderstood and abused – should certainly visit it. The content of the abbey, as opposed to its form or the immediate purposes for which it was designed, is very similar to that of the Unité d'Habitation. It is very hard indeed to take account of the nine centuries that separate them.

I do not know how to describe, without recourse to drawing, the complex simplicity of the abbey. It is like the human body. During the French Revolution it was sacked and was never refurnished: yet its nakedness is no more than a logical conclusion to the Cistercian rule which condemned decoration. Children were playing in the cloister, as in the pool on the roof, and running the length of the nave. They were never dwarfed by the structure. The abbey buildings are functional because they were concerned with supplying the means rather than suggesting the end. The end is up to those who inhabit it. The means allow them to realize themselves and so to discover their purpose. This seems as true of the children today as of the monks then. Such architecture offers only tranquillity and human proportion. For myself I find in its discretion everything which I can recognize as spiritual. The power of functionalism does not lie in its utility, but in its moral example: an example of trust, the refusal to exhort.

Our third visit was to the bay where he died. If you follow a scrubby footpath along the side of the railway, eastwards from the station of Roquebrune, you come to a café and hotel built of wood and corrugated roofing. In most respects it is a shack like hundreds of others built over the beaches of the Côte d'Azur – a cross between a houseboat and a gimcrack stage. But this one was built according to the advice of Le Corbusier because *le patron* was an old friend. Some of the proportions and the colour scheme are recognizably his. And on the outside wooden wall, facing the sea, he painted his emblem of the six-foot man who acted as modular and measure for all his architecture.

We sat on the planked terrace and drank coffee. As I watched the sea below, it seemed for one moment that the barely visible waves, looking like ripples, were the last sign of the body that had sunk there a week before. It seemed for one moment as though the sea might recognize more than the architecture of dyke and breakwater. A pathetic illusion.

Across the bay you can see Monte Carlo. If the light is diffused, the silhouette of the mountains coming down to the sea can look like a Claude Lorrain. If the light is hard, you see the commerce of the architecture on those mountains. Particularly noticeable is a four-star hotel built on the very edge of a precipice. Vulgar and strident as it is, it would never have been built without Corbusier's initial example. And the same applies to a score of other buildings lower down on the slopes. All of them exhort to wealth.

Then I noticed near the modular man the imprint of a hand. A deliberate imprint, forming part of the decoration. It was a few feet from a Coca-Cola advertisement: several hundred feet above the sea: and it faced the buildings that exhorted to wealth. It was probably Le Corbusier's hand. But it could stand for his memorial if it was any man's.

Victor Serge

Victor Serge was born in Belgium in 1890. His parents were Russian émigrés who fled Russia as a result of his father's revolutionary activities.

On the walls of our humble and makeshift lodgings there were always portraits of men who had been hanged. The conversations of grown-ups dealt with trials, executions, escapes, and Siberian highways, with great ideas incessantly argued over, and with the latest books about these ideas.

Serge left home at fifteen, was quickly disillusioned by the Belgian socialist party, and became an anarchist. In Paris he edited the paper *L'Anarchie* and in 1912 was arrested and sentenced to five years' solitary confinement for being associated with the Bonnot gang who were terrorizing Paris. (One of the recurring features of Serge's life was his 'guilt' by association with those whom he refused to condemn or betray but did not necessarily agree with.)

After his release from prison he went to Barcelona where he became a syndicalist agitator. His one idea following the October revolution was to return to his own country – where he had never yet been – and to work for and defend the revolution. On his way through France he was interned as a suspect Bolshevik. In Petrograd he worked closely with Zinoviev on the founding of the Communist International, and joined the Communist Party. By 1923 he belonged to the Trotskyist left opposition – which at that time was still treated as a loyal opposition. In 1927 he was expelled from the party and afterwards imprisoned and exiled. His life was probably saved by the intercession of certain French writers on his behalf. Deprived of Soviet citizenship, he was allowed to leave the U.S.S.R. In the late thirties, he arrived back in Paris without papers. He broke with the Trotskyists because he considered the Fourth International sectarian and ineffective. He escaped the Gestapo at the last moment in 1941, by sailing to Mexico. There he died, penniless, in 1947.

Serge wrote about twenty books – books of political comment, history, novels, poems, autobiography. All are related to his own experiences.

Writing, as distinct from agitational journalism, was for Serge a secondary activity, only resorted to when more direct action was impossible. He began writing his serious books in 1928 when his position in the U.S.S.R. was extremely precarious and he was awaiting arrest. He saw writing

as a means of expressing to men what most of them live inwardly without being able to express, as a means of communion, a testimony to the vast flow of life through us, whose essential aspect we must try to fix for the benefit of those who will come after us.

It was an ambitious view, and it was justified. We, who come after, indeed have the benefit.

I know of no other writer with whom Serge can be very usefully compared. The essence of the man and his books is to be found in his attitude to the truth. There have of course been many scrupulously honest writers. But for Serge the value of the truth extended far beyond the simple (or complex) telling of it.

His *Memoirs*[1] open with the following sentence:

Even before I emerged from childhood, I seem to have experienced, deeply at heart, that paradoxical feeling which was to

---

1. Victor Serge, *Memoirs of a Revolutionary 1901–1941*, ed. and trans. Peter Sedgwick, Oxford University Press, 1963.

dominate me all through the first part of my life: that of living in a world without any possible escape, in which there was nothing for it but to fight for an impossible escape.

The truth for Serge was what he found in his search for the 'impossible'; it was never a mere description of the given as it appears to appear.

Early on, I learned from the Russian intelligentsia that the only meaning of life is conscious participation in the making of history. ... It follows that one must range oneself actively against everything that diminishes man, and involve oneself in all struggles which tend to liberate and enlarge him. ... This conviction has brought me, as it has brought others, to a somewhat unusual destiny: but we were, and still are, in line with the development of history, and it is now obvious that, during an entire epoch, millions of individual destinies will follow the paths along which we were the first to travel.

He recognized the forces of history traversing his time and chose to inhabit them, entering into them through both action and imagination. Yet general truths could never obliterate particular ones for him. He never saw anybody as an anonymous agent of historical forces. He could not write even of a passer-by without feeling the tension between the passer-by's inner and outer life. He identified himself imaginatively with everyone he encountered – workers, peasants, judges, crooks, rich lawyers, seamstresses, spies, traitors, heroes. It was methodologically impossible for a stereotype to occur in Serge's writing. The nature of his imagination forbade it.

Such a wide-ranging and ready sympathy combined with his sense of historical destiny might have made Serge a latter-day, inevitably fifth-rate, Tolstoy. (Inevitably because Tolstoy's view of the world was spontaneously possible only for a few decades.) But Serge was not primarily a creative writer. He wrote in order to report on what he had seen as a consequence of his actions. All his life these actions were those of a socialist revolutionary. Unlike Malraux or Koestler in their political novels, Serge was never writing about a phase of his life that was over; writing was never for him a form of renegation. Those with whom he imaginatively identified himself – whether enemies or comrades – were those on whom his life could depend. Thus, just as his imagination precluded stereotypes, his situation precluded any form of sentimental liberalism.

The truth for Serge was something to be undergone. And, if I understand him rightly, in a rather special way. Despite his very considerable intelligence and courage, Serge never proved himself a revolutionary leader. He was always, more or less, among the rank and file. This may have been partly the result of a reluctance to take any final responsibility of command (here his early anarchism corresponded with a temperamental weakness); but it was also the result of a deliberate choice concerning the category of truth he sought. If the role of the proletariat was to be as historic as Marx had declared, it was the truth of *their* experience, between the possible and the impossible, which must be judged crucial, which must define the only proper meaning of social justice.

Birth of Our Power, a novel,[2] refers to the Russian Revolution, and the book is written in the first person plural. The identity of this *we* changes.

We suffocated, about 30 of us, from seven in the morning to 6.30 at night, in the Gambert y Pia print shop.

– this in Barcelona on the eve of an abortive uprising in 1917.

We had a quiet little room with four cots, the walls papered with maps, a table loaded with books. There were always a few of us there, poring over the endlessly annotated, commented, summarized texts. There Saint-Just, Robespierre, Jacques Roux, Babeuf, Blanqui, Bakunin, were spoken of as if they had just come down to take a stroll under the trees.

– this is a group of revolutionaries thrown together in an internment camp in France in 1918.

---

2. Victor Serge, *Birth of Our Power*, trans. Richard Greeman, Gollancz, 1968.

The times when it was necessary for us to know how to accept prison, exile, poverty and – the best and strongest of us – death itself are in the past. From now on we must persist obstinately in living and only consent to everything for that.

– these are the defenders of Petrograd in the winter of 1919, starving, without fuel, the White Army closing in, nine miles away. It might be more accurate to say that the identity of Serge's *we* multiplies rather than changes.

His belief that the truth must be actively pursued, his sense of history, his power of imaginative identification, his decision to remain within the mass – this is what equipped Serge to be an exceptional witness of events. His evidence seems to carry the weight of collective experiences which he never renders abstract but which always remain precise and existential. Perhaps no other writer has been so genuine a spokesman for others.

A large part of Serge's testimony has acquired a further value. The supreme event of his life was the Russian Revolution. Everything before 1917 is attendant upon it. The revolution itself, in all its extraordinary diversity of triumphs and desperations, has no precedent. Everything that happens afterwards Serge refers back in one way or another to the opportunities taken and lost between 1917 and 1927. Very few witnesses of that decade survive to give evidence. Of the few who did, most were concerned with self-justification. Serge's testimony has become unique.

His political judgement of events can often be questioned. He tended to criticize rather than to propose. He contributed little to the theory of revolution. But on behalf of thousands of those who made, and lived through, the Russian Revolution, he set down his evidence. The possible conclusions to be drawn from this cannot be compressed into a short essay. Many of them relate to the central question of why the first successful socialist revolution occurred in an industrially backward country. Bolshevism was itself an expression of this fact – as was also the bureaucracy and the autonomous secret police which it created. Years before Stalin's dictatorship and the so-called cult of personality, this bureaucracy tended towards a totalitarianism which inevitably weakened revolutionary morale.

For Serge the first warning came with the Kronstadt uprising of 1921. Significantly, he recognized that the uprising had to be put down; what shocked him, even more than the unnecessary brutality with which this was done, was the fact that the truth about the revolt was systematically suppressed.

In 1967, the fiftieth anniversary celebrations of the Russian Revolution revealed how grossly Soviet history continues to be falsified. This falsification, which deprives not only Soviet citizens but people all over the world of the benefit of learning from certain crucial mistakes (and achievements) of the revolution, can be said to be a counter-revolutionary act. The official criteria of the U.S.S.R. are no longer those by which all revolutionary activities in the world are forced to be judged. Such is the context in which Serge is likely to be read. His life and its choices demonstrate an exemplary truth to which he was prophetically sensitive and which we should now accept as axiomatic. Institutions can be defended by lies, revolutions never.

Alexander Herzen

Many times in moments of weakness and despair, when the cup of bitterness was too full, when my whole life seemed to me nothing but one prolonged blunder, when I doubted of myself, of 'the last thing, all that is left', those words came into my head: 'Why did I not take the gun from the workman and stay at the barricades?' Struck down by a sudden bullet, I should have borne two or three beliefs with me to the grave.

Alexander Herzen died in 1870. He was fifty-eight. Most of what we read of his was written during the preceding two decades. This brings us straight away to the crux of the matter. On the one hand why does Herzen seem so peculiarly modern? And on the other hand how do we (or at least some of us) differ from him because we belong to the middle of our own century? If we cannot answer these questions and come to terms with what lies behind them, we should logically accept the despair which overtook Herzen and helped to kill him.

In England many readers must have been introduced to Herzen through E. H. Carr's book *The Romantic Exiles*.[1] It tells the very readable story of the private lives in exile of Herzen, his life-long friend Ogarev, and Bakunin; it tells it accurately and sympathetically. But despite my respect for Carr's later works as an historian, this early book seems to me to falsify by being

---

1. E. H. Carr, *The Romantic Exiles*, Gollancz, 1933; Penguin Books, 1968.

over-urbane. It presents the three men and the women with whom they were in love as though they were self-evidently *foreign*: as though there were an inevitable distinction between their unbalance and our balance. We are shown them as through a sheet of aquarium glass.

Herzen was the illegitimate son of a rich Moscow aristocrat. His father acknowledged him and later left him his very considerable fortune. But his childhood was bleak. The first volume of his *Memoirs*[2] opens with his nurse telling him about Moscow burning in 1812, the year of his own birth: a description very similar to Tolstoy's in *War and Peace*. (There are certain resemblances in character and circumstances between Herzen and Pierre Bezukhov.)

He was fourteen when the plot of the Decembrists was uncovered. He was present at the religious service in the Kremlin which commemorated the execution of the five leaders. And he swore then that to avenge these five he would devote his whole life to fighting 'the throne, the altar and the cannon'.

At Moscow University he and his friend Ogarev were among the most outspoken critics of the regime in the name of a kind of Saint-Simonist socialism. In 1834 he was arrested for these opinions (he was never involved in any actual conspiracy) and after nine months in prison was exiled to Vyatka.

Through the influence of his father he obtained in 1838 a government post in St Petersburg. But an indiscreet sentence about the police in a letter which was opened by the censor cost him another year of exile in Novgorod. After the death of his father in 1846 he left Russia for Paris and never returned. Living in Nice, Paris, Geneva, London, he became the friend and supporter of Mazzini, Bakunin, Orsini, Proudhon, Garibaldi, Kossuth, Louis Blanc and many other well-known and less-known revolutionary patriots. He offered them intelligent – even if increasingly sceptical – friendship, money, and the good offices of his occasional influence in certain official quarters.

---

2. *My Past and Thoughts: The Memoirs of Alexander Herzen*, trans. Constance Garnett, first published by Chatto & Windus, 1924–7, revised edition Chatto & Windus, 4 vols., 1968.

For ten years from 1857 Herzen and Ogarev edited *The Bell*, a monthly magazine which, printed in the Russian language in London (later Geneva) and distributed half secretly and half openly in Russia, became the first effective instrument of revolutionary propaganda directed against the Russian autocracy. The first four years of its life were the most important. In 1861 Alexander II met one of its principal demands – the freeing of the serfs. In the same year Herzen wrote passionately in support of an anti-Russian Polish uprising. *The Bell* ceased to be a unifying focal point. The young left found it merely liberal; the centre condemned it as unpatriotic.

Herzen died in Paris, disillusioned, worn out, lonely, fourteen months before the Paris Commune was proclaimed.

The easiest charge to bring against him is that he was a dilettante. But this depends on the role you wish to accord him. He was neither a political leader, nor a revolutionary activist, nor a political philosopher, and least of all a fighter obeying orders. Men in each of these categories trusted him and were grateful to him. But he was not of them. He himself only half realized what his true role was. It was to pay homage to, to exemplify, and to record the spirit of the year 1848 and its aftermath.

Our historical vocation, our work, consists in this: that by our disillusionment, by our sufferings, we reach resignation and humility in face of the truth, and spare following generations from these afflictions.

Throughout the four volumes of Herzen's *Memoirs*, which begin with his childhood and often refer to the late 1860s when he was still writing them, one feels the fatal gravitational pull of the year 1848. Towards it, all aspirations lead: from it, all disappointments arise.

One feels this all the more strongly because of a strange personal coincidence. The year 1848, besides being the year of revolution and its defeat, was the year in which Herzen's hitherto romantic and idealized marriage began to be destroyed, and the agony of its destruction continued through the four years of France's mounting political corruption and confusion. Finally Herzen's young wife, as a consequence of her sufferings during those years, died on 2 May 1852, the very Sunday of the guaranteed election whose coming and whose democratic threat so haunted Napoleon III that he had to forestall them with his coup d'état of 2 December 1851.

Herzen never recovered from the tragedy of his marriage. It turned him, at the age of forty, into a kind of elderly stoic: sceptical, limited in ambition, consoled to some degree by the memories of his youth, capable of appreciating the energy of others but incapable of fully committing himself, withdrawn.

His *Memoirs* are brilliantly discursive and in a characteristically Russian manner continually move between the personal and the public, the historical and the introspective. And so what they offer is an extraordinarily contradictory, deeply cut but homogeneous cross-section through a life lived and history observed. The writer's nostalgia for the purity of his youthful aspirations gives a contrary dimension to the bloated revival of the Napoleonic legend; his scepticism illumines in the same negative way the profound vulgarity of the Second Empire; his aloofness throws into relief the new 'democracy' of commerce; his aristocratic assumptions reveal the measure of the French bourgeois triumph. And all the while he mixes with men who persist with different visions of liberation and revolutionary change.

Herzen and Marx were mutually disagreeable about each other. Yet it is hard to imagine a work more complementary to Marx's *Eighteenth Brumaire* than Herzen's *Memoirs*. The memoirs encompass the experience – or a very great part of it – which Marx's great model essay explains.

To return now to the original question. Why do the *Memoirs* strike us as peculiarly modern? First, because no socialist revolution since 1848 has yet succeeded in a highly industrialized capitalist society. Political events often still follow the same pattern. For example, the manner in which during the crisis of May 1968 de Gaulle was able to manoeuvre and lever the electorate and the constitution was remarkably similar to Louis

Napoleon's. Furthermore there are many prophetic pages in Herzen about what he calls 'the great trade routes' of consumer societies. Secondly, because Herzen's style – perhaps because he was an exile writing for friends – is remarkably free of nineteenth-century *public* rhetoric; in this respect, if in no other, he somewhat resembles Stendhal. Thirdly, because his attitude towards authority and therefore towards most social situations is profoundly un-bourgeois – the temper of his reactions is libertarian in the broadest sense of the term – his sympathies are not with those who maintain order but with those who recognize the arbitrariness of that order.

In so far as they can be demonstrated in a single passage, these characteristics are evident in the following:

This time he led me into a big office. There a tall, stout, rosy-cheeked gentleman was sitting in a big easy-chair at a huge table. He was one of those persons who are always hot, with white flesh, fat but flabby, plump, carefully tended hands, a necktie reduced to a minimum, colourless eyes and the jovial expression which is usually found in men who are completely immersed in love for their own wellbeing, and who can have recourse, coldly and without great effort, to extraordinary infamies.

'You wished to see the prefect,' he said to me; 'but he asks you to excuse him; he has been obliged to go out on very important business. If I can do anything in any way for your pleasure I ask nothing better. Here is an easy-chair: will you sit down?'

All this he brought out smoothly, very politely, screwing up his eyes a little and smiling with the little cushions of flesh which adorned his cheekbones. 'Well, this fellow has been in the service for a long time,' I thought.

'You surely know what I've come about.' He made that gentle movement of the head which everyone makes on beginning to swim, and did not answer.

'I have received an order to leave within three days. Since I know that your minister has the right of expulsion without giving a reason or holding an inquiry, I am not going to inquire why I am being expelled ...'

Yet why, finally, does Herzen belong to a different historical period? How are we able to avoid sharing his despair?

To answer this fully one would have to treat of numerous world-historical developments. But there is an answer in microcosm. Compare the quotations from Herzen with this typical one from the *Eighteenth Brumaire of Louis Bonaparte*:

Finally, the culminating point of the '*idées Napoléoniennes*' is the preponderance of the *army*. The army was the *point d'honneur* of the peasants, it was they themselves transformed into heroes, defending their new possessions against the outer world, glorifying their recently won nationality, plundering and revolutionizing the world. The uniform was their own state dress; war was their poetry; the smallholding, extended and rounded off in imagination, was their fatherland, and patriotism the ideal form of the property sense.

The substance of what Marx is saying here, although brilliant, is beside our purpose, but not the manner of seeing and thinking. Every articulation of the thought involves a connection between opposites. Simply to call this dialectical may be to miss the point. The words do not accumulate to confirm one another; each articulation supersedes the preceding one. One might argue that this is in the nature of writing itself; in life one begins at the beginning: in literature one begins at the end. But in Marx's mode of thinking the degree to which each superseding phase of the thought modifies the orientation of the preceding phase is new, because it plays upon a new notion of discontinuity. The model is no longer an edifice constructed stone by stone or phase by phase, but a pivotal balance like that of a pair of scales or a see-saw. The total of the phases no longer covers an extensive area, but instead defines a single point occupying no space at all. From paragraph to paragraph one proceeds by leaps from point to point.

Many Marxists and anti-Marxists have been so anxious to prove or disprove the letter of Marx's prophecies that they have ignored one of the ways in which he was most profoundly and incontrovertibly prophetic. The mode of discontinuity demonstrated by Marx's thinking has now become an essential part of the modern means of communication. Discontinuity is now intrinsic to our view of reality.

For Herzen continuity was the condition of civilization. This continuity is implicit in his manner of relating and writing. Each phase confirms the next. He is never aware of the force of what is *not* being said (which is perhaps a test for judging truly modern writers). A serious break in continuity means for him chaos, disintegration, barbarism. He sees revolution as the culminating point of long-cherished ideals and aspirations. He underestimates the revolutionary element of explosive desperation. And this is because he is blind to the gaping discontinuities within society, within the world. He is fully aware of the terrible inequalities which exist, but he does not see that they are such that, as between classes, as between the privileged and the exploited, everything changes its entire value and meaning. Finally he despairs at the recalcitrance of a monolithic mankind.

This is not to suggest that political despair can no longer exist. At times it may be even more total, but it will be less final. Today such despair borders on the revolutionary recognition that continuity in the world, as it is, is impossible and intolerable.

Walter Benjamin

Walter Benjamin was born of a bourgeois Jewish family in Berlin in 1892. He studied philosophy and became a kind of literary critic – a kind such as had never quite existed before. Every page, every object which attracted his attention, contained, he believed, a coded testament addressed to the present: coded so that its message should not become a straight highway across the intervening period blocked with the traffic of direct causality, the military convoys of progress and the gigantic pantechnicons of inherited institutionalized ideas.

He was at one and the same time a romantic antiquarian and an aberrant Marxist revolutionary. The structuring of his thought was theological and Talmudic; his aspirations were materialist and dialectical. The resulting tension is typically revealed in such a sentence as: 'The concept of life is given its due only if everything that has a history of its own, and is not merely the setting for history, is credited with life.'

The two friends who probably influenced him most were Gerhard Scholem, a Zionist professor of Jewish mysticism in Jerusalem, and Bertolt Brecht. His life style was that of a financially independent nineteenth-century 'man of letters', yet he was never free of severe financial difficulties. As a writer he was obsessed with giving the objective existence of his subject its full weight (his dream was to compose a book entirely of quotations); yet he was incapable of writing a sentence which does not demand that one accept his own highly idiosyncratic procedure of thought. For example: 'What seems paradoxical about everything that is justly called beautiful is the fact that it appears.'

The contradictions of Walter Benjamin – and I have listed only some of them above – continually interrupted his work and career. He never wrote the full-length book he intended on Paris at the time of the Second Empire, seen architecturally, sociologically, culturally, psychologically, as the quintessential locus of mid-nineteenth-century capitalism. Most of what he wrote was fragmentary and aphoristic. During his lifetime his work reached a very small public and every 'school' of thought – such as might have encouraged and promoted him – treated him as an unreliable eclectic. He was a man whose originality precluded his reaching whatever was defined by his contemporaries as achievement. He was treated, except by a few personal friends, as a failure. Photographs show the face of a man rendered slow and heavy by the burden of his own existence, a burden made almost overwhelming by the rapid instantaneous brilliance of his scarcely controllable insights.

In 1940 he killed himself for fear of being captured by the Nazis while trying to cross the French frontier into Spain. It is unlikely that he would have been captured. But from a reading of his works it appears likely that suicide may have seemed a natural end for him. He was very conscious of the degree to which a life is given form by its death; and he may have decided to choose that form for himself, bequeathing to life his contradictions still intact.

Fifteen years after Benjamin's death a two-volume edition of his writings was published in Germany and he acquired a posthumous public reputation. In the last five years this reputation has begun to become international and now there are frequent references to him in articles, conversation, criticism and political discussions.

Why is Benjamin more than a literary critic? And why has his work had to wait nearly half a century to begin to find its proper audience? In trying to answer these two questions, we will perhaps recognize more clearly the need in us which

Benjamin now answers and which, never at home in his own time, he foresaw.

The antiquarian and the revolutionary can have two things in common: their rejection of the present as given and their awareness that history has allotted them a task. For them both history is vocational. Benjamin's attitude as a critic to the books or poems or films he criticized was that of a thinker who needed a fixed object before him in historic time, in order thereby to measure time (which he was convinced was not homogeneous) and to grasp the import of the specific passage of time which separated him and the work, to redeem, as he would say, that time from meaninglessness.

Only that historian will have the gift of fanning the spark of hope in the past who is firmly convinced that *even the dead* will not be safe from the enemy (the ruling class) if he wins. And this enemy has not ceased to be victorious.

Benjamin's hypersensitivity to the dimension of time was not, however, limited to the scale of historical generalization or prophecy. He was equally sensitive to the time scale of a life –

A la Recherche du temps perdu is the constant attempt to charge an entire lifetime with the utmost awareness. Proust's method is actualization, not reflexion. He is filled with the insight that none of us has time to live the true dramas of the life that we are destined for. This is what ages us – this and nothing else. The wrinkles and creases on our faces are the registration of the great passions, vices, insights that called on us; but we, the masters, were not home.

– or to the effect of a second. He is writing about the transformation of consciousness brought about by the film:

Our taverns and our metropolitan streets, our offices and furnished rooms, our railroad stations and our factories appeared to have us locked up hopelessly. Then came the film and burst this prison-world asunder by the dynamite of the tenth of a second, so that now, in the midst of its far-flung ruins and debris, we calmly and adventurously go travelling. With the close-up, space expands; with slow motion, movement is extended ...

I do not wish to give the impression that Benjamin used works of art or literature as convenient illustrations to already formulated arguments. The principle that works of art are not for use but only for judgement, that the critic is an impartial go-between between the utilitarian and the ineffable, this principle, with all its subtler and still current variations, represents no more than a claim by the privileged that their love of passive pleasure must be considered disinterested! Works of art await use. But their real usefulness lies in what they actually are – which may be quite distinct from what they once were – rather than in what it may be convenient to believe they are. In this sense Benjamin used works of art very realistically. The passage of time which so intrigued him did not end at the exterior surface of the work, it entered into it and there led him into its 'after-life'. In this after-life, which begins when the work has reached 'the age of its fame', the separatedness and isolated identity of the individual work is transcended just as was meant to happen to the soul in the traditional Christian heaven. The work enters the totality of what the present consciously inherits from the past, and in entering that totality it changes it. The after-life of Baudelaire's poetry is not only coexistent with Jeanne Duval, Edgar Allen Poe and Constantin Guys but also, for example, with Haussmann's boulevards, the first department stores, Engels's descriptions of the urban proletariat and the birth of the modern drawing-room in the 1830s which Benjamin described as follows:

For the private citizen, for the first time the living-space became distinguished from the place of work. The former constituted itself as the interior. The counting-house was its complement. The private citizen who in the counting-house took reality into account required of the interior that it should maintain him in his illusions. This necessity was all the more pressing since he had no intention of adding social preoccupations to his business ones. In the creation of his private environment he suppressed them both. From this sprang the phantasmagorias of the interior. This represented the universe for the private citizen. In it, he assembled the distant in space and in time. His drawing-room was a box in the world theatre.

Perhaps it is now a little clearer why Benjamin was more than a literary critic. But one more point needs to be made. His attitude to works of art was never a mechanically social–historical one. He never tried to seek simple causal relations between the social forces of a period and a given work. He did not want to explain the appearance of the work; he wanted to discover the place that its existence needed to occupy in our knowledge. He did not wish to encourage a love of literature; he wanted the art of the past to realize itself in the choices men make today in deciding their own historical role.

Why is it only now that Benjamin begins to be appreciated as a thinker, and why is his influence likely to increase still further in the 1970s? The awakened interest in Benjamin co-incides with Marxism's current re-examination of itself; this re-examination is occurring all over the world, even where it is treated as a crime against the state.

Many developments have led to the need for re-examinations: the extent and degree of the pauperization and violence which imperialism and neo-colonialism inflict upon an ever-increasing majority in the world; the virtual depoliticization of the people of the Soviet Union: the re-emergence of the question of revo-lutionary *democracy* as primary; the achievements of China's *peasant* revolution; the fact that the proletariats of consumer societies are now less likely to arrive at revolutionary con-sciousness through the pursuit of their directly economic self-interests than through a wider and more generalized sense of pointless deprivation and frustration; the realization that socialism, let alone communism, cannot be fully achieved in one country so long as capitalism exists as a global system, and so on.

What the re-examinations will entail, both in terms of theory and political practice, cannot be foreseen in advance or from outside the specific territories involved. But we can begin to define the interregnum – the period of re-examination – in rela-tion to what actually preceded it, whilst leaving sensibly aside the claims and counter-claims concerning what Marx himself really meant.

The interregnum is anti-deterministic, both as regards the present being determined by the past and the future by the present. It is sceptical of so-called historical laws, as it is also sceptical of any supra-historical value, implied by the notion of overall Progress or Civilization. It is aware that excessive personal political power always depends for its survival upon appeals to an impersonal destiny: that every true revolutionary act must derive from a personal hope of being able to contest in that act the world as it is. The interregnum exists in an invisible world, where time is short, and where the immorality of the conviction that ends justify means lies in the arrogance of the assumption that time is always on one's own side and that, therefore, the present moment – the time of the Now, as Benjamin called it – can be compromised or forgotten or denied.

Benjamin was not a systematic thinker. He achieved no new synthesis. But at a time when most of his contemporaries still accepted logics that hid the facts, he foresaw our interregnum. And it is in this context that thoughts like the following from his *Theses on the Philosophy of History* apply to our present preoccupations:

The true picture of the past flits by. The past can be seized only as an image which flashes up at the instant when it can be recognized and is never seen again. 'The truth will not run away from us': in the historical outlook of historicism these words of Gottfried Keller mark the exact point where historical materialism cuts through historicism. For every image of the past that is not recognized by the present as one of its own concerns threatens to disappear irretrievably.

A historical materialist cannot do without the notion of a present which is not a transition, but in which time stands still and has come to a stop. For this notion defines the present in which he himself is writing history.

Whoever has emerged victorious participates to this day in the triumphal procession in which the present rulers step over those who are lying prostrate. According to traditional practice, the spoils are carried along in the procession. They are called cultural treasures, and a historical materialist views them with cautious detachment. For without exception the cultural treasures he surveys have an origin which he cannot contemplate without horror. They owe their existence not only to the efforts of the great minds and talents who have created them, but also to the anonymous toil of their contemporaries. There is no document of civilization which is not at the same time a document of barbarism.

Success and Failure

Notes from an
Exhibition on Romanticism
at the Tate Gallery, 1959

Romantic Notebooks

It was with a kind of shame-faced surprise that I realized how great a painter Constable was. Shame-faced because after all one ought to have realized it before. In an exhibition at the Tate, in 1959, he shared the honours with Goya – born thirty years earlier. (Not learning dates is disastrous; comparative dates are an unfailing stimulus to thought. I only discovered the other day that the Danish astronomer Römer was the first man to suggest that light was not instantaneous but had a fixed velocity. This was in 1675. Rembrandt died in 1669.)

It was a good idea to hang the sketches for the *Leaping Horse* and *Salisbury Cathedral* next to the finished canvases. I must say I agree with Constable's contemporaries rather than his later admirers: the finished versions seem to me much better. Admittedly the sky in the final *Leaping Horse* has gone a bit steamy, but the organization of the painting as a whole is so much tauter. Constable constructed his landscapes much more than people think – he didn't just tear leaves out of nature. What misleads people is the extraordinary skill with which he painted landscape surfaces, comparable to Rubens's skill in painting flesh. And landscape surfaces are of course a question of light. The light in a Constable masterpiece is like water dripping off the gunwale of a boat as it drives through the sea. It suggests the way the whole scene is surging through the day, dipping through sun and cloud. By comparison the light of most other landscape painters is either like a fountain, playing prettily up and down for no purpose, or like water running flatly out of a tap.

Compare the Constables with the landscapes of Caspar David Friedrich. The Friedrichs are indeed admirable. But for almost entirely negative reasons. He looked at the German landscape with a kind of artless honesty. Wordsworth would surely have admired him. And through his eyes we look at the pine-forests in the snow or the bare hill in the dusk, and say to ourselves, 'How such scenes humble us, how small the mark we make upon them.' Whereas in front of a Constable we are aware of mastery – like seeing a mountain through the eyes of a man who has climbed it. In art it isn't just the moral virtue of humility that is needed – if it were, Friedrich would be a master; rather it is a healthy respect for the difficulties of the job, a caution maintained in order to achieve victory, not just a turning of the other cheek.

*

My personal *bêtes noires*: Samuel Palmer with his landscapes like furnished wombs; Landseer's *The Hunting of Chevy Chase* – like fox furs at a cocktail party round a tired social lion; Wright of Derby's portrait of Sir Brooke Boothby with his long, gauche body reclining on the grass, his suede volume and his face like a stupid widow's in a Restoration comedy, but even more like a representative of the British Council; Etty expiring on the body of *Hero Expiring on the Body of Leander*.

*

The two most difficult pictures to appreciate – the equestrian portraits by David of Napoleon and Stanislas-Kostka Potocki. All that once told for them now tells against them – the heroic prance, the manes like the locks of Greek goddesses, the tailoring and the grooming. But what paintings they are! They move me as they once moved Léger and as Légers move me now. In these pictures even the shadows fall for man. They have a clarity which inspires supreme confidence. This clarity is the result of their formal organization in an almost abstract sense. But the all-important difference between these and literally abstract works is that here the order has been imposed on reality. As soon as a system of geometry ceases to explain the phenomena we know, it has to be discarded. Geometry is concerned with patterns, but the last thing it is is pattern-making.

*

In the gallery of portraits there is only one man who is not posing: Don Ramon Satué, painted by Goya. All the others act; he watches. The drama is within himself. I cannot fully explain how Goya expresses his extraordinary psychological insight, an insight which separates him from all his contemporaries and all his predecessors. That is to say, I don't know how he communicates his discoveries *through* his painting. It is as if Goya were never in front of his subject, but always behind it – as if he were disinterested for himself, invisible, yet always present and profoundly involved – like a ghost. In this way he shows us prisoners demonstrating all the few movements that are possible when your ankles and wrists are manacled; two soldiers carting off a woman to rape her, the front one carrying her legs like an awkward, over-heavy mattress; a young girl on a balcony beside an old woman, the differences between them not just those which any man would notice, but rather those caused by the young girl's idea of herself. No one is aware of Goya. He doesn't even haunt us. He simply shows us our own breath on the mirror.

*

The talent to be single-minded – that is the rarity. Other talents are as common as roses. Géricault was a clumsy painter and frantically impatient. Delacroix had ten times as much skill – and was ten times as diffuse in his aims. Consequently Géricault was great in himself, representing and demonstrating a particular kind of ambition in painting; whilst in Delacroix there

are only magnificent details – like the light on the torso of
the *Woman with the Parrot*, a square section of light limited
by the window frame we can't see. Géricault wanted above all
to produce tangible images, to be committed to the physical
reality. For this reason he painted soldiers. For this reason he
painted the horses that he rode until they killed him. For this
reason he painted the inmates of the asylum, the survivors of
The Raft, the dying. In these studies there is little psychological
understanding and even less philanthropy. What there is is a
passionate self-identification, a desire to be all that is suffering,
mortal and therefore sentient. To put it crudely – as he himself
would have liked it – this paid off. At the end of his short life
he painted *The Lime Kiln*: two outhouses, a few carthorses,
some smoke and mud. This small canvas is the only one that
tells us truly what the texture of life was like in the first half of
the nineteenth century. That smoke is what Blake smelt. That
corner is where a dozen Chartists met. That level of scientific
development was what couldn't save Keats.

*

Turner is often thought of as the great painter of natural
forces – water, wind and fire. But was he? When you look at
The Burning of the Houses of Parliament, *The Destruction of
Sodom*, *The Slave Ship*, *Hannibal Crossing the Alps*, you find
yourself thinking that it's all the same force, which isn't a
natural force at all but a philosophical one. Turner was more a
painter of ideas than is usually realized. And like many of his
nineteenth-century contemporaries he was obsessed by the idea
of destiny. (What natural selection meant for Darwin and
the class struggle meant for Marx, the whirlpool meant for
Turner.)

I think this explains why his figures are so frequently like
Jonahs, being 'sucked away' by the water or light. And also it
explains the apparent contrast between his pedantic exercises
in the manner of Claude and the seeming boldness of his later
works: in fact none of his work was based on great, first-hand
visual discoveries: his ideas and fantasies simply became more

independent and eccentric. I don't mean this to sound disparaging. Turner was repetitive, at times bombastic and probably over-estimated during his lifetime, but at his best he was still incomparable. The *Houses of Parliament* canvas and *The Slave Ship* are unforgettable. He organized compositions such as had never been conceived before, substituting a plume of smoke for a pillar, waves for hills, fire for drapery. But it is important to understand what kind of artist he was. He extended the possibilities of painting in terms of subject matter, and in this way was a forerunner not only of Impressionism but also of Expressionism. He did not, however, establish a new way of seeing – as did Constable, or Courbet or Cézanne.

*

Cézanne's copy after Delacroix's *La Barque de Dante* is a very small canvas, and yet momentous in its example. In it one can see the whole struggle which lay behind Cézanne's renunciation of his own Romanticism. Foothold by foothold he climbs out of the pit to which Romanticism by that date was bound to condemn him. The boat, the rough sea, Dante's red cloak – all the Romantic ingredients are there, and yet he reinterprets Delacroix in order to do away with everything that is mysterious, in order to establish a logic and clarity utterly opposed to Romanticism. He traces the undulations of form across a torso, and so anxious is he to reveal and explain every variation that the torso becomes far wider than it naturally would be. (Was it such widening, the result of his punctilious, clumsy integrity, that first suggested to Cézanne the advantage of having more than one viewpoint, because later he certainly widened out forms quite deliberately?) The painting makes one wonder what nineteenth-century Romanticism bequeathed to us. Abstract Expressionism is of course a pure form of latter-day Romanticism. But the bequest is fortunately more positive than that. Leaving aside all that the Romantics did historically by establishing new subjects, they changed the nature of culture even for those who have no wish to follow them. They separated fervour from ambition. They questioned immediate success and success has never been quite the same since. Cézanne could never have borne the apparent failure of his life's work unless he had been sustained by the Romanticism he was working to overthrow.

Drawings by Watteau

Delicacy in art is not necessarily the opposite of strength. A water-colour on silk can have a more powerful effect on the spectator than a ten-foot figure in bronze. Most of Watteau's drawings are so delicate, so tentative, that they almost appear to have been done in secret; as though he were drawing a butterfly that had alighted on a leaf in front of him and was frightened that the movement or noise of his chalk on the paper would scare it away. Yet at the same time they are drawings which reveal an enormous power of observation and feeling.

This contrast gives us a clue to Watteau's temperament and the underlying theme of his art. Although he mostly painted clowns, harlequins, fêtes and what we would now call fancy-dress balls, his theme was tragic: the theme of mortality. He suffered from tuberculosis and probably sensed his own early death at the age of thirty-seven. Possibly he also sensed that the world of aristocratic elegance he was employed to paint was also doomed. The courtiers assemble for *The Embarkation for Cythera* (one of his most famous paintings), but the poignancy of the occasion is due to the implication that when they get there it will not be the legendary place they expect – the guillotines will be falling. (Some critics suggest that the courtiers are *returning* from Cythera; but either way there is a poignant contrast between the legendary and the real.) I do not mean that Watteau actually foresaw the French Revolution or painted prophesies. If he had, his works might be less important today than they are, because the prophesies would now be outdated. The theme of his art was simply change, transcience, the brevity of each moment – poised like the butterfly.

Such a theme could have led him to sentimentality and wispy nostalgia. But it was at this point that his ruthless observation of reality turned him into a great artist. I say ruthless because an artist's observation is not just a question of his using his eyes; it is the result of his honesty, of his fighting with himself to understand what he sees. Look at his self-portrait. It is a slightly feminine face: the gentle eyes, like the eyes of a woman painted by Rubens, the mouth full for pleasure, the fine ear tuned to hear romantic songs or the romantic echo of the sea in the shell that is the subject of another one of his drawings. But look again further, for behind the delicate skin and the impression of dalliance is the skull. Its implications are only whispered, by the dark accent under the right cheek bone, the shadows round the eyes, the drawing of the ear that emphasizes the temple in front of it. Yet this whisper, like a stage whisper, is all the more striking because it is not a shout. 'But,' you may object, 'every drawing of a head discloses a skull because the form of any head depends upon the skull.' Of course. There is, however, all the difference in the world between a skull as structure and a skull as a presence. Just as eyes can gaze through a mask, thus belying the disguise, so in this drawing bone seems to gaze through the very flesh, as thin in places as silk.

In a drawing of a woman with a mantle over her head Watteau makes the same comment by opposite means. Here instead of contrasting the flesh with the bone beneath it, he contrasts it with the cloth that is over it. How easy it is to imagine this mantle preserved in a museum – and the wearer dead. The contrast between the face and the drapery is like the contrast between the clouds in the sky above and the cliff and buildings beneath, in a landscape drawing. The line of the woman's mouth is as transient as the silhouette of a bird in flight.

On a sketch-book page with two drawings of a child's head on it, there is also a marvellous study of a pair of hands tying a ribbon. And here analysis breaks down. It is impossible to explain why that loosely tied knot in the ribbon can so easily be transformed into a symbol of the loosely tied knot of human life; but such a transformation is not far-fetched and certainly coincides with the mood of the whole page.

I do not want to suggest that Watteau was always consciously concerned with mortality, that he was morbidly concerned with death. Not at all. To his contemporary patrons this aspect of his work was probably invisible. He never enjoyed great success, but he was appreciated for his skill – very serious in, for example, his portrait of a Persian diplomat – his elegance, and for what would then have seemed his romantic languor. And today one can also consider other aspects of his work: for instance, his masterly technique of drawing.

He usually drew with a chalk – either red or black. The softness of this medium enabled him to achieve the gentle, undulating sense of movement that is typical of his drawing. He described as no other artist has done the way silk falls and the way the light falls on the falling silk. His boats ride on the swell of the sea and the light glances along their hulls with the same undulating rhythm. His studies of animals are full of the *fluency* of animal movement. Everything has its tidal movement, slow or edging – look at the cats' fur, the children's hair, the convolutions of the shell, the cascade of the mantle, the whirlpool of the three grotesque faces, the gentle river-bend of the nude flowing to the floor, the delta-like folds across the Persian's gown. Everything is in flux. But within this flux, Watteau placed his accents, his marks of certainty that are impervious to every current. These marks make a cheek turn, a thumb articulate with a wrist, a breast press against an arm, an eye fit into its socket, a doorway have depth, or a mantle circle a head. They cut into every drawing, like slits in silk, to reveal the anatomy beneath the sheen.

The mantle will outlast the woman whose head it covers. The line of her mouth is as elusive as a bird. But the blacks either side of her neck make her head solid, precise, turnable, energetic, and thus – alive. It is the dark, accented lines which give the figure or the form life by momentarily checking the flow of the drawing as a whole.

On another level, human consciousness is such a momentary check against the natural rhythm of birth and death. And, in the same way, Watteau's consciousness of mortality, far from being morbid, increases one's awareness of life.

Fernand Léger

Since the middle of the last century all artists of any worth have been forced to consider the future because their works have been misunderstood in the present. The very concept of the avant-garde suggests this. The qualitative meaning that the word *modern* has acquired suggests it too. *Modern Art*, for those who have produced it, has meant not the art of today, as opposed to yesterday: but the art of tomorrow as opposed to the conservative tastes of today. Every important painter since 1848 has had to rely upon his faith in the future. The fact that he has believed that the future will be different and *better* has been the result of his awareness (sometimes fully conscious and sometimes only dimly sensed) of living in a time of profound social change. *From the middle of the last century socialism has promised the alternative which has kept the future open, which has made the power (and the philistinism) of the ruling classes seem finite.* It would be absurd to suggest that all the great painters of the last century were socialists; but what is certainly true is that all of them made innovations in the hope of serving a richer future.

Fernand Léger (1881–1955) was unique in that he made his vision of this future the theme of his art.

*

Léger's subjects are cities, machinery, workers at work, cyclists, picnickers, swimmers, women in kitchens, the circus, acrobats, still-lifes – often of functional objects such as keys, umbrellas, pincers – and landscapes. A similar list of Picasso's recurring subjects might be as follows: bullfights, the minotaur, goddesses, women in armchairs, mandolins, skulls, owls, clowns, goats, fawns, other painters' paintings. In his preoccupations Picasso does not belong to the twentieth century. It is in the use to which he puts his temperament that Picasso is a modern man. The other major painters of the same generation – Braque, Matisse, Chagall, Rouault – have all been concerned with very specialized subjects. Braque, for instance, with the interior of his studio; Chagall with the Russian memories of his youth. No other painter of his generation except Léger has consistently included in his work the objects and materials with which everybody who now lives in a city is surrounded every day of his life. In the work of what other artist could you find cars, metal frames, templates, girders, electric wires, number plates, road signs, gas stoves, functional furniture, bicycles, tents, keys, locks, cheap cups and saucers?

Léger then is exceptional because his art is full of direct references to modern urban life. But this could not in itself make him an important painter. The function of painting is not that of a pictorial encyclopedia. We must go further and now ask: what do these references add up to? What is Léger's interest in the tools, artefacts and ornaments of the twentieth-century city?

*

When one studies an artist's life work as a whole, one usually finds that he has an underlying, constant theme, a kind of hidden but *continuous* subject. For example, Géricault's continuous subject was endurance. Rembrandt's continuous subject was the process of ageing. The continuous subject reflects the bias of the artist's imagination; it reveals that area of experience to which his temperament forces him to return again and again, and from which he creates certain standards of interest with which to judge ordinary disparate subjects as they present themselves to him. There is hardly a painting by Rembrandt where the significance of growing older is not in some way emphasized. The continuous subject of Matisse is the balm of leisure. The continuous subject of Picasso is the cycle of creation and destruction. The continuous subject of Léger is mechanization. He cannot paint a landscape without including in it the base of a pylon or some telegraph wires. He cannot paint a tree without placing sawn planks or posts next to it. Whenever he paints a natural object, he juxtaposes it deliberately with a manufactured one – as though the comparison increased the value of each. Only when he paints a woman, naked, is he content to let her remain incomparable.

A number of twentieth-century artists have been interested by machines – although, surprising as it may seem, the majority have not. The Futurists in Italy, Mondrian and the de Stijl group in Holland, the Constructivists in Russia, Wyndham Lewis and the Vorticists in England, artists like Roger de la Fresnaye and Robert Delaunay in France, all constructed for themselves aesthetic theories based on the machine, but not one of them thought of the machine as a means of production, making inevitable revolutionary changes in the relations between men. Instead they saw it as a god, a 'symbol' of modern life, the means with which to satisfy a personal lust for power, a Frankenstein's monster, or a fascinating enigma. They treated the machine as though it were a new star in the sky, although they disagreed about interpreting its portents. Only Léger was different. Only Léger saw the machine for what it is – a tool: a tool both practically and historically in the hands of men.

*

This is perhaps the best place to examine the frequently made accusation that Léger sacrifices the human to the mechanical and that his figures are as 'cold' as robots. I have heard this argument in Bond Street – put forward by those who, if they pay their money, expect art to console them for the way the world is going; but I have also heard it in Moscow, put forward by art experts who want to judge Léger by the standards of Repin. The misunderstanding arises because Léger is something so rare in recent European art that we have almost forgotten the existence of the category of art to which he belongs. He is an *epic* painter. That is not to say that he paints illustrations to Homer. It is to say that he sees his constant subject of *mechanization* as a human epic, an unfolding adventure of which man is the hero. If the word was not discredited one could equally say that he was a monumental painter. He is not concerned with individual psychology or with nuances of sensation: he is concerned with action and conquest. Because the standards by which we judge painting have been created since the Renaissance and because in general this has been the period of the bourgeois discovery of the individual, there have been very few epic painters. In an extraordinarily complex way Michelangelo was one, and if one compares Léger with Michelangelo, from whom he learnt a great deal, one sees how 'traditional' Léger suddenly becomes. But the best test of all is to place Léger beside the fifth-century Greek sculptors. Naturally there are enormous differences. But the quality of emotions implied and *the distance at which the artist stands from the personality of his subject* – these are very similar. The figures, for example, in *Les Perroquets* are no 'colder' or more impersonal than the Doryphorus of Polyclitus. It is absurd to apply the same standards to all categories of art, and it betrays an essential vulgarization of taste to do so. The epic artist struggles to find an image for the whole of mankind. The lyric artist struggles to present the world in the image of his own individualized experience. They both face reality, but they stand back to back.

*

Léger's attitude to mechanization did not stay the same all his life. It changed and developed as his political and historical understanding increased. Very roughly his work can be divided into three periods. I will try briefly to put into words the attitude suggested by each period so as to make it easier to grasp his *general* approach and the consistent direction of his thinking.

In his early work, up to about 1918, he was fascinated (it is worth remembering that he came from a family of Norman farmers) by the basic material of modern industry – steel. He became a Cubist, but for him, unlike most of the other Cubists, the attraction of Cubism was not in its intellectual system but in its use of essentially manufactured *metallic* shapes. The turning, the polishing, the grinding, the cutting of steel, were all processes which fired the young Léger with a sense of modernity and a new kind of beauty. The cleanness and strength of the new material may also have suggested a symbolic contrast with the hypocrisy and corruption of the bourgeois world that plunged with self-congratulation and inane confidence into the 1914 war. I am of course simplifying and I don't want to mislead as a result. Léger did not paint pictures of steel. He painted and drew nudes, portraits, soldiers, guns, aeroplanes, trees, a wedding. But in all his work at this time he uses shapes (and often colours) which suggest metal and a new awareness of speed and mechanical strength. All the artists of that period were aware of living on the threshold of a new world. They knew they were heralds. But it was typical of Léger that the new was epitomized for him by a new *material*.

*

The second period in Léger's work lasted roughly from 1920 to 1930. His interest shifted from basic materials to finished, machine-made products. He began to paint still lifes, interiors, street scenes, workshops, all contributing to the same idea : the idea of the mechanized city. In many of the paintings, figures are introduced : women in modern kitchens with children, men with machines. The relationship of the figures to their environment is very important. It is this that prevents anyone suspecting that Léger is only celebrating commodity goods for their own sake. These modern kitchens are not advertisements for paints, linoleum or up-to-date bungalows. They are an attempt to show (but in terms of painting and not lectures) how modern technology and modern means of production can enable men to build the environment they need, *so that nature and the material world can become fully humanized.* In these paintings it is as though Léger is saying : It is no longer necessary to separate man from what he makes, for he now has the power to make all that he needs, so that what he has and what he makes will become an extension of himself. And this was based, in Léger's mind, on the fact that for the first time in history, we have the productive means to create a world of plenty.

*

The third period lasted roughly from 1930 to Léger's death in 1955. Here the centre of interest moved again; this time from the means of production to productive relations. During these twenty-five years he painted such subjects as cyclists, picnickers, acrobats, swimmers diving, building-workers. At first these subjects may seem mysteriously irrelevant to what I have just said. But let me explain further. All these subjects involve groups of people, and in every case these people are depicted in such a way that no one can doubt that they are modern workers. One could, more generally, say therefore that in this period Léger's recurring subjects were workers at work and at leisure. They are not of course documentary paintings. Further, they make no direct comment at all on working conditions at the time at which they were painted. Like almost every picture Léger painted, they are affirmative, gay, happy and, by comparison with the works of most of his contemporaries, strangely carefree. You may ask : What is the significance of these paintings? Can they do nothing but smile?

I believe that their significance is really very obvious, and has been so little understood only because most people have not bothered to trace Léger's development even as sketchily as we are doing now. Léger knew that new means of production make new social relations inevitable; he knew that industrialization, which originally only capitalism could implement, had already created a working class which would eventually destroy capitalism and establish socialism. For Léger this process (which one describes in abstract language) became implicit in the very sight of a pair of pliers, an earphone, a reel of unused film. And in the paintings of his last period he was prophetically celebrating the liberation of man from the intolerable contradictions

of the late capitalist world. I want to emphasize that this interpretation is not the result of special pleading. It is those who
wish to deny it who must close their eyes to the facts. In painting after painting the same theme is stressed. Invariably there
is a group of figures, invariably they are connected by easy
movement one with another, invariably the meaning of this
connection is emphasized by the very tender and gentle
gestures of their hands, invariably the modern equipment, the
tackle they are using, is shown as a kind of confirmation of the
century, and invariably the figures have moved into a new
freer environment. The campers are in the country, the divers
are in the air, the acrobats are weightless, the building-workers
are in the clouds. These are paintings about freedom: that
freedom which is the result of the aggregate of human skills
when the major contradictions in the relations between men
have been removed.

*

To discuss an artist's style in words and to trace his stylistic
development is always a clumsy process. Nevertheless I should
like to make a few observations about the way Léger painted
because, unless the form of his art is considered, any evaluation
of its content becomes one-sided and distorted; also because
Léger is a very clear example of how, when an artist is *certain*
about what he wants to express, this *certainty* reveals itself as
logically in his style as in his themes or content.

I have already referred to Léger's debt to Cubism and his very
special (indeed unique) use of the language of the Cubists.
Cubism was for him the only way in which he could demonstrate the quality of the new materials and machines which
struck him so forcibly. Léger was a man who always preferred
to begin with something tangible (I shall refer later to the effect
of this on his style). He himself always referred to his subjects
as 'objects'. During the Renaissance a number of painters were
driven by a scientific passion. I think it would be true to say
that Léger was the first artist to express the passion of the
technologists. And this began with his seizing on the style of

Cubism in order to communicate his excitement about the potentiality of new materials.

*

In the second period of his work, when his interest shifted to machine-made products, the style in which he painted is a proof of how thoroughly he was aware of what he was saying. He realized (in 1918!) that mass production was bound to create new aesthetic values. It is hard for us now, surrounded by unprecedented commercial vulgarity, not to confuse the new values of mass production with the gimmicks of the salesmen, but they are not of course the same thing. Mass production turns many old aesthetic values into purely snob values. (Every woman now can have a plastic handbag which is in every way as good as a leather one: the qualities of a good leather one become therefore only the attributes of a status symbol.) The qualities of the mass-produced object are bound at first to be contrasted with the qualities of the hand-made object: their 'anonymity' will be contrasted with 'individuality', and their regularity with 'interesting' irregularity. (As pottery has become mass-produced, 'artistic' pottery, in order to emphasize and give a spurious value to its being hand-made, has become wobblier, rougher and more and more irregular.)

Léger made it a cardinal point of his style at this time to celebrate the special aesthetic value of the mass-produced object in the actual way he painted. His colours are flat and hard. His shapes are regular and fixed. There is a minimum of gesture and a minimum of textural interest (texture in painting is the easiest way to evoke 'personality'). As one looks at these paintings one has the illusion that they too could exist in their hundreds of thousands. The whole idea of a painting being a jewel-like and unique private possession is destroyed. On the contrary, a painting, we are reminded, is an image made by a man for other men and can be judged by its efficiency. Such a view of art may be partisan and one-sided, but so is any view of art held by any practising artist. The important point is that in the way he painted these pictures Léger strove to prove the argument which was their content: the argument that modern means of production should be welcomed (and not regretted as vulgar, soulless or cheap) because they offered men their first chance to create a civilization not exclusive to a minority, not founded on scarcity.

*

There are three points worth making about the style of Léger's third period. He now has to deal with far more complex and variegated subjects – whole groups of figures, figures in landscapes, etc. It is essential to his purpose that these subjects appear unified: the cloud and the woman's shoulder, the leaf and the bird's wing, the rope and the arm, must all be seen in the same way, must all be thought to exist under the same conditions. Léger now introduced light into his painting to create this unity of condition. By light I do not mean anything mysterious; I mean simply light and shade. Until the third period Léger mostly used flat local colours and the forms were established by line and colour rather than by tone. Now the forms become much more solid and sculptural because light and shade play upon them to reveal their receding and parallel planes, their rises and hollows. But the play of the light and shade does more than this: it also allows the artist to create an overall pattern, regardless of where one object or figure stops and another begins. Light passes into shade and shade into light, alternately, a little like the black and white squares of a chessboard. It is by this device that Léger is able to *equate* a cloud with a limb, a tree with a sprig, a stream with hair; and it is by the same device that he can bind a group of figures together, turning them into one *unit* in the same way as the whole chessboard can be considered one unit rather than each square. In his later work Léger used the element of light (which means nothing without shade) to suggest the essential *wholeness* of experience for which all men long and which they call freedom. The other artist to use light in a similar way was Michelangelo, and even a superficial comparison between the drawings of the two artists will reveal their closeness in this respect. The all-important difference is that for Michelangelo freedom meant lonely individuality and was therefore tragic, whereas for Léger it meant a classless society and was therefore triumphant.

*

The second point I want to make about Léger's style in his third period concerns the special use to which he discovered he could put colour. This did not happen until about the last ten years of his life. In a sense, it was a development which grew out of the use of light and shade which I have just described. He began to paint bands of colour across the features or figures of his subject. The result was a little like seeing the subject through a flag which, although quite transparent in places, imposed occasional strips or circles of colour on the scene behind. In fact it was not an arbitrary imposition: the colour strips were always designed in precise relation to the forms behind them. It is as though Léger now wanted to turn his paintings into emblems. He was no longer concerned with his subjects as they existed but with his subjects as they *could* exist. They are, if you like, paintings in the conditional mood. *La Grande Parade* represents what pleasure, entertainments, popular culture could mean. *Les Constructeurs* represents what work could mean. *Les Campeurs* represents what being at home in the world could mean. This might have led Léger to sentimental idealization and utopian dreams. It did not because Léger understood the historical process which has released and will increasingly release human potentiality. These last 'conditional mood' paintings of Léger's were not made to console and lull. They were made to remind men of what they are capable. *He did not deceive us by painting them as though the scenes already existed.* He painted them as hopes. And one of the ways in which he made this clear (he did not employ the same method in all his last pictures) was to use colour to make the pictures *emblematic.* Here I am using the word in its two senses, thinking of an emblem as both a sign and an allegory. In discussions on twentieth-century art, references are often made to *symbols.* It is usually forgotten that symbols must by definition be accessible.

In art, a private symbol is a contradiction in terms. Léger's emblems are among the few true symbols created in our time.

*

The last point I want to make about Léger's later work has nothing to do, like the first two points, with any stylistic innovation, but with a tendency which, although inherent in all Léger's painting, became stronger and more obvious and conscious as time passed: the tendency to visualize everything he wanted to paint *in terms of its being able to be handled*. His world is literally *a substantial* world: the very opposite of the world of the Impressionists. I have already said that Léger allowed no special value to the hand-made as opposed to the machine-made product. But the human hand itself filled him with awe. He made many drawings of hands. One of his favourite juxtapositions was to put a hand in front of, or beside, a face; as though to convey that without the hand all that makes the human eye human would never have occurred. He believed that man could be manager of his world and he recognized the Latin root of the word manager. *Manus.* Hand. He seized upon this truth as a metaphor, in his struggle against all cloudy mystification. Léger's clouds are in fact like pillows, his flowers are like egg-cups, his leaves are like spoons. And for the same reason he frequently introduces ladders and ropes into his pictures. He wanted to construct a world where the link between man's imagination and his ability to fashion and control with his hands was always emphasized. This, I am certain, is the principal explanation of why he simplified and stylized objects and landscapes in the way he did. He wanted to make everything he included in his art tangible and unmysterious: not because he was a mechanical nineteenth-century rationalist, but because he was so impressed by the greater mystery: the mystery of man's insatiable desire to hold and understand.

*

This is perhaps the best place to refer to the artists who influenced Léger: the artists who helped him to develop the means with which to express his unusual vision. I have already mentioned Michelangelo: for Léger he was *the* example of an artist who created an heroic, epic art based exclusively on man. Picasso and Braque, who invented Cubism, were also indispensable examples. Cubism may have meant something different to its inventors (theirs was perhaps a more consciously art-historical approach and was more closely connected with an admiration for African art) but nevertheless Cubism supplied Léger with his twentieth-century visual language. The last important influence was that of the Douanier Rousseau: the naïve Sunday painter who was treated as a joke or, later, thought to be 'delightful', but who believed himself to be a realist.

It would be foolish to exaggerate the realist element in Rousseau if one is using the word realist in its usual sense. Rousseau was quite uninterested in social issues or politics. His realism, as he believed it to be, was in no sense a protest against a specific set of social or ideological lies. But nevertheless there are elements in Rousseau's art which in a long historical perspective can be seen to have extended the possibilities of painting certain aspects of reality, to use them and transform them for his own purpose.

I will try briefly to explain what these elements were – for the connection between Léger and Rousseau is not yet sufficiently recognized. Rousseau can be termed an amateur artist in so far as he was untrained and both his social and financial position precluded him from having any place at all in the official cultural hierarchy of France. Measured by official standards he was not only totally unqualified to be an artist but also pathetically uncultured. All that he inherited was the usual stale deposit of petit-bourgeois clichés. His imagination, his imaginative experience, was always in conflict with his received culture. (If I may add a personal parenthesis, I would suggest that such conflicts have not yet been properly understood or described; which is one of the reasons why I chose such a conflict as the theme of my novel *Corker's Freedom*.[1])

---

1. John Berger, *Corker's Freedom*, Methuen, 1964.

Every picture that Rousseau painted was a testimony to the existence of an alternative, unrecognized, indeed as yet unformulated culture. This gave his work a curious, self-sufficient and uninhibited conviction. (A little similar in this, though in nothing else, to some of the works of William Blake.) Rousseau had no method to rely on if his imagination failed him : he had no art with which to distract attention, if the *idea* he was trying to communicate was weak. The *idea* of any given picture was all that he had. (One begins to realize the intensity of these ideas by the story of how he became terrified in his little Parisian room when he was painting a tiger in the jungle.) One might say – exaggerating with a paradox – that Rousseau made all the other artists of his time look like mere virtuosos. And it was probably the strength of Rousseau's 'artlessness' which first appealed to Léger, for Léger also was an artist with surprisingly little facility, for whom the *ideas* of his art were also constant and primary, and whose work was designed to testify to the existence of an alternative, unrecognized culture.

There was, then, a moral affinity between Rousseau and Léger. There was also a certain affinity of method. Rousseau's style had very little to do with the Fine Arts as they were then recognized : as little to do with the fine arts as the circus has with the Comédie Française. Rousseau's models were postcards, cheap stage scenery, shop signs, posters, fairground and café decorations. When he paints a goddess, a nude, it has far more to do – iconographically but not of course emotionally – with the booth of any Fat Lady at a fair than with a Venus by Titian. He made an art of visual wonder out of the visual scraps sold to and foisted upon the petty bourgeoisie. It has always seemed over-romantic to me to call such scraps popular art : one might just as well call second-hand clothes popular *couture*! But the important point is that Rousseau showed that it was possible to make works of art using the visual vocabulary of the streets of the Parisian suburbs instead of that of the museums. Rousseau of course used such a vocabulary because he knew no other. Léger chose a similar vocabulary because of what he wanted to say. Rousseau's spirit was nostalgic (he

looked back to a time when the world was as innocent as he)
and his ambience was that of the nineteenth century. Léger's
spirit was prophetic (he looked forward to the time when everyone would understand what he understood) and the atmosphere
of his work belongs to this century. But nevertheless as painters
they often both use similar visual prototypes. The posed group
photograph as taken by any small-town photographer; the placing of simple theatrical props to conjure up a whole scene –
Rousseau makes a jungle out of plants in pots, Léger makes a
countryside out of a few logs : the clear-cut poster where everything must be defined – so that it can be read from a distance –
and mystery must never creep into the method of drawing :
flags and banners to make a celebration : brightly coloured
prints of uniforms or dresses – in the pictures of Rousseau and
Léger all the clothes worn are easily identifiable and there is a
suggested pride in the wearing of them which belongs essentially to the city street. There is also a similarity in the way both
artists painted the human head itself. Both tend to enlarge and
simplify the features, eyes, nose, mouth, and in doing this, because the mass of people think of a head as a face and a face
as a sequence of features to be read like signs – 'shifty eyes',
'smiling mouth' – both come far nearer to the popular imagination of the storyteller, the clown, the singer, the actor, than to
the 'ideal proportions' of the 'Fine' artist.

Lastly, one further element in Rousseau's art which seems to
have been important for Léger : its happiness. Rousseau's paintings are affirmative and certain : they reject and dispel all
doubt and anxiety : they express none of the sense of alienation that haunted Degas, Lautrec, Seurat, Van Gogh, Gauguin,
Picasso. The probable reason for this is simple but surprising:
Rousseau was so innocent, so idealistic that it was the rest of
the world and its standards which struck him as absurd, never
his own unlikely vision. His confidence and credulity and good-
naturedness survived, not because he was treated well – he was
treated appallingly – but because he was able to dismiss the
corruption of the world around him as an absurd accident.
Léger also wanted to produce an art which was positive and

hopeful. His reasoning was very different; it was based on the acceptance and understanding of facts rather than their rejection; but except for Rousseau, there was no other nineteenth- or twentieth-century artist to whom he could look for support and whose fundamental attitude was one of celebration.

*

In a certain sense Léger's art is extremely easy to appreciate, and all efforts to explain it therefore run the danger of becoming pretentious. There is less obscurity in Léger's work than in that of any of his famous contemporaries. The difficulties are not intrinsic. They arise from our conditioned prejudices.

We inherit the Romantic myth of the genius and therefore find his work 'mechanical' and 'lacking in individuality'. We expect a popular artist to use the style of debased magazine illustration, and therefore find his work 'formalistic'. We expect socialist art to be a protest and so find his work 'lacking in contradiction'. (The contradiction is in fact between what he shows to be possible and what he knew existed.) We expect his work to be 'modern' and therefore fail to see that it is often tender in the simplest manner possible. We are used to thinking of art in an 'intimate' context and therefore find his epic, monumental style 'crude' and 'oversimplified'.

I would like to end with a quotation from Léger himself. Everything I have said is only a clumsy elaboration of this text.

I am certain that we are not making woolly prophecies: our vision is very like the reality of tomorrow. We must create a society without frenzy, a society that is calm and ordered, that knows how to live naturally within the Beautiful, without protestations or romanticism, quite naturally. We are going towards it; we must bend our efforts towards that goal. It is a religion more universal than the others, made of tangible, definite, human joys, free from the troubled, disappointment-filled mysticism of the old ideals which are slowly disappearing every day, leaving the ground free for us to construct our religion of the Future.

A Belief in Uniforms
(Lovis Corinth)

Let us be clear. The critic in my view can teach very little about painting as such : for that, go to museums and studios. What he can do is to try to reveal and describe causes and consequences, and so be a guide to action. He is neither a final judge nor a purveyor of armchair appreciation. A fine passage in a particular work is bound to mean less to him *as a critic* than the story of a life's work. He is a moralist applauding talent turned to maximum human advantage, condemning wasted talent. The harshness of his judgements is not meant to be Olympian but useful; if bad consequences are emphasized, fewer may take the paths that lead to them.

I emphasize this because what I want to say about Lovis Corinth's paintings is harsh – despite his great talent and despite his personal tragedy. Corinth was born in East Prussia in 1858 and died in 1925. In 1911 he had a stroke which left him literally trembling for the rest of his life, and which changed the character of his work. He began as a nineteenth-century pre-Impressionist painter producing portraits, landscapes and subject pictures such as *The Temptation of St Anthony*. Later, as a result of seeing Rembrandt, Hals, Manet and the Impressionists, his work became lighter, looser and generally more 'expressive'. After his stroke it became looser still and its mood changed: frenzy taking the place of bravura.

In 1896 he painted himself like a healthy young bullock side by side with a skeleton; in 1901 in a flamboyant black hat, with a gold stud in his dressy shirt and a girl's head on his shoulder; in 1912 – after his stroke – like a tragic actor; in 1920 like a proud officer of a defeated army; in 1925 like a patient who knows he will never leave the ward alive. Progressively the face becomes more ravaged, the paint wilder and more emphatic, the touch more masterly. But – and this is what one gradually realizes with a shock – the painting becomes no more profound. The content of all of them is equally commonplace. The early portraits are flamboyant or melodramatic because their stories are contrived and theatrical. In the late ones the truth behind them has indeed become dramatic and tragic but the artist can no longer rise to the challenge – he has cried 'Wolf!' too often.

Nor is this just true of the self-portraits. It applies to his late works, and it is on these that his mounting reputation depends. The late landscapes are brilliantly painted, but think of Soutines or Kokoschkas and they seem empty – like 'modern' pictures painted *over* picture postcards. Or compare the very early portrait of Paul Gorge, patiently, carefully painted – a young man's tentatively idealized vision of another young man – with the very late portrait of Georg Brandes, an old man's mask in a wild blizzard. Technically they are as different as an early Rembrandt from a late one. But here has the wildness added anything? Does its strong implication of increased suffering and experience connect with any new discovery or perspective of vision as it does in the late works of Milton or Beethoven or Turner? Unfortunately not: the hand trembles, the mind races, incoherence is avoided, but nothing is added.

I cannot pretend to be able to explain fully the causes of Corinth's failure, but I am certain that they are connected with something very evident: his seduction by the rhetorical. In 1909 he wrote about art:

Egotistical as a goddess, who stands in all her beauty and allows herself to be worshipped by her true purists ... great art has only one fatherland: heaven ruled by divine power from eternity to eternity.

All his life he appears to have equated such high-sounding

abstractions with superficial gestures: or to put it another way – like so many Germans of his time he believed in uniforms. He admired Rembrandt and so he painted himself in a Rembrandt hat. He admired Hals and so he made a virtue of being seen leading a wild life. He liked women so he painted their skin like satin. He respected courage and patriotism and so in 1917 he painted a strutting Black Hussar who might have been used as a recruiting poster. He strove after dignity and so he painted his children in poses like Junkers. He saw *through* nothing. And if all this seems too literary, the same is true of his styles as a painter. First, he was an impressionist in manner and yet never understood the relationship between colour and light. Later he was an expressionist in manner and yet never got beyond the brush strokes to change the forms themselves with expression – as, for instance, Manet did. And so, finally, when all the gestures and manners and masks failed him, when he was reduced to the desperate state of the Rembrandt and the Hals he admired so much, and he turned to his high-sounding abstractions, they also failed him. All was empty. The hand trembled, the mind raced, incoherence was avoided, but nothing could be added.

Thicker than Water
(Corot)

Any critic who attacks Corot does so at his own risk. This is not because Corot was a giant. Clearly he wasn't. It is because in one way or another Corot has won his modest way into the hearts of all those who love painting. For the very sentimental, those for whom all art is a Swan Lake, there are the nymphs beneath the birches (silver); for the realists there are his pellucid landscape sketches coming between Constable and the Impressionists; for the romantics there are his nudes in the grass studio; for the classicists there are his Italianate muses in costume; and for the moralists there is the man himself, his humility, his great generosity, his keeping of Daumier after that dangerous seer had gone blind, his support for Millet's widow, his friendliness and helpfulness to all but the pretentious.

In fact I have no wish to attack Corot. To attack such a man is a form of historical hooliganism. What I do want to do is define his art and give his gifts their proper name. What I have to say is not original. But it is too often forgotten.

Corot was initially a weak draughtsman. He got by with making notations. A little mark here connected with a little mark there. He was unable to grasp his subjects. He was like a mouse trying to come to terms with an elephant. In his early Italian landscape sketches, which he painted on the spot and which certain Corot purists claim as his best work, this always seems to me to be very evident. There is also their marvellous tonal accuracy which allows them to cup the air in their hands.

But Corot's eye for tone was again an eye for comparison: this tone here with that tone there. It is still a form of piecemeal notation, of matching and pinning. True, the influence of Poussin makes him stop before one sense rather than another, but it does not embolden him to take any liberties for the sake of art with what Nature presents him.

Up to about 1840 you can see the same thing in his figure paintings. Even in his exquisite portraits of children. I nevertheless say 'exquisite' because the large burly Corot is on his hands and knees, on exactly the same level as his models, putting their small shapes down on to the canvas as tentatively as a small girl might enter a dark room, and such matter-of-fact gentleness is exquisite. But the painting is still frail; frail like a much darned garment. It is still piecemeal mending and stitching.

Then in the middle 1840s, when Corot himself is nearly fifty, he achieves mastery in his craft. To himself the change was perhaps imperceptible. But to us it is clear. It is no longer a question of stitching. He can now cut the material to his own measure. He now sees his figures complete from their very inception. Consequently they have their due weight. Their patient hands really lie in their laps as they dream or read. In his own shy way he can now even afford to be extravagant. He pins distracting, eye-catching decorations upon them, a garland of leaves catching the light, a flutter of loose material by the bodice, an emphasized red stripe in the skirt, and these charming frivolities do not destroy the form or seriousness of the figure as a whole.

In his landscapes he intensifies the atmosphere. His earlier landscapes are topographical in so far as everyone can plan his own route across them. In the landscapes of this period you must follow Corot. You must enter at that moment of delight at which he entered. (This question of Corot's paintings recapturing the *specific* moment of discovery is far more relevant to his relationship with the Impressionists than the mere fact that he painted out of doors; it also relates him to later painters like Bonnard and Sickert.)

Within ten years of acquiring this mastery, Corot became successful. And, instead of using his mastery, instead of making discoveries that could really have extended human awareness (as Géricault had done and Courbet was doing), he relapsed. He started his prodigious production of *salon* nymphs and glades. These were gauze and chiffon work, tacked together with flimsy, loose threads. They had neither the virtue of the darning nor the energy of the cutting period. They were consolations. He wrote:

> In the next room there is a pretty girl who comes and goes at my will. She is Folly, my invisible companion, whose youth is eternal and whose fidelity never wearies.

Why was Corot at first so excessively tentative, and then why, when he could have taken huge steps forward, did he draw back? It would be quite unjust to say that he sold out. Despite his great success, he still believed in what he was doing. As a man he still impressed everyone by his purity. And out of his sales, whilst living modestly himself, he financed all his good works and charities.

No, the answer is more subtle and less insulting. Corot remained a petit-bourgeois. Matching, pinning, sewing, he was never quite able to shake off the effect of his father's drapery business and his mother's dress-shop.

In 1846 when Corot was decorated with the Legion of Honour, his father – according to Théophile Sylvestre – at first thought the cross was for himself:

> When he realized that the government had deigned to cast a benevolent eye on his son, who at fifty was still not earning enough to pay for his colours, he said: 'My son – a man who has been decorated has duties towards society. I hope that you will understand them. Your negligent dress is unsuitable for one who wears the red ribbon in his buttonhole.' A little later he said to his wife: 'I think we ought to give a little more money to Camille.'

Corot was certainly not the epitome of the petit-bourgeois, as was his father. Indeed this is specifically denied by those who knew him. 'His naïve familiarity stops at exactly where that of the jovial commercial traveller would start.' He must have hated his family's way of life. But his reaction to it was to absent himself in dreams, in modest celibacy, in virtue – just as he absents his favourite models in reverie. I am not suggesting he was a prig – if he were, how could he have been a friend of Daumier's? He was a petit-bourgeois only in his refusal to speculate on how the world could be changed. This explains why he was timid without being a coward. Instead of questioning, he set out to make his own peace, to avoid all contradictions. He knew it himself: 'Delacroix is an eagle and I'm only a lark. I sing little songs in my grey clouds.' He reveals it unconsciously when he says: 'Charity is a still more beautiful thing than talent. Besides, one benefits the other. If you have a kind heart, your work will show it.' How comfortably without contradictions that 'Besides' is!

Corot was tentative as an artist for so long because his true but excessive modesty was his answer to his class's hypocritical obsequiousness. After all he was not really a mouse trying to come to terms with an elephant. As a landscape artist he should have been a man imposing order on nature. He drew back halfway through his career because to have gone on would have meant being involved in revolutionary changes. Impressionism was an art with a totally new basis, and it was Impressionism that stared him in the face – it was his own art that was leading him to it. His devotion to Poussin combined with his determination to be faithful to nature could conceivably even have led him beyond Impressionism to prophesy Cézanne. There are hints in Corot's work of so much that was to come later, but they are the unconscious hints of a man who preferred not to see what was happening, what was changing around him.

He knew after all what had befallen Daumier, Géricault, Millet, even Delacroix, and he might have guessed what was going to happen to the Impressionists. Nevertheless he could still, in the second half of the nineteenth century, write:

If painting is a madness, it is a sweet madness which men should not merely forgive but seek out. Seeing my bright looks and my health, I defy anyone to find traces of worry, ambition or remorse, which hollow the faces of so many poor mortals. That is why one should love the art which procures calm, moral contentment and even health for those who know how to balance their lives.

For others of the same class it has been vegetarianism, spiritualism, teetotalism . . .

Corot was a lovable man. At his best he was an artist of minor genius, comparable to, say, Manet. And let me add – with the due modesty that ought to precede such a statement – that Corot has contributed to many people's happiness.

The *Actual* and the *Desired*

The Moment of Cubism

I would like to dedicate this essay to Barbara Niven who prompted it nearly twenty years ago in an ABC teashop off the Grays Inn Road.

> Certains hommes sont des collines
> Qui s'élèvent d'entre les hommes
> Et voient au loin tout l'avenir
> Mieux que s'il était le présent
> Plus net que s'il était passé.
>
> APOLLINAIRE

The things that Picasso and I said to one another during those years will never be said again, and even if they were, no one would understand them any more. It was like being roped together on a mountain. GEORGES BRAQUE

There are happy moments, but no happy periods in history. ARNOLD HAUSER

The work of art is therefore only a halt in the becoming and not a frozen aim on its own. EL LISSITZKY

I find it hard to believe that the most extreme Cubist works were painted over fifty years ago. It is true that I would not expect them to have been painted today. They are both too optimistic and too revolutionary for that. Perhaps in a way I am surprised that they have been painted at all. It would seem more likely that they were yet to be painted.

Do I make things unnecessarily complicated? Would it not be more helpful to say simply: the few great Cubist works were painted between 1907 and 1914? And perhaps to qualify this by adding that a few more, by Juan Gris, were painted a little later?

And anyway is it not nonsense to think of Cubism having not yet taken place when we are surrounded in daily life by the apparent effects of Cubism? All modern design, architecture and town planning seem inconceivable without the initial example of Cubism.

Nevertheless I must insist on the sensation I have in front of the works themselves: the sensation that the works and I, as I look at them, are caught, pinned down, in an enclave of time, waiting to be released and to continue a journey that began in 1907.

Cubism was a style of painting which evolved very quickly, and whose various stages can be fairly specifically defined.[1] Yet there were also Cubist poets, Cubist sculptors, and later on so-called Cubist designers and architects. Certain original stylistic features of Cubism can be found in the pioneer works of other movements: Suprematism, Constructivism, Futurism, Vorticism, the de Stijl movement.

The question thus arises: can Cubism be adequately defined as a style? It seems unlikely. Nor can it be defined as a policy. There was never any Cubist manifesto. The opinions and outlook of Picasso, Braque, Léger or Juan Gris were clearly very different even during the few years when their paintings had many features in common. Is it not enough that the category of Cubism includes those works that are now generally agreed to be within it? This is enough for dealers, collectors, and cataloguers who go by the name of art historians. But it is not, I believe, enough for you or me.

---

1. See John Golding, *Cubism*, Faber & Faber, 1959.

Even those whom the stylistic category satisfies are wont to say that Cubism constituted a revolutionary change in the history of art. Later we shall analyse this change in detail. The concept of painting as it had existed since the Renaissance was overthrown. The idea of art holding up a mirror to nature became a nostalgic one: a means of diminishing instead of interpreting reality.

If the word revolution is used seriously and not merely as an epithet for this season's novelties, it implies a process. No revolution is simply the result of personal originality. The maximum that such originality can achieve is madness: madness is revolutionary freedom confined to the self.

Cubism cannot be explained in terms of the genius of its exponents. And this is emphasized by the fact that most of them became less profound artists when they ceased to be Cubists. Even Braque and Picasso never surpassed the works of their Cubist period: and a great deal of their later work was inferior.

The story of how Cubism happened in terms of painting and of the leading protagonists has been told many times. The protagonists themselves found it extremely difficult – both at the time and afterwards – to explain the meaning of what they were doing.

To the Cubists, Cubism was spontaneous. To us it is part of history. But a curiously unfinished part. Cubism should be considered not as a stylistic category but as a moment (even if a moment lasting six or seven years) experienced by a certain number of people. A strangely placed moment.

It was a moment in which the promises of the future were more substantial than the present. With the important exception of the avant-garde artists during a few years after 1917 in Moscow, the confidence of the Cubists has never since been equalled among artists.

D. H. Kahnweiler, who was a friend of the Cubists and their dealer, has written:

I lived those seven crucial years from 1907 to 1914 with my painter friends ... what occurred at that time in the plastic arts will be understood only if one bears in mind that a new epoch was being born, in which man (all mankind in fact) was undergoing a transformation more radical than any other known within historical times.[2]

What was the nature of this transformation? I have outlined elsewhere[3] the relation between Cubism and the economic, technological and scientific developments of the period. There seems little point in repeating this here: rather, I would like to try to push a little further our definition of the philosophic meaning of these developments and their coincidence.

An interlocking world system of imperialism; opposed to it, a socialist international; the founding of modern physics, physiology and sociology; the increasing use of electricity, the invention of radio and the cinema; the beginnings of mass production; the publishing of mass-circulation newspapers; the new structural possibilities offered by the availability of steel and aluminium; the rapid development of chemical industries and the production of synthetic materials; the appearance of the motor-car and the aeroplane: what did all this mean?

The question may seem so vast that it leads to despair. Yet there are rare historical moments to which such a question can perhaps be applied. These are moments of convergence, when numerous developments enter a period of similar qualitative change, before diverging into a multiplicity of new terms. Few of those who live through such a moment can grasp the full significance of the qualitative change taking place: but everybody is aware of the times changing: the future, instead of offering continuity, appears to advance towards them.

This was surely the case in Europe from about 1900 to 1914 – the reaction of many people to their own awareness of change is to pretend to ignore it.

---

2. D. H. Kahnweiler, *Cubism*, Éditions Braun, Paris, 1950.

3. In John Berger, *The Success and Failure of Picasso*, Penguin Books, 1965.

Apollinaire, who was the greatest and most representative poet of the Cubist movement, repeatedly refers to the future in his poetry.

> Where my youth fell
> You see the flame of the future
> You must know that I speak today
> To tell the whole world
> That the art of prophecy is born at last.[4]

The developments which converged at the beginning of the twentieth century in Europe changed the meaning of both time and space. All, in different ways, some inhuman and others full of promise, offered a liberation from the immediate, from the rigid distinction between absence and presence. The concept of the field, first put forward by Faraday when wrestling with the problem – as defined in traditional terms – of 'action at a distance', entered now, unacknowledged, into all modes of planning and calculation and even into many modes of feeling. There was a startling extension through time and space of human power and knowledge. For the first time the world, as a totality, ceased to be an abstraction and became *realizable*.

If Apollinaire was the greatest Cubist poet, Blaise Cendrars was the first. His poem 'Les Pâques à New York' (1912) had a profound influence on Apollinaire and demonstrated to him how radically one could break with tradition. The three major poems of Cendrars at this time were all concerned with travelling – but travelling in a new sense across a *realizable* globe. In 'Le Panama ou Les Aventures de Mes Sept Oncles' he writes :

> Poetry dates from today
> The milky way round my neck
> The two hemispheres on my eyes
> At full speed
> There are no more breakdowns
> If I had the time to save a little money I'd
> be flying in the air show

---

4. All translations of Apollinaire by Anna Bostock and John Berger.

> I have reserved my seat in the first train through
>   the tunnel under the Channel
> I am the first pilot to cross the Atlantic solo
> 900 millions

The 900 millions probably refers to the then estimated popula·
tion of the world.

It is important to see how philosophically far-reaching were
the consequences of this change and why it can be termed
qualitative. It was not merely a question of faster transport,
quicker messages, a more complex scientific vocabulary, larger
accumulations of capital, wider markets, international organizations, etc. The process of the secularization of the world was at
last complete. Arguments against the existence of God had
achieved little. But now man was able to extend *himself* in-
definitely beyond the immediate : he took over the territory in
space and time where God had been presumed to exist.

'Zone', the poem that Apollinaire wrote under the immediate
influence of Cendrars, contains the following lines :

> Christ pupil of the eye
> Twentieth pupil of the centuries knows how
> This century changed into a bird ascends like Jesus
> Devils in pits raise their heads to watch it
> They say it's imitating Simon Magus of Judea
> If it can fly we'll call it the fly one
> Angels swing past its trapeze
> Icarus Enoch Elias Apollonius of Tyana
> Hover round the first aeroplane
> Dispersing at times to let through the priests
> As they bear the Holy Eucharist
> Forever ascending and raising the Host ...

The second consequence concerned the relation of the self to
the secularized world. There was no longer any essential discontinuity between the individual and the general. The invisible
and the multiple no longer intervened between each individual
and the world. It was becoming more and more difficult to think
in terms of having been *placed* in the world. A man was part
of the world and indivisible from it. In an entirely original

sense, which remains at the basis of modern consciousness, a man *was* the world which he inherited.

Again, Apollinaire expresses this:

> I have known since then the bouquet of the world
> I am drunk from having drunk the universe whole.

All the previous spiritual problems of religion and morality would now be increasingly concentrated in a man's choice of attitude to the existing state of the world considered as his own existing state.

It is now only against the world, within his own consciousness, that he can measure his stature. He is enhanced or diminished according to how he acts towards the enhancement or diminishment of the world. His self apart from the world, his self wrenched from its global context – the sum of all existing social contexts – is a mere biological accident. The secularization of the world exacts its price as well as offering the privilege of a choice, clearer than any in history.

Apollinaire:

> I am everywhere or rather I start to be everywhere
> It is I who am starting this thing of the centuries
>   to come.

As soon as more than one man says this, or feels it, or aspires towards feeling it – and one must remember that the notion and the feeling are the consequence of numerous material developments impinging upon millions of lives – as soon as this happens, the unity of the world has been proposed.

The term *unity of the world* can acquire a dangerously utopian aura. But only if it is thought to be politically applicable to the world as it is. A *sine qua non* for the unity of the world is the end of exploitation. The evasion of this fact is what renders the term utopian.

Meanwhile the term has other significations. In many respects (the Declaration of Human Rights, military strategy, communication, etc.) the world since 1900 has been treated as a single unit. The unity of the world has received *de facto* recognition.

Today we know that the world should be unified, just as we know that all men should have equal rights. In so far as a man denies this or acquiesces in its denial, he denies the unity of his own self. Hence the profound psychological sickness of the imperialist countries, hence the corruption implicit in so much of their learning – when knowledge is used to deny knowledge.

At the moment of Cubism, no denials were necessary. It was a moment of prophecy, but prophecy as the basis of a transformation that had actually begun.

Apollinaire :

> Already I hear the shrill sound of the friend's voice to come
> Who walks with you in Europe
> Whilst never leaving America ...

I do not wish to suggest a general period of ebullient optimism. It was a period of poverty, exploitation, fear and desperation. The majority could only be concerned with the means of their survival, and millions did not survive. But for those who asked questions, there were new positive answers whose authenticity seemed to be guaranteed by the existence of new forces.

The socialist movements in Europe (with the exception of that in Germany and sections of the trade union movement in the United States) were convinced that they were on the eve of revolution and that the revolution would spread to become a world revolution. This belief was shared even by those who disagreed about the political means necessary – by syndicalists, parliamentarians, communists and anarchists.

A particular kind of suffering was coming to an end: the suffering of hopelessness and defeat. People now believed, if not for themselves then for the future, in victory. The belief was often strongest where the conditions were worst. Everyone who was exploited or downtrodden and who had the strength left to ask about the purpose of his miserable life was able to hear in answer the echo of declarations like that of Lucheni, the Italian anarchist who stabbed the Empress of Austria in 1898: 'The hour is not far distant when a new sun will shine upon all men alike', or like that of Kalyaev in 1905 who, on being sentenced to death for the assassination of the Governor-General of Moscow, told the Court 'to learn to look the advancing revolution straight in the eye'.

An end was in sight. The limitless, which until now had always reminded men of the unattainability of their hopes, became suddenly an encouragement. The world became a starting point.

The small circle of Cubist painters and writers were not directly involved in politics. They did not think in political terms. Yet they were concerned with a revolutionary transformation of the world. How was this possible? Again we find the answer in the historical timing of the Cubist movement. It was not then essential for a man's intellectual integrity to make a political choice. Many developments, as they converged to undergo an equivalent qualitative change, appeared to promise a transformed world. The promise was an overall one.

'All is possible,' wrote André Salmon, another Cubist poet, 'everything is realizable everywhere and with everything.'

Imperialism had begun the process of unifying the world. Mass production promised eventually a world of plenty. Mass circulation newspapers promised informed democracy. The aeroplane promised to make the dream of Icarus real. The terrible contradictions born of the convergence were not yet clear. They became evident in 1914 and they were first politically polarized by the Russian Revolution of 1917. El Lissitzky, one of the great innovators of Russian revolutionary art until this art was suppressed, implies in a biographical note how the moment of political choice came from the conditions of the Cubist moment:

The Film of El's Life till 1926[5]

BIRTH: My generation was born a few dozen years before the Great October Revolution.

---

5. *El Lissitzky*, Verlag der Kunst, Dresden, 1967, p. 235 (trans. A.B.).

ANCESTORS: A few centuries ago our ancestors had the luck to make the great voyages of discovery.

WE: We, the grandchildren of Columbus, are creating the epoch of the most glorious inventions. They have made our globe very small, but have expanded our space and intensified our time.

SENSATIONS: My life is accompanied by unprecedented sensations. Barely five years old I had the rubber leads of Edison's phonograph stuck in my ears.
Eight years, and I was chasing after the first electric tram in Smolensk, the diabolical force which drove the peasant horses out of the town.

COMPRESSION OF MATTER: The steam engine rocked my cradle. In the meantime it has gone the way of all ichthyosauruses. Machines are ceasing to have fat bellies full of intestines. Already we have the compressed skulls of dynamos with their electric brains. Matter and mind are directly transmitted through crankshafts and thus made to work. Gravity and inertia are being overcome.

1918: In 1918 in Moscow before my eyes the short-circuit sparked which split the world in half.
This stroke drove our present apart like a wedge between yesterday and tomorrow. My work too forms part of driving the wedge further in. One belongs here or there: there is no middle.

The Cubist moment ended in France in 1914. With the war a new kind of suffering was born. Men were forced to face for the first time the full horror – not of hell, or damnation, or a lost battle, or famine, or plague – but the full horror of what stood in the way of their own progress. And they were forced to face this in terms of their own responsibility, not in terms of a simple confrontation as between clearly defined enemies.

The scale of the waste and the irrationality and the degree to which men could be persuaded and forced to deny their own interests led to the belief that there were incomprehensible and blind forces at work. But since these forces could no longer be accommodated by religion, and since there was no ritual by which they could be approached or appeased, each man had to live with them *within himself*, as best he could. Within him they destroyed his will and confidence.

On the last page of *All Quiet on the Western Front* the hero thinks:

I am very quiet. Let the months and years come, they can take nothing from me, they can take nothing more. I am so alone, and so without hope that I can confront them without fear. The life that has borne me through these years is still in my hands and my eyes. Whether I have subdued it, I know not. But so long as it is there it will seek its own way out, heedless of the will that is within me.[6]

The new kind of suffering which was born in 1914 and has persisted in Western Europe until the present day is an inverted suffering. Men fought within themselves about the meaning of events, identity, hope. This was the negative possibility implicit in the new relation of the self to the world. The life they experienced became a chaos within them. They became lost within themselves.

Instead of apprehending (in however simple and direct a way) the processes which were rendering their own destinies identical with the world's, they submitted to the new condition passively. That is to say the world, which was nevertheless indivisibly part of them, reverted *in their minds* to being the old world which was separate from them and opposed to them: it was as though they had been forced to devour God, heaven and hell and live forever with the fragments inside themselves. It was indeed a new and terrible form of suffering and it coincided with the widespread, deliberate use of false ideological propaganda as a weapon. Such propaganda preserves within people outdated structures of feeling and thinking whilst forcing new experiences upon them. It transforms them into puppets −

6. E. M. Remarque, *All Quiet on the Western Front*, trans. A. W. Wheen, Mayflower-Dell Paperback, New York, 1963.

whilst most of the strain brought about by the transformation remains politically harmless as inevitably *incoherent* frustration. The only purpose of such propaganda is to make people deny and then abandon the selves which otherwise their own experience would create.

In 'La Jolie Rousse', Apollinaire's last long poem (he died in 1918), his vision of the future, after his experience of the war, has become a source of suffering as much as of hope. How can he reconcile what he has seen with what he once foresaw? From now on there can be no unpolitical prophecies.

> We are not your enemies
> We want to take over vast strange territories
> Where the flowering mystery waits to be picked
> Where there are fires and colours never yet seen
> A thousand imponderable apparitions
> Which must be given reality
> We wish to explore the vast domain of goodness
> where everything is silent
> And time can be pursued or brought back
> Pity us who fight continually on the frontiers
> Of the infinite and the future
> Pity for our mistakes pity for our sins.
>
> The violence of summer is here
> My youth like the spring is dead
> Now, O sun, is the time of scorching Reason
> Laugh then laugh at me
> Men from everywhere and more particularly here
> For there are so many things I dare not tell you
> So many things you will not let me say
> Have pity on me.

We can now begin to understand the central paradox of Cubism. The spirit of Cubism was objective. Hence its calm and its comparative anonymity as between artists. Hence also the accuracy of its technical prophecies. I live in a satellite city that has been built during the last five years. The character of the pattern of what I now see out of the window as I write can be traced directly back to the Cubist pictures of 1911 and 1912.

Yet the Cubist spirit seems to us today to be curiously distant and disengaged.

This is because the Cubists took no account of politics *as we have since experienced them.* In common with even their experienced political contemporaries, they did not imagine and did not foresee the extent, depth and duration of the suffering which would be involved in the political struggle to realize what had so clearly become possible and what has since become imperative.

The Cubists imagined the world transformed, but not the process of transformation.

Cubism changed the nature of the relationship between the painted image and reality, and by so doing it expressed a new relationship between man and reality.

Many writers have pointed out that Cubism marked a break in the history of art comparable to that of the Renaissance in relation to medieval art. That is not to say that Cubism can be equated with the Renaissance. The confidence of the Renaissance lasted for about sixty years (approximately from 1420 to 1480): that of Cubism lasted about six years. However, the Renaissance remains a point of departure for appreciating Cubism.

The function of the painter is to render with lines and colours, on a given panel or wall, the visible surface of any body, so that at a certain distance and from a certain position it appears in relief and just like the body itself.[7]

It was not, of course, as simple as that. There were the mathematical problems of linear perspective which Alberti himself solved. There was the question of choice – that is to say the question of the artist doing justice to nature by choosing to represent what was typical of nature at her best.

---

7. Quoted in Anthony Blunt, *Artistic Theory in Italy, 1450–1600,* Oxford Paperback, 1962.

Yet the artist's relation to nature was comparable to that of the scientist. Like the scientist, the artist applied reason and method to the study of the world. He observed and ordered his findings. The parallelism of the two disciplines is later demonstrated by the example of Leonardo.

Although often employed far less accurately during the following centuries, the metaphorical model for the function of painting at this time was *the mirror*. Alberti cites Narcissus, when he sees himself reflected in the water, as the first painter. The mirror renders the appearances of nature and simultaneously delivers them into the hands of man.

It is extremely hard to reconstruct the attitudes of the past. In the light of more recent developments and the questions raised by them, we tend to iron out the ambiguities which may have existed before the questions were formed. In the early Renaissance, for example, the humanist view and a medieval Christian view could still be easily combined. Man became the equal of God, but both retained their traditional positions. Arnold Hauser writes of the early Renaissance:

> The seat of God was the centre round which the heavenly spheres revolved, the earth was the centre of the material universe, and man himself a self-contained microcosm round which, as it were, revolved the whole of nature, just as the celestial bodies revolved round that fixed star, the earth.[8]

Thus man could observe nature around him on every side and be enhanced both by what he observed and by his own ability to observe. He had no need to consider that he was essentially part of that nature. *Man was the eye for which reality had been made visual*: the ideal eye, the eye of the viewing-point of Renaissance perspective. The human greatness of this eye lay in its ability to reflect and contain, like a mirror, what was.

---

8. See Arnold Hauser's *Mannerism*, Routledge, London, 1965, p. 44: an essential book for anybody concerned with the problematic nature of contemporary art, and its historical roots.

The Copernican revolution, Protestantism, the Counter-Reformation, destroyed the Renaissance position. With this destruction modern subjectivity was born. The artist becomes primarily concerned with creation. His own genius takes the place of nature as the marvel. It is the gift of his genius, his 'spirit', his 'grace' which makes him god-like. At the same time the equality between man and god is totally destroyed. Mystery enters art to emphasize the inequality. A century after Alberti's claim that art and science are parallel activities, Michelangelo speaks – no longer of imitating nature – but of imitating Christ:

In order to imitate in some degree the venerable image of Our Lord, it is not enough to be a painter, a great and skilful master; I believe that one must further be of blameless life, even if possible a saint, that the Holy Spirit may inspire one's understanding.[9]

It would take us too far from our field even to attempt to trace the history of art from Michelangelo onwards – Mannerism, the baroque, seventeenth- and eighteenth-century classicism. What is relevant to our purpose is that, from Michelangelo until the French Revolution, the metaphorical model for the function of painting becomes the *theatre stage*. It may seem unlikely that the same model works for a visionary like El Greco, a Stoic like Poussin (who actually worked from stage models he built himself) and a middle-class moralist like Chardin. Yet all the artists of these two centuries shared certain assumptions. For them all the power of art lay in its *artificiality*. That is to say they were concerned with constructing comprehensive examples of some truth such as could not be met with in such an ecstatic, pointed, sublime or meaningful way in life itself.

Painting became a schematic art. The painter's task was no longer to represent or imitate what existed; it was to summarize experience. Nature is now what man has to redeem himself from. The artist becomes responsible not simply for the means of conveying a truth, but also for the truth itself. Painting

---

9. Quoted in Anthony Blunt, op. cit.

ceases to be a branch of natural science and becomes a branch of the moral sciences.

In the theatre the spectator faces events from whose consequences he is immune : he may be affected emotionally and morally but he is physically removed, protected, separate, from what is happening before his eyes. What is happening is artificial. It is *he* who now represents nature – not the work of art. And if, at the same time, it is from himself that he must redeem himself, this represents the contradiction of the Cartesian division which prophetically or actually so dominated these two centuries.

Rousseau, Kant and the French Revolution – or rather, all the developments which lay behind the thought of the philosophers and the actions of the Revolution – made it impossible to go on believing in constructed order as against natural chaos. The metaphorical model changed again, and once more it applies over a long period despite dramatic changes of style. The new model is that of the *personal account*. Nature no longer confirms or enhances the artist as he investigates it. Nor is he any longer concerned with creating 'artificial' examples, for these depend upon the common recognition of certain moral values. He is now alone, surrounded by nature, from which his own experience separates him.

Nature is what he sees *through* his experience. There is thus in all nineteenth-century art – from the 'pathetic fallacy' of the Romantics to the 'optics' of the Impressionists – considerable confusion about where the artist's experience stops and nature begins. The artist's personal account is his attempt to make his experience as real as nature, which he can never reach, by communicating it to others. The considerable suffering of most nineteenth-century artists arose out of this contradiction : because they were alienated from nature, they needed to present *themselves* as nature to others.

Speech, as the recounting of experience and the means of making it real, preoccupied the Romantics. Hence their constant comparisons between paintings and poetry. Géricault, whose *Raft of the Medusa* was the first painting of a contemporary event consciously based on eye-witness accounts, wrote in 1821 :

How I should like to be able to show our cleverest painters several portraits, which are such close resemblances to nature, whose easy pose leaves nothing to be desired, and of which one can really say that all they lack is the power of speech.

In 1850 Delacroix wrote :

I have told myself a hundred times that painting – that is to say, the material thing called painting – was no more than the pretext, the bridge between the mind of the painter and that of the spectator ...

For Corot experience was a far less flamboyant and more modest affair than for the Romantics. But nevertheless he still emphasized how essential the personal and the relative are to art. In 1865 he wrote :

Reality is one part of art: feeling completes it ... before any site and any object, abandon yourself to your first impression. If you have really been touched, you will convey to others the sincerity of your emotion.[10]

Zola, who was one of the first defenders of the Impressionists, defined a work of art as 'a corner of nature seen through a temperament'. The definition applies to the whole of the nineteenth century and is another way of describing the same metaphorical model.

Monet was the most theoretical of the Impressionists and the most anxious to break through the century's barrier of subjectivity. For him (at least theoretically) the role of his temperament was reduced to that of the process of perception. He speaks of a 'close fusion' with nature. But the result of this fusion, however harmonious, is a sense of powerlessness – which suggests that, bereft of his subjectivity, he has nothing to put in its place. Nature is no longer a field for study, it has

---

10. *Artists on Art*, ed. R. J. Goldwater and M. Treves, Pantheon Books, New York, 1945.

become an overwhelming force. One way or another the confrontation between the artist and nature in the nineteenth century is an unequal one. Either the heart of man or the grandeur of nature dominates. 'I have painted for half a century,' wrote Monet,

and will soon have passed my sixty-ninth year, but, far from decreasing, my sensitivity has sharpened with age. As long as constant contact with the outside world can sustain the ardour of my curiosity, and my hand remains the quick and faithful servant of my perception, I have nothing to fear from old age. I have no other wish than a close fusion with nature, and I desire no other fate than (according to Goethe) to have worked and lived in harmony with her rules. Beside her grandeur, her power and her immortality, the human creature seems but a miserable atom.

I am well aware of the schematic nature of this brief survey. Is not Delacroix in some senses a transitional figure between the eighteenth and nineteenth centuries? And was not Raphael another transitional figure who confounds such simple categories? The scheme, however, is true enough to help us appreciate the nature of the change which Cubism represented.

The metaphorical model of Cubism is the *diagram*: the diagram being a visible, symbolic representation of invisible processes, forces, structures. A diagram need not eschew certain aspects of appearances: but these too will be treated symbolically as *signs*, not as imitations or re-creations.

The model of the *diagram* differs from that of the *mirror* in that it suggests a concern with what is not self-evident. It differs from the model of the *theatre stage* in that it does not have to concentrate upon climaxes but can reveal the continuous. It differs from the model of the *personal account* in that it aims at a general truth.

The Renaissance artist imitated nature. The Mannerist and Classic artist reconstructed examples from nature in order to transcend nature. The nineteenth-century artist experienced nature. The Cubist realized that his awareness of nature was part of nature.

Heisenberg speaks as a modern physicist:

Natural science does not simply describe and explain nature; it is part of the interplay between nature and ourselves: it describes nature as exposed to our method of questioning.[11]

Similarly, the frontal facing of nature became inadequate in art.

How did the Cubists express their intimation of the new relation existing between man and nature?

1   *By Their Use of Space*

Cubism broke the illusionist three-dimensional space which had existed in painting since the Renaissance. It did not destroy it. Nor did it muffle it – as Gauguin and the Pont-Aven school had done. It broke its continuity. There is space in a Cubist painting in that one form can be inferred to be behind another. But the relation between any two forms does not, as it does in illusionist space, establish the rule for all the spatial relationships between all the forms portrayed in the picture. This is possible without a nightmarish deformation of space, because the two-dimensional surface of the picture is always there as arbiter and resolver of different claims. The picture surface acts in a Cubist painting as the constant which allows us to appreciate the variables. Before and after every sortie of our imagination into the problematic spaces and through the interconnections of a Cubist painting, we find our gaze resettled on the picture surface, aware once more of two-dimensional shapes on a two-dimensional board or canvas.

This makes it impossible to *confront* the objects or forms in a Cubist work. Not only because of the multiplicity of viewpoints – so that, say, a view of a table from below is combined with a view of the table from above and from the side – but also because the forms portrayed never present themselves as a totality. The totality is the surface of the picture, *which is now the origin and sum of all that one sees*. The viewing-point of

---

11. Werner Heisenberg, *Physics and Philosophy*, Allen & Unwin, 1959, p. 75.

Renaissance perspective, fixed and outside the picture, but to which everything within the picture was drawn, has become a field of vision which is the picture itself.

It took Picasso and Braque three years to arrive at this extraordinary transformation. In most of their pictures from 1907 to 1910 there are still compromises with Renaissance space. The effect of this is to deform the subject. The figure or landscape becomes the construction, instead of the construction being the picture acting as an expression of the relation between viewer and subject.[12]

After 1910 all references to appearances are made as signs on the picture surface. A circle for a top of a bottle, a lozenge for an eye, letters for a newspaper, a volute for the head of a violin, etc. Collage was an extension of the same principle. Part of the actual or imitation surface of an object was stuck on to the surface of the picture as a sign referring to, but not imitating, its appearance. A little later painting borrowed from this experience of collage, so that, say, a pair of lips or a bunch of grapes might be referred to by a drawing which 'pretended' to be on a piece of white paper stuck on to the picture surface.

2 *By Their Treatment of Form*

It was this which gave the Cubists their name. They were said to paint everything in *cubes*. Afterwards this was connected with the remark attributed to Cézanne : 'Treat nature by the cylinder, by the sphere, the cone, everything in proper perspective . . .' And from then on the misunderstanding has continued – encouraged, let it be said, by a lot of confused assertions by some of the lesser Cubists themselves.

The misunderstanding is that the Cubists wanted to simplify – for the sake of simplification. In some of the Picassos and Braques of 1908 it may look as though this is the case. Before finding their new vision, they had to jettison traditional com-

---

12. For a similar analysis of Cubism, written thirty years earlier but unknown to the author at the time of writing, see Max Raphael's great work, *The Demands of Art*, Routledge, 1969, p. 162.

plexities. But their aim was to arrive at a far more complex image of reality than had ever been attempted in painting before.

To appreciate this we must abandon a habit of centuries: the habit of looking at every object or body as though it were complete in itself, its completeness making it separate. The Cubists were concerned with the interaction between objects.

They reduced forms to a combination of cubes, cones, cylinders – or, later, to arrangements of flatly articulated facets or planes with sharp edges – so that the elements of any one form were interchangeable with another, whether a hill, a woman, a violin, a carafe, a table or a hand. Thus, as against the Cubist discontinuity of space, they created a continuity of structure. Yet when we talk of the Cubist discontinuity of space, it is only to distinguish it from the convention of linear Renaissance perspective.

Space is part of the continuity of the events within it. It is in itself an event, comparable with other events. It is not a mere container. And this is what the few Cubist masterpieces show us. The space between objects is part of the same structure as the objects themselves. The forms are simply reversed so that, say, the top of a head is a convex element and the adjacent space which it does not fill is a concave element.

The Cubists created the possibility of art revealing processes instead of static entities. The content of their art consists of various modes of interaction: the interaction between different aspects of the same event, between empty space and filled space, between structure and movement, between the seer and the thing seen.

Rather than ask of a Cubist picture: Is it true? or: Is it sincere? one should ask: Does it continue?

Today it is easy to see that, since Cubism, painting has become more and more diagrammatic, even when there has been no direct Cubist influence – as, say, in Surrealism. Eddie Wolfram in an article about Francis Bacon writes:

Painting today functions directly as a conceptual activity in philosophical terms and the art object acts only as a cypher reference to tangible reality.[13]

This was part of the Cubist prophecy. But only part. Byzantine art might equally well be accommodated within Wolfram's definition. To understand the full Cubist prophecy we must examine the content of their art.

A Cubist painting like Picasso's *Bottle and Glasses* of 1911 is two-dimensional in so far as one's eye comes back again and again to the surface of the picture. We start from the surface, we follow a sequence of forms which leads into the picture, and then suddenly we arrive back at the surface again and deposit our newly acquired knowledge upon it, before making another foray. This is why I called the Cubist picture surface the origin and sum of all that we can see in the picture. There is nothing decorative about such two-dimensionality, nor is it merely an area offering possibilities of juxtaposition for dissociated images – as in the case of much recent neo-Dadaist or Pop art. We begin with the surface, but since everything in the picture refers back to the surface we begin with the conclusion. We then search – not for an explanation, as we do if presented with an image with a single, predominant meaning (a man laughing, a mountain, a reclining nude), but for some understanding of the configuration of events whose interaction is the conclusion from which we began. When we 'deposit our newly acquired knowledge upon the picture surface', what we in fact do is to find the sign for what we have just discovered: a sign which was always there but which previously we could not read.

To make the point clearer it is worth comparing a Cubist picture with any work in the Renaissance tradition. Let us say Pollaiuolo's *Martyrdom of St Sebastian*. In front of the Pollaiuolo the spectator completes the picture. It is the spectator who draws the conclusions and infers all except the aesthetic rela-

---

13. Eddie Wolfram, *Art and Artists*, London, September 1966.

154

tions between the pieces of evidence offered – the archers, the martyr, the plain laid out behind, etc. It is he who through his reading of what is portrayed seals its unity of meaning. The work is presented to him. One has the feeling almost that St Sebastian was martyred so that he should be able to explain this picture. The complexity of the forms and the scale of the space depicted enhance the sense of achievement, of grasp.

In a Cubist picture, the conclusion and the connections are given. They are what the picture is made of. They are its content. The spectator has to find his place *within* this content whilst the complexity of the forms and the 'discontinuity' of the space remind him that his view from that place is bound to be only partial.

Such content and its functioning was prophetic because it coincided with the new scientific view of nature which rejected simple causality and the single permanent all-seeing viewpoint. Heisenberg writes:

One may say that the human ability to understand may be in a certain sense unlimited. But the existing scientific concepts cover always only a very limited part of reality, and the other part that has not yet been understood is infinite. Whenever we proceed from the known to the unknown we may hope to understand, but we may have to learn at the same time a new meaning of the word understanding.[14]

Such a notion implies a change in the methodology of research and invention. W. Grey Walter, the physiologist, writes:

Classical physiology, as we have seen, tolerated only one single unknown quantity in its equations – in any experiment there could be only one thing at a time under investigation. ... We cannot extract one independent variable in the classical manner; we have to deal with the interaction of many unknowns and variables, all the time. ... In practice, this implies that not one but many – as many as possible – observations must be made at once and compared with

---

14. Werner Heisenberg, op. cit., p. 172.

one another, and that whenever possible a simple known variable should be used to modify the several complex unknowns so that their tendencies and interdependence can be assessed.[15]

The best Cubist works of 1910, 1911 and 1912 were sustained and precise models for the method of searching and testing described above. That is to say, they force the senses and imagination of the spectator to calculate, omit, doubt and conclude according to a pattern which closely resembles the one involved in scientific observation. The difference is a question of appeal. Because the act of looking at a picture is far less concentrated, the picture can appeal to wider and more various areas of the spectator's previous experience. Art is concerned with memory: experiment is concerned with predictions.

Outside the modern laboratory, the need to adapt oneself constantly to presented totalities – rather than making inventories or supplying a transcendental meaning as in front of the Pollaiuolo – is a feature of modern experience which affects everybody through the mass media and modern communication systems.

Marshall McLuhan is a manic exaggerator, but he has seen certain truths clearly:

In the electric age, when our central nervous system is technologically extended to involve us in the whole of mankind and to incorporate the whole of mankind in us, we necessarily participate, in depth, in the consequences of our every action.... The aspiration of our time for wholeness, empathy and depth of awareness is a natural adjunct of electric technology. The age of mechanical industry that preceded us found vehement assertion of private outlook the natural mode of expression.... The mark of our time is its revolution against imposed patterns. We are suddenly eager to have things and people declare their beings totally.[16]

The Cubists were the first artists to attempt to paint totalities rather than agglomerations.

---

15. W. Grey Walter, *The Living Brain*, Duckworth, 1953; Penguin Books, 1961, p. 69.

16. Marshall McLuhan, *Understanding Media*, McGraw-Hill, New York, 1964; Routledge & Kegan Paul, 1964, pp. 4 and 5.

I must emphasize again that the Cubists were not aware of all that we are now reading into their art. Picasso and Braque and Léger kept silent because they knew that they might be doing more than they knew. The lesser Cubists tended to believe that their break with tradition had freed them from the bondage of appearances so that they might deal with some kind of spiritual essence. The idea that their art coincided with the implications of certain new scientific and technological developments was entertained but never fully worked out. There is no evidence at all that they recognized as such the qualitative change which had taken place in the world. It is for these reasons that I have constantly referred to their *intimation* of a transformed world: it amounted to no more than that.

One cannot explain the exact dates of the maximum Cubist achievement. Why 1910 to 1912 rather than 1905 to 1907? Nor is it possible to explain *exactly* why certain artists, at exactly the same time, arrived at a very different view of the world – artists ranging from Bonnard to Duchamp or de Chirico. To do so we would need to know an *impossible* amount about each separate individual development. (In that impossibility – which is an absolute one – lies our freedom from determinism.)

We have to work with partial explanations. With the advantage of sixty years' hindsight, the correlations I have tried to establish between Cubism and the rest of history seem to me to be undeniable. The precise route of the connections remains unknown. They do not inform us about the intentions of the artists: they do not explain exactly why Cubism took place in the manner it did: but they do help to disclose the widest possible continuing meaning of Cubism.

Two more reservations. Because Cubism represented so fundamental a revolution in the history of art, I have had to discuss it as though it were pure theory. Only in this way could I make its revolutionary content clear. But naturally it was not pure theory. It was nothing like so neat, consistent or reduced. There are Cubist paintings full of anomalies and marvellous gratuitous tenderness and confused excitement. We see the beginning in the light of the conclusions it suggested. But it was only a beginning, and a beginning cut short.

For all their insight into the inadequacy of appearances and of the frontal view of nature, the Cubists used such appearances as their means of reference to nature. In the maelstrom of their new constructions, their liaison with the events which provoked them is shown by way of a simple, almost naïve reference to a pipe stuck in the 'sitter's' mouth, a bunch of grapes, a fruit dish or the title of a daily newspaper. Even in some of the most 'hermetic' paintings – for example Braque's *Le Portugais* – you can find naturalistic allusions to details of the subject's appearance, such as the buttons on the musician's jacket, buried intact within the construction. There are only a very few works – for instance Picasso's *Le Modèle* of 1912 – where such allusions have been totally dispensed with.

The difficulties were probably both intellectual and sentimental. The naturalistic allusions seemed necessary in order to offer a measure for judging the transformation. Perhaps also the Cubists were reluctant to part with appearances because they suspected that in art they could never be the same again. The details are smuggled in and hidden as mementoes.

The second reservation concerns the social content of Cubism – or, rather, its lack of it. One cannot expect of a Cubist painting the same kind of social content as one finds in a Brueghel or a Courbet. The mass media and the arrival of new publics have profoundly changed the social role of the Fine Arts. It remains true, however, that the Cubists – during the moment of Cubism – were unconcerned about the personalized human and social implications of what they were doing. This, I think, is because they had to simplify. The problem before them was so complex that their manner of stating it and their trying to solve it absorbed all their attention. As innovators they wanted to make their experiments in the simplest possible conditions; consequently, they took as subjects whatever was at hand and made least demands. The content of these works is the relation between the seer and the seen. This relation is only possible given the fact that the seer inherits a precise historical, economic and social situation. Otherwise they become meaningless. They do not illustrate a human or social situation, they posit it.

I spoke of the continuing meaning of Cubism. To some degree this meaning has changed and will change again according to the needs of the present. The bearings we read with the aid of Cubism vary according to our position. What is the reading now?

It is being more and more urgently claimed that 'the modern tradition' begins with Jarry, Duchamp and the Dadaists. This confers legitimacy upon the recent developments of neo-Dadaism, auto-destructive art, happenings, etc. The claim implies that what separates the characteristic art of the twentieth century from the art of all previous centuries is its acceptance of unreason, its social desperation, its extreme subjectivity and its forced dependence upon existential experience.

Hans Arp, one of the original Dadaist spokesmen, wrote:

The Renaissance taught men the haughty exaltation of their reason. Modern times, with their science and technology, turned men towards megalomania. The confusion of our epoch results from this over-estimation of reason.

And elsewhere:

The law of chance, which embraces all other laws and is as unfathomable to us as the depths from which all life arises, can only be comprehended by complete surrender to the Unconscious.[17]

Arp's statements are repeated today with a slightly modified vocabulary by all contemporary apologists of outrageous art. (I use the word outrageous descriptively and not in a pejorative sense.)

---

17. Quoted in Hans Richter, *Dada*, Thames & Hudson, London, 1965, p. 55.

During the intervening years, the Surrealists, Picasso, de Chirico, Miró, Klee, Dubuffet, the Abstract Expressionists and many others can be drafted into the same tradition : the tradition whose aim is to cheat the world of its hollow triumphs, and disclose its pain.

The example of Cubism forces us to recognize that this is a one-sided interpretation of history. Outrageous art has many earlier precedents. In periods of doubt and transition the majority of artists have always tended to be preoccupied with the fantastic, the uncontrollable and the horrific. The greater extremism of contemporary artists is the result of their having no fixed social role; to some degree they can create their own. Thus there is no precedent in art history for, say, auto-destructive art. But there are precedents for the spirit of it in the history of other activities : heretical religions, alchemy, witchcraft, etc.

The real break with tradition, or the real reformation of that tradition, occurred with Cubism itself. The modern tradition, based on a qualitatively different relationship being established between man and the world, began, not in despair, but in affirmation.

The proof that this was the objective role of Cubism lies in the fact that, however much its spirit was rejected, it supplied to all later movements the primary means of their own liberation. That is to say, it re-created the syntax of art so that it could accommodate modern experience. The proposition that a work of art is a new object and not simply the expression of its subject, the structuring of a picture to admit the coexistence of different modes of space and time, the inclusion in a work of art of extraneous objects, the dislocation of forms to reveal movement or change, the combining of hitherto separate and distinct media, the diagrammatic use of appearances – these were the revolutionary innovations of Cubism.

It would be foolish to underestimate the achievements of post-Cubist art. Nevertheless it is fair to say that in general the art of the post-Cubist period has been anxious and highly subjective. What the evidence of Cubism should prevent us doing is concluding from this that anxiety and extreme subjectivity constitute the nature of modern art. They constitute the nature of art in a period of extreme ideological confusion and inverted political frustration.

During the first decade of this century a transformed world became theoretically possible and the necessary forces of change could already be recognized as existing. Cubism was the art which reflected the possibility of this transformed world and the confidence it inspired. Thus, in a certain sense, it was the most modern art – as it was also the most philosophically complex – which has yet existed.

The vision of the Cubist moment still coincides with what is technologically possible. Yet three quarters of the world remain undernourished and the foreseeable growth of the world's population is outstripping the production of food. Meanwhile millions of the privileged are the prisoners of their own sense of increasing powerlessness.

The political struggle will be gigantic in its range and duration. The transformed world will not arrive as the Cubists imagined it. It will be born of a longer and more terrible history. We cannot see the end of the present period of political inversion, famine and exploitation. But the moment of Cubism reminds us that, if we are to be representative of our century – and not merely its passive creatures – the aim of achieving that end must constantly inform our consciousness and decisions.

The moment at which a piece of music begins provides a clue to the nature of all art. The incongruity of that moment, compared to the uncounted, unperceived silence which preceded it, is the secret of art. What is the meaning of that incongruity and the shock which accompanies it? It is to be found in the distinction between the actual and the desirable. All art is an attempt to define and make *unnatural* this distinction.

For a long time it was thought that art was the imitation and celebration of nature. The confusion arose because the concept of nature itself was a projection of the desired. Now that we have cleansed our view of nature, we see that art is an expression of our sense of the inadequacy of the given – which we are not obliged to accept with gratitude. Art mediates between our good fortune and our disappointment. Sometimes it mounts to a pitch of horror. Sometimes it gives permanent value and meaning to the ephemeral. Sometimes it describes the desired.

Thus art, however free or anarchic its mode of expression, is always a plea for greater control and an example, within the artificial limits of a 'medium', of the advantages of such control. Theories about the artist's inspiration are all projections back on to the artist of the effect which his work has upon us. The only inspiration which exists is the intimation of our own potential. Inspiration is the mirror image of history : by means of it we can see our past, while turning our back upon it. And it is precisely this which happens at the instant when a piece of music begins. We suddenly become aware of the previous silence at the same moment as our attention is concentrated upon following sequences and resolutions which will contain the desired.

The Cubist moment was such a beginning, defining desires which are still unmet.

Questioning the Visible

Drawing

For the artist drawing is discovery. And that is not just a slick phrase, it is quite literally true. It is the actual act of drawing that forces the artist to look at the object in front of him, to dissect it in his mind's eye and put it together again; or, if he is drawing from memory, that forces him to dredge his own mind, to discover the content of his own store of past observations. It is a platitude in the teaching of drawing that the heart of the matter lies in the specific process of looking. A line, an area of tone, is not really important because it records what you have seen, but because of what it will lead you on to see. Following up its logic in order to check its accuracy, you find confirmation or denial in the object itself or in your memory of it. Each confirmation or denial brings you closer to the object, until finally you are, as it were, inside it: the contours you have drawn no longer marking the edge of what you have seen, but the edge of what you have become. Perhaps that sounds needlessly metaphysical. Another way of putting it would be to say that each mark you make on the paper is a stepping-stone from which you proceed to the next, until you have crossed your subject as though it were a river, have put it behind you.

This is quite different from the later process of painting a 'finished' canvas or carving a statue. Here you do not pass through your subject, but try to re-create it and house yourself in it. Each brush-mark or chisel-stroke is no longer a stepping-stone, but a stone to be fitted into a planned edifice. A drawing is an autobiographical record of one's discovery of an event – seen, remembered or imagined. A 'finished' work is an attempt to construct an event in itself. It is significant in this respect that only when the artist gained a relatively high standard of individual 'autobiographical' freedom, did drawings, as we now understand them, begin to exist. In a hieratic, anonymous tradition they are unnecessary. (I should perhaps point out here that I am talking about *working* drawings – although a working drawing need not necessarily be made for a specific project. I do not mean linear designs, illustrations, caricatures, certain portraits or graphic works which may be 'finished' productions in their own right.)

A number of technical factors often enlarge this distinction between a working drawing and a 'finished' work : the longer time needed to paint a canvas or carve a block : the larger scale of the job : the problem of simultaneously managing colour, quality of pigment, tone, texture, grain, and so on – the 'shorthand' of drawing is relatively simple and direct. But nevertheless the fundamental distinction is in the working of the artist's mind. A drawing is essentially a private work, related only to the artist's own needs; a 'finished' statue or canvas is essentially a public, *presented* work – related far more directly to the demands of communication.

It follows from this that there is an equal distinction from the point of view of the spectator. In front of a painting or statue he tends to identify himself with the subject, to interpret the images for their own sake; in front of a drawing he identifies himself with the artist, using the images to gain the conscious experience of seeing as though through the artist's own eyes.

As I looked down at the clean page in my sketchbook I was more conscious of its height than its breadth. The top and bottom edges were the critical ones, for between them I had to reconstruct the way he rose up from the floor, or, thinking in the opposite direction, the way that he was held down to the floor. The energy of the pose was primarily vertical. All the small lateral movements of the arms, the twisted neck, the leg which was not supporting his weight, were related to that vertical force, as the trailing and overhanging branches of a tree are related to the vertical shaft of the trunk. My first lines had to express that; had to make him stand like a skittle, but at the same time had to imply that, unlike a skittle, he was capable of movement, capable of readjusting his balance if the floor tilted, capable for a few seconds of leaping up into the air against the vertical force of gravity. This capability of movement, this irregular and temporary rather than uniform and permanent tension of his body, would have to be expressed in relation to the side edges of the paper, to the variations on either side of the straight line between the pit of his neck and the heel of his weight-bearing leg.

I looked for the variations. His left leg supported his weight and therefore the left, far side of his body was tense, either straight or angular; the near, right side was comparatively relaxed and flowing. Arbitrary lateral lines taken across his body ran from curves to sharp points – as streams flow from hills to sharp, compressed gulleys in the cliff-face. But of course it was not as simple as that. On his near, relaxed side his fist was clenched and the hardness of his knuckles recalled the hard line of his ribs on the other side – like a cairn on the hills recalling the cliffs.

I now began to see the white surface of the paper, on which I was going to draw, in a different way. From being a clean flat page it became an empty space. Its whiteness became an area of limitless, opaque light, possible to move through but not to see through. I knew that when I drew a line on it – or *through* it – I should have to control the line, not like the driver of a car, on one plane: but like a pilot in the air; movement in all three dimensions being possible.

Yet, when I made a mark, somewhere beneath the near ribs, the nature of the page changed again. The area of opaque light suddenly ceased to be limitless. The whole page was changed by what I had drawn just as the water in a glass tank is changed immediately you put a fish in it. It is then only the fish that you look at. The water merely becomes the condition of its life and the area in which it can swim.

Then, when I crossed the body to mark the outline of the far shoulder, yet another change occurred. It was not simply like putting another fish into the tank. The second line altered the nature of the first. Whereas before the first line had been aimless, now its meaning was fixed and made certain by the second line. Together they held down the edges of the area between them, and the area, straining under the force which had once given the whole page the potentiality of depth, heaved itself up into a suggestion of solid form. The drawing had begun.

The third dimension, the solidity of the chair, the body, the tree, is, at least as far as our senses are concerned, the very proof of our existence. It constitutes the difference between the word and the world. As I looked at the model I marvelled at the simple fact that he *was* solid, that he occupied space, that he was more than the sum total of ten thousand visions of him from ten thousand different viewpoints. In my drawing, which was inevitably a vision from just one point of view, I hoped eventually to imply this limitless number of other facets. But now it was simply a question of building and refining forms until their tensions began to be like those I could see in the model. It would of course be easy by some mistaken over-emphasis to burst the whole thing like a balloon; or it might collapse like too-thin clay on a potter's wheel; or it might become irrevocably misshapen and lose its centre of gravity. Nevertheless, the thing was there. The infinite, opaque possibilities of the blank page had been made particular and lucid. My task now was to coordinate and measure : not to measure by inches as one might measure an ounce of sultanas by counting them, but to measure by rhythm, mass and displacement : to gauge distances and angles as a bird flying through a trellis of branches; to visualize the ground plan like an architect; to feel the pressure of my lines and scribbles towards the uttermost surface of the paper, as a sailor feels the slackness or tautness of his sail in order to tack close or far from the surface of the wind.

I judged the height of the ear in relation to the eyes, the angles of the crooked triangle of the two nipples and the navel, the lateral lines of the shoulders and hips – sloping towards each other so that they would eventually meet, the relative position of the knuckles of the far hand directly above the toes of the far foot. I looked, however, not only for these linear proportions, the angles and lengths of these imaginary pieces of string stretched from one point to another, but also for the relationships of planes, of receding and advancing surfaces.

Just as looking over the haphazard roofs of an unplanned city you find identical angles of recession in the gables and dormer-windows of quite different houses – so that if you extended any particular plane through all the intermediary ones, it would eventually coincide perfectly with another; in exactly the same way you find extensions of identical planes in different parts of the body. The plane, falling away from the summit of the stomach to the groin, coincided with that which led backwards from the near knee to the sharp, outside edge of the calf. One of the gentle, inside planes, high up on the thigh of the same leg, coincided with a small plane leading away and around the outline of the far pectoral muscle.

And so, as some sort of unity was shaped and the lines accumulated on the paper, I again became aware of the real tensions of the pose. But this time more subtly. It was no longer a question of just realizing the main, vertical stance. I had become involved more intimately with the figure. Even the smaller facts had acquired an urgency and I had to resist the temptation to make every line over-emphatic. I entered into the receding spaces and yielded to the oncoming forms. Also, I was correcting: drawing over and across the earlier lines to re-establish proportions or to find a way of expressing less obvious discoveries. I saw that the line down the centre of the torso, from the pit of the neck, between the nipples, over the navel and between the legs, was like the keel of a boat, that the ribs formed a hull and that the near, relaxed leg dragged on its forward movement like a trailing oar. I saw that the arms hanging either side were like the shafts of a cart, and that the outside curve of the weight-bearing thigh was like the ironed rim of a figure on a crucifix. Yet such images, although I have chosen them carefully, distort what I am trying to describe. I saw and recognized quite ordinary anatomical facts; but I also felt them physically – as if, in a sense, *my* nervous system inhabited *his* body.

A few of the things I recognized I can describe more directly. I noticed how at the foot of the hard, clenched, weight-bearing leg, there was clear space beneath the arch of the instep. I noticed how subtly the straight under-wall of the stomach elided into the attenuated, joining planes of thigh and hip. I noticed the contrast between the hardness of the elbow and the vulnerable tenderness of the inside of the arm at the same level.

Then, quite soon, the drawing reached its point of crisis. Which is to say that what I had drawn began to interest me as much as what I could still discover. There is a stage in every drawing when this happens. And I call it a point of crisis because at that moment the success or failure of the drawing has really been decided. One now begins to draw according to the demands, the needs, of the drawing. If the drawing is already in some small way true, then these demands will probably correspond to what one might still discover by actual searching. If the drawing is basically false, they will accentuate its wrongness.

I looked at my drawing trying to see what had been distorted; which lines or scribbles of tones had lost their original and necessary emphasis, as others had surrounded them; which spontaneous gestures had evaded a problem, and which had been instinctively right. Yet even this process was only partly conscious. In some places I could clearly see that a passage was clumsy and needed checking; in others, I allowed my pencil to hover around – rather like the stick of a water-diviner. One form would pull, forcing the pencil to make a scribble of tone which could re-emphasize its recession; another would jab the pencil into restressing a line which could bring it further forward.

Now when I looked at the model to check a form, I looked in a different way. I looked, as it were, with more connivance: to find only what I wanted to find.

Then the end. Simultaneously ambition and disillusion. Even

170

as in my mind's eye I saw my drawing and the actual man coincide – so that, for a moment, he was no longer a man posing but an inhabitant of my half-created world, a unique expression of my experience, even as I saw this in my mind's eye, I saw in fact how inadequate, fragmentary, clumsy my small drawing was.

I turned over the page and began another drawing, starting from where the last one had left off. A man standing, his weight rather more on one leg than the other . . .

Dedicated to
Sven Blomberg

Painting a Landscape

The first thing my eye questions when I wake up is the small square of sky above the fig tree in the top left-hand corner of the window. If it is blue I am satisfied. It is as though its blueness is a sign that I have had enough sleep. When it is grey and opaque I have to reconcile myself to not seeing either of the landscapes on which I am working.

The house belongs to a painter with whom I often stay. I know the district well. Any peasant born in the village knows it a thousand times better. I can compare it to other very different landscapes, both real and painted. This means that I can name its elements more precisely. For me it is unique not because I have always known it, but because I can compare it.

When I am not here I might dream of this landscape. In my dream I would recognize it. I would recognize it, not in terms of previous events, but by its colour, the forms of its hills, its textures and its scale. I would recognize it before I could distinguish between a cherry and an apricot tree. Sometimes perhaps I would recognize it just by virtue of the sky above it — the range of its blues across its immense distance, and the characteristic deployment of the clouds whose shadows pass across the plain. The sharp edges of these shadows reveal what is literally the lie of the land. The shadows of the clouds are like hands large enough to examine the recumbent body.

But all this amounts to only a generalized image. It concerns a district, not a place. The subjects of the paintings are far more particular. As soon as I begin looking at a field, an escarpment or an orchard as though in it there was some code to be deciphered, it becomes unfamiliar. Even the result – that is to say the 'message' transmitted – remains mysterious. I can never be sure what my own painting says. And this is not just because of the problem of finding words to describe formal revelations: it is because the longer you spend with them, the more mysterious all visual images become.

What is this painting of a landscape? It is said that landscape painting has died a natural death. Certainly there are no great modern landscapes comparable to those of the past. But what of those which are not comparable? Which are not even landscapes? For that is the point: the genre has changed beyond recognition. Cubism when it broke painting broke the landscape too. It is unlikely that the specific appearance of a given landscape will ever again be the aim of an important painter. But it can well be his starting point. Landscape painting must now be subsumed under Painting. That is all that natural death means.

I am painting from nature. What I do between times in the studio is only marginal. I am aware as I walk across the rocks or through the oakwoods whose leaves, just unfurled, are pink at their tips, membrane pink, and white-green at their base as the sea can be, with my folding easel and paint box, I am aware of apparently being a nineteenth-century figure. Yet in my head, in my conditioned eye, it also seems that I have the benefit of all experimental twentieth-century art to date. What is in my head – as the result of three generations of artists – would have been beyond the reckoning of Pissarro or Gauguin. Even what I see in a Pissarro would have surprised the old man himself.

As I work I am faithful to what I see in front of me, because only by being faithful, by constantly checking, correcting, analysing what I can see and how it changes as the day progresses can I discover forms and structures too complex and varied to be invented out of my head or reconstructed from vague memories. The messages are not the kind that can be sent to oneself.

173

Yet to a third party (the landscape is the second) what is on the canvas is scarcely readable as a landscape. The 'legibility' of the image is something which must be approached with extreme caution. The cult of obscurity is sentimental nonsense. But the kind of clarity which two centuries of art encouraged people to expect, the clarity of maximum resemblance, is irrevocably outdated. This is not the result of a mere change of fashion but a development in our understanding of reality. Objects no longer confront us. Rather, relationships surround us. These can only be illustrated diagrammatically. Even in front of a Rembrandt we are bound to be far more conscious than before of its diagrammatic aspect.

A work of art is not the same thing as a scientific model. But it stands in an equivalent relationship to reality. Once it was useful to think of art as a mirror. It no longer is – because our view of nature has changed. Today to hold a mirror up to nature is only to diminish the world.

The most difficult thing of all, painting on the spot, is to look at your canvas. Your glance constantly moves between the scene itself and the marks on the canvas : but these glances tend to arrive loaded, and return empty. The largest part of the great, heroic self-discipline of Cézanne lay precisely in this. He was able to look at his painting, in process of being constructed, as patiently and objectively as at the subject which was complete. It sounds very easy : it is as easy as walking on water.

The marks on the canvas must have a life of their own. We must be made aware of their independence. This is why their logic and their needs must be so carefully assessed. Given their independence *and* their relation to reality – given, that is, the artist's ability to include his own work as part of the reality he is studying – the image will act as a metaphor. The alternative is for it to be either a false statement or a meaningless exclamation : naturalism or primitivism of one kind or another.

The nature of the metaphor depends on innumerable varying factors; but its *raison d'être* is always the same : it is what connects the event and the artist's judgement of it : it is the means of rendering the subject and its meaning visually inseparable. The thing interpreted becomes the interpretation.

This is why the balance of the metaphor is so difficult to sustain. Every work begins as an obvious metaphor. This explains the modern taste for the 'liveliness' of the sketch, as distinct from the finished painting. As the work progresses, the temptation either to efface oneself before nature or else to return to the abstraction of what is already known becomes harder and harder.

The pretension of what I am trying to do from my rock seems overwhelming. The sunlight already claims the canvas by making the colours apparently fade.

The light is so strong that my shadow seems to have more substance than the earth itself. Thus the long dry grass, which the shadow falls on, looks like the straw stuffing of my shadow-body.

In a field near the house I found an old drawing on yellowed paper. On one side was a student's life-drawing, a reclining nude with large very round breasts, emphasized by the clumsiness of the drawing. On the other side were attached eight or nine small white-shelled snails.

*

Last night the season changed. The spring became early summer. But this did not happen under the usual clear sky and brilliant stars. It was in a mist with distant thunder that the cicadas began to sing, the frogs to croak louder than ever before this year, the nightingales to crack their tinned liquid songs open more and more blatantly. At this moment of precise change – which was also the moment of dusk – the whole landscape lay indeterminate and confused like an adolescent's dream in a mist of spunk. Clarity is rare.

Nevertheless there are moments of painting when it seems that the pretensions are justified. However short-lived, there are moments of triumph, incomparable in my experience to moments achieved in any other activity. They are usually short-lived because they depend upon a correspondence existing between the totality of relations between the marks on the canvas and those deducible in the landscape : as soon as one more mark is added or an existing mark modified, this correspondence is liable to collapse utterly. The process of painting is the process of trying to re-achieve at a higher level of complexity a previous unity which has been lost. As one leaves the central area of the painting and paints towards the edges of the canvas this becomes more and more difficult. Then one's memory of the original blank white canvas becomes more and more seductive.

During the moments of triumph one has the sensation of having mastered the landscape according to its own rules and similtaneously of having been liberated from the hegemony of all rules. Some might describe the position as god-like. But there is a common experience which it resembles : the experience of every child who imagines that he is able to fly.

The child distinguishes between the fantasy and the fact. But the distinction is of no importance. The metaphor allows him to imagine the familiar world from above, and his own liberation from it. The actual experience of flying would do no more.

The motive for the metaphor is perhaps born of the dreams of childhood whose power continues in later life. The sexual content assumed to exist in dreams about flying is closely connected to the sexual content of landscape.

But the possible relevance of the metaphor involves our modern approach to reality itself. Liberated from its role as a narrative medium, painting, of all the arts, is the closest to philosophy.

Making lustreless marks upon a tiny canvas in front of a landscape that has been cultivated for centuries and in view of the fact that such cultivation has and still demands lives of the hardest labour, I ask myself what is it to be close to philosophy ?

Imagine a cubic metre of space : empty it of your conception of that space : what you are then left with is like death.

The other day I saw a lorry carting blocks of stone, white in the sunlight, from the quarries on the other side of the village. On top of the blocks was a wooden box with tools in it. On top of them, carefully placed so that it should not blow away, lay a sprig of cherry blossom. In the rockface is buried the promise of dynamite: in the dynamite the promise of space: in the space grows the promise of a tree: in the core of the tree the promise of blossom. That was the relationship between the spray and the blocks of stone on the lorry.

The white blossom on the trees, seen from above the reddish earth, is slightly stained with viridian. But the white of the canvas between the marks of paint upon it is more vibrant. The blossom, which the slightest wind may now blow away, is fixed in space: the white canvas is the field of the diagram.

In the evening S and I hang our unfinished paintings on the kitchen wall. They are distorted by the lamplight with its emphatic shadows and its yellow preponderance: nevertheless we can look at them to prove them wrong. We look at them suddenly from moment to moment as though to catch them unawares. A dozen people talk round the kitchen table. Maybe S and I are more silent than usual. I notice that when the woman opposite S is talking to him, he pretends to be attentive but in fact keeps on glancing beyond her at his painting on the wall. He quizzes it. On his face is that expression otherwise peculiar to self-portraits: a quizzical, sceptical look of inquiry.

I too can't prevent my eyes from straying towards my canvas. If I was absolutely convinced that the canvas was finished, I wouldn't give it a glance. It is only its shortcomings that fascinate me. In these I can see the possibilities of a more accurate metaphor: I can feel all that has escaped me. And it is the consequent sense of the near impossibility of the task which allows me to take pleasure in the little that I have temporarily achieved.

Understanding a Photograph

For over a century, photographers and their apologists have argued that photography deserves to be considered a fine art. It is hard to know how far the apologetics have succeeded. Certainly the vast majority of people do not consider photography an art, even whilst they practise, enjoy, use and value it. The argument of apologists (and I myself have been among them) has been a little academic.

It now seems clear that photography deserves to be considered as though it were *not* a fine art. It looks as though photography (whatever kind of activity it may be) is going to outlive painting and sculpture as we have thought of them since the Renaissance. It now seems fortunate that few museums have had sufficient initiative to open photographic departments, for it means that few photographs have been preserved in sacred isolation, it means that the public have not come to think of any photographs as being *beyond* them. (Museums function like homes of the nobility to which the public at certain hours are admitted as visitors. The class nature of the 'nobility' may vary, but as soon as a work is placed in a museum it acquires the *mystery* of a way of life which excludes the mass.)

Let me be clear. Painting and sculpture as we know them are not dying of any stylistic disease, of anything diagnosed by the professionally horrified as cultural decadence; they are dying because, in the world as it is, no work of art can survive and not become a valuable property. And this implies the death of painting and sculpture because property, as once it was not, is now inevitably opposed to all other values. People believe in property, but in essence they only believe in the illusion of protection which property gives. All works of fine art, whatever their content, whatever the sensibility of an individual spectator, must now be reckoned as no more than props for the confidence of the world spirit of conservatism.

By their nature, photographs have little or no property value because they have no rarity value. The very principle of photography is that the resulting image is not unique, but on the contrary infinitely reproducible. Thus, in twentieth-century terms, photographs are records of things seen. Let us consider them no closer to works of art than cardiograms. We shall then be freer of illusions. Our mistake has been to categorize things as art by considering certain phases of the process of creation. But logically this can make all man-made objects art. It is more useful to categorize art by what has become its social function. It functions as property. Accordingly, photographs are mostly outside the category.

Photographs bear witness to a human choice being exercised in a given situation. A photograph is a result of the photographer's decision that it is worth recording that this particular event or this particular object has been seen. If everything that existed were continually being photographed, every photograph would become meaningless. A photograph celebrates neither the event itself nor the faculty of sight in itself. A photograph is already a message about the event it records. The urgency of this message is not entirely dependent on the urgency of the event, but neither can it be entirely independent from it. At its simplest, the message, decoded, means : *I have decided that seeing this is worth recording.*

This is equally true of very memorable photographs and the most banal snapshots. What distinguishes the one from the other is the degree to which the photograph explains the message, the degree to which the photograph makes the photographer's decision transparent and comprehensible. Thus we come to the little-understood paradox of the photograph. The photograph is an automatic record through the mediation of light of a given event: yet it uses the *given* event to *explain* its recording. Photography is the process of rendering observation self-conscious.

We must rid ourselves of a confusion brought about by continually comparing photography with the fine arts. Every handbook on photography talks about composition. The good photograph is the well-composed one. Yet this is true only in so far as we think of photographic images imitating painted ones. Painting is an art of arrangement: therefore it is reasonable to demand that there is some kind of order in what is arranged. Every relation between forms in a painting is to some degree adaptable to the painter's purpose. This is not the case with photography. (Unless we include those absurd studio works in which the photographer arranges every detail of his subject before he takes the picture.) Composition in the profound, formative sense of the word cannot enter into photography.

The formal arrangement of a photograph explains nothing. The events portrayed are in themselves mysterious or explicable according to the spectator's knowledge of them prior to his seeing the photograph. What then gives the photograph as photograph meaning? What makes its minimal message – *I have decided that seeing this is worth recording* – large and vibrant?

The true content of a photograph is invisible, for it derives from a play, not with form, but with time. One might argue that photography is as close to music as to painting. I have said that a photograph bears witness to a human choice being exercised. This choice is not between photographing x and y: but between photographing at x moment or at y moment. The objects recorded in any photograph (from the most effective to the most commonplace) carry approximately the same weight, the same conviction. What varies is the intensity with which we are made aware of the poles of absence and presence. Between these two poles photography finds its proper meaning. (The most popular use of the photograph is as a memento of the absent.)

A photograph, whilst recording what has been seen, always and by its nature refers to what is not seen. It isolates, preserves and presents a moment taken from a continuum. The power of a painting depends upon its internal references. Its reference to the natural world beyond the limits of the painted surface is never direct; it deals in equivalents. Or, to put it another way: painting interprets the world, translating it into its own language. But photography has no language of its own. One learns to read photographs as one learns to read footprints or cardiograms. The language in which photography deals is the language of events. All its references are external to itself. Hence the continuum.

A movie director can manipulate time as a painter can manipulate the confluence of the events he depicts. Not so the still photographer. The only decision he can take is as regards the moment he chooses to isolate. Yet this apparent limitation gives the photograph its unique power. *What it shows invokes what is not shown.* One can look at any photograph to appreciate the truth of this. The immediate relation between what is present and what is absent is particular to each photograph: it may be that of ice to sun, of grief to a tragedy, of a smile to a pleasure, of a body to love, of a winning race-horse to the race it has run.

A photograph is effective when the chosen moment which it records contains a quantum of truth which is generally applicable, which is as revealing about what is absent from the photograph as about what is present in it. The nature of this quantum of truth, and the ways in which it can be discerned, vary greatly. It may be found in an expression, an action, a juxtaposition, a visual ambiguity, a configuration. Nor can this truth ever be independent of the spectator. For the man with a Polyfoto of his girl in his pocket, the quantum of truth in an 'impersonal' photograph must still depend upon the general categories already in the spectator's mind.

All this may seem close to the old principle of art transforming the particular into the universal. But photography does not deal in constructs. There is no transforming in photography. There is only decision, only focus. The minimal message of a photograph may be less simple than we first thought. Instead of it being: *I have decided that seeing this is worth recording,* we may now decode it as: *The degree to which I believe this is worth looking at can be judged by all that I am willingly not showing because it is contained within it.*

Why complicate in this way an experience which we have many times every day – the experience of looking at a photograph? Because the simplicity with which we usually treat the experience is wasteful and confusing. We think of photographs as works of art, as evidence of a particular truth, as likenesses, as news items. Every photograph is in fact a means of testing, confirming and constructing a total view of reality. Hence the crucial role of photography in ideological struggle. Hence the necessity of our understanding a weapon which we can use and which can be used against us.

The Political Uses of
Photo-Montage

John Heartfield, whose real name was Helmut Herzfelde, was born in Berlin in 1891. His father was an unsuccessful poet and anarchist. Threatened with prison for public sacrilege, the father fled from Germany and settled in Austria. Both parents died when Helmut was eight. He was brought up by the peasant mayor of the village on the outskirts of which the Herzfelde family had been living in a forest hut. He had no more than a primary education.

As a youth he got a job in a relative's bookshop and from there worked his way to art school in Munich, where he quickly came to the conclusion that the Fine Arts were an anachronism. He adopted the English name Heartfield in defiance of German wartime patriotism. In 1916 he started with his brother Wieland a dissenting left-wing magazine, and, with George Grosz, invented the technique of photo-montage. (Raoul Hausmann claims to have invented it elsewhere at the same time.) In 1918 Heartfield became a founder member of the German Communist Party. In 1920 he played a leading role in the Berlin Dada Fair. Until 1924 he worked in films and for the theatre. Thereafter he worked as a graphic propagandist for the German communist press and between about 1927 and 1937 became internationally famous for the wit and force of his photo-montage posters and cartoons.

He remained a communist, living after the war in East Berlin, until his death in 1968. During the second half of his life, none of his published work was in any way comparable in originality or passion to the best of his work done in the decade 1927–37. The latter offers a rare example outside the Soviet Union during the revolutionary years of an artist committing his imagination wholly to the service of a mass political struggle.

What are the qualities of this work? What conclusions may we draw from them? First, a general quality.

There is a Heartfield cartoon of Streicher standing on a pavement beside the inert body of a beaten-up Jew. The caption reads: 'A Pan-German'. Streicher stands in his Nazi uniform, hands behind his back, eyes looking straight ahead, with an expression that neither denies nor affirms what has happened at his feet. It is literally and metaphorically beneath his notice. On his jacket are a few slight traces of dirt or blood. They are scarcely enough to incriminate him – in different circumstances they would seem insignificant. All that they do is slightly to soil his tunic.

In Heartfield's best critical works there is a sense of everything having been soiled – even though it is not possible, as it is in the Streicher cartoon, to explain exactly why or how. The greyness, the very tonality of the photographic prints suggests it, as do the folds of the grey clothes, the outlines of the frozen gestures, the half-shadows on the pale faces, the textures of the street walls, of the medical overalls, of the black silk hats. Apart from what they depict, the images themselves are sordid: or, more precisely, they express disgust at their own sordidness.

One finds a comparable physical disgust suggested in nearly all modern political cartoons which have survived their immediate purpose. It does not require a Nazi Germany to provoke such disgust. One sees this quality at its clearest and simplest in the great political portrait caricatures of Daumier. It represents the deepest universal reaction to the stuff of modern politics. And we should understand why.

It is disgust at that particular kind of sordidness which exudes from those who now wield individual political power. This sordidness is not a confirmation of the abstract moral belief that all power corrupts. It is a specific historical and political phenomenon. It could not occur in a theocracy or a secure feudal society. It must await the principle of modern democracy and then the cynical manipulating of that principle. It is endemic in, but by no means exclusive to, latter-day bourgeois politics and advanced capitalism. It is nurtured from the gulf between the aims a politician claims and the actions he has in fact already decided upon.

It is not born of personal deception or hypocrisy as such. Rather, it is born of the manipulator's assurance, of his own indifference to the flagrant contradiction which he himself displays between words and actions, between noble sentiments and routine practice. It resides in his complacent trust in the hidden undemocratic power of the state. Before each public appearance he knows that his words are only for those whom they can persuade, and that with those whom they do not there are other ways of dealing. Note this sordidness when watching the next party political broadcast.

What is the particular quality of Heartfield's best work? It stems from the originality and aptness of his use of photo-montage. In Heartfield's hands the technique becomes a subtle but vivid means of political education, and more precisely of Marxist education.

With his scissors he cuts out events and objects from the scenes to which they originally belonged. He then arranges them in a new, unexpected, discontinuous scene to make a political point – for example, parliament is being placed in a wooden coffin. But this much might be achieved by a drawing or even a verbal slogan. The peculiar advantage of photo-montage lies in the fact that everything which has been cut out keeps its familiar photographic appearance. We are still looking first at *things* and only afterwards at symbols.

But because these things have been shifted, because the natural continuities within which they normally exist have been broken, and because they have now been arranged to transmit an unexpected message, we are made conscious of the arbitrariness of their continuous normal message. Their ideological covering or disguise, which fits them so well when they are in their proper place that it becomes indistinguishable from their appearances, is abruptly revealed for what it is. Appearances themselves are suddenly showing us how they deceive us.

Two simple examples. (There are many more complex ones.) A photograph of Hitler returning the Nazi salute at a mass meeting (which we do not see). Behind him, and much larger than he is, the faceless figure of a man. This man is discreetly passing a wad of banknotes into Hitler's open hand raised above his head. The message of the cartoon (October 1932) is that Hitler is being supported and financed by the big industrialists. But, more subtly, Hitler's charismatic gesture is being divested of its accepted current meaning.

A cartoon of one month later. Two broken skeletons lying in a crater of mud on the Western Front, photographed from above. Everything has disintegrated except for the nailed boots which are still on their feet, and, although muddy, are in wearable condition. The caption reads : 'And again?' Underneath there is a dialogue between the two dead soldiers about how other men are already lining up to take their place. What is being visually contested here is the power and virility normally accorded by Germans to the sight of jackboots.

Those interested in the future didactic use of photo-montage for social and political comment should, I am sure, experiment further with this ability of the technique to *demystify things.* Heartfield's genius lay in his discovery of this possibility.

Photo-montage is at its weakest when it is purely symbolic, when it uses its own means to further rhetorical mystification. Heartfield's work is not always free from this. The weakness reflects deep political contradictions.

For several years before 1933, communist policy towards the Nazis on the one hand and the German social-democrats on the other was both confused and arbitrary. In 1928, after the fall of Bukharin and under Stalin's pressure, the Comintern decided to designate all social democrats as 'social fascists' – there is a Heartfield cartoon of 1931 in which he shows an S.P.D. leader with the face of a snarling tiger. As a result of this arbitrary scheme of simplified moral clairvoyance being imposed from Moscow on local contradictory facts, any chance of the German communists influencing or collaborating with the 9,000,000 S.P.D. voters who were mostly workers and potential anti-Nazis was forfeited. It is possible that with a different strategy the German working class might have prevented the rise of Hitler.

Heartfield accepted the party line, apparently without any misgivings. But among his works there is a clear distinction between those which demystify and those which exhort with simplified moral rhetoric. Those which demystify treat of the rise of Nazism in Germany – a social-historical phenomenon with which Heartfield was tragically and intimately familiar; those which exhort are concerned with global generalizations which he inherited ready-made from elsewhere.

Again, two examples. A cartoon of 1935 shows a minuscule Goebbels standing on a copy of *Mein Kampf*, putting out his hand in a gesture of dismissal. 'Away with these degenerate sub-humans,' he says – a quotation from a speech he made at Nuremberg. Towering above him as giants, making his gesture pathetically absurd, is a line of impassive Red Army soldiers with rifles at the ready. The effect of such a cartoon on all but loyal communists could only have been to confirm the Nazi lie that the U.S.S.R. represented a threat to Germany. In ideological contrasts, as distinct from reality, there is only a paper-thin division between thesis and antithesis; a single reflex can turn black into white.

A poster for the First of May 1937 celebrating the Popular Front in France. An arm holding a red flag and sprigs of cherry blossom; a vague background of clouds (?), sea waves (?), mountains (?). A caption from the *Marseillaise*: '*Liberté, liberté chérie, combats avec tes défenseurs!*' Everything about this poster is as symbolic as it is soon to be demonstrated politically false.

I doubt whether we are in a position to make moral judgements about Heartfield's integrity. We would need to know and to feel the pressures, both from within and without, under which he worked during that decade of increasing menace and terrible betrayals. But, thanks to his example, and that of other artists such as Mayakovsky or Tatlin, there is one issue which we should be able to see more clearly than was possible earlier.

It concerns the principal type of moral leverage applied to committed artists and propagandists in order to persuade them to suppress or distort their own original imaginative impulses. I am not speaking now of intimidation but of moral and political argument. Often such arguments were advanced by the artist himself against his own imagination.

The moral leverage was gained through asking questions concerning utility and effectiveness. Am I being useful enough? Is my work effective enough? These questions were closely connected with the belief that a work of art or a work of propaganda (the distinction is of little importance here) was a *weapon* of political struggle. Works of imagination can exert great political and social influence. Politically revolutionary artists hope to integrate their work into a mass struggle. But the influence of their work cannot be determined, either by the artist or by a political commissar, in advance. And it is here that we can see that to compare a work of imagination with a weapon is to resort to a dangerous and far-fetched metaphor.

The effectiveness of a weapon can be estimated quantitatively. Its performance is isolable and repeatable. One chooses a weapon for a situation. The effectiveness of a work of imagination cannot be estimated quantitatively. Its performance is not isolatable or repeatable. It changes with circumstances. It creates its own situation. There is no *foreseeable* quantitative correlation between the quality of a work of imagination and its effectiveness. And this is part of its nature because it is intended to operate within a field of subjective interactions which are interminable and immeasurable. This is not to grant to art an ineffable value; it is only to emphasize that the imagination, when true to its impulse, is continually and inevitably questioning the existing category of usefulness. It is ahead of that part of the social self which asks the question. It must deny itself in order to answer the question in its own terms. By way of this denial revolutionary artists have been persuaded to compromise, and to do so in vain – as I have indicated in the case of John Heartfield.

It is lies that can be qualified as useful or useless; the lie is surrounded by what has not been said and its usefulness or not can be gauged according to what has been hidden. The truth is always first discovered in open space.

The Sight of a Man

There are reports that many thousands of monumental sculptures have been recently put up in the towns and villages of China. These sculptures depict local groups of workers or peasants achieving some revolutionary feat – often a production record. The sculptural style is so naturalistic as to suggest the figures being cast from life. The apotheosis of the living heroes is as immediate as possible. They can straight away look at themselves in the monument, not as in a mirror, but as from the outside, as others in history may see them.

From here it is impossible to judge the effect of these works on the masses in China. But one can make a number of general comments. The conscious aim behind the policy decision in Peking to produce these monuments is not different in kind – though leading to a cruder practice – from the unformulated aims of nearly all the patrons of European art since the Renaissance. The aim is to isolate and *reproduce* an aspect of reality in order to award it an outside prize, to confer upon it a value which is not intrinsic to it but which derives from an abstract religious or historical schema. Thus, appearances are abstracted from nature and society, through the imitative faculty of art, and used to dress, to clothe a social-moral-historical ideal. When the schema is not abstract and does not have to be imposed on social life, it has no need of the borrowed clothes of appearances.

The distinction between works produced according to an

190

abstract schema and those rare works which extend, as distinct from transposing, the experience of the spectator, is that the latter never remove appearances from the essential and specific body of meaning behind them. (They never flay their subjects.) They deny the validity of any outside prize. One must add, however, that such masterpieces have as yet contributed nothing directly to solving the problems of revolutionary political organization and education. It is impossible to oppose them directly to the Chinese monuments. These monuments need not be assessed as art but they can be considered as things to be seen. And it is at this point that – somewhat surprisingly – the example of Cézanne may be relevant.

Millions of words have been written in psychological and aesthetic studies about Cézanne yet their conclusions lack the gravity of the works. Everyone is agreed that Cézanne's paintings appear to be different from those of any painter who preceded him; whilst the works of those who came after seem scarcely comparable, for they were produced out of the profound crisis which Cézanne (and probably also Van Gogh) half foresaw and helped to provoke.

What then made Cézanne's painting different? Nothing less than his view of the visible. He questioned and finally rejected the belief, which was axiomatic to the whole Renaissance tradition, that things are seen for what they are, that their visibility belongs to them. According to this tradition, to make a likeness was to reconstitute a truth; even fantastic painters, like Bosch, treated visibility in the same way; their only difference was that they conferred visibility upon imagined constructions. To be visible was to be there, to make visible was to make there. Reality (nature) consisted of an infinite number of sights; the duty of the artist was to bring together and arrange sights. The artist captured appearances and in capturing them preserved a truth. The world offered its visibility to men as a tree offers its reflection to water. The mediation of optics did not alter this fundamental relation. The visible remained the *object* of every man's vision.

Cézanne, intensely introspective yet determinedly objective, propelled forward by continual self-doubt, born at a time when it was possible for a painter to recognize and give equal weight to his *petite sensation* on the one hand and *nature* on the other, Cézanne, who consciously strove towards a new synthesis between art and nature, who wanted to renew the European tradition, in fact destroyed for ever the foundation of that tradition by insisting, more and more radically as his work developed, that visibility is as much an extension of ourselves as it is a quality-in-itself of things. Through Cézanne we recognize that a visible world begins and ends with the life of each man, that millions of these visible worlds correspond in so many respects that from the correspondences we can construct *the* visible world, but that this world of appearances is inseparable from each one of us: and each one of us constitutes its centre.

What I am saying may become clearer if related to the actual landscapes in which Cézanne found his 'motifs'. I have been to many places to see how they compare to a painter's concentrated vision of them (Courbet's Jura, Van Gogh's southern Holland, Piero's Umbria, Poussin's Rome, etc.); but the experience of visiting and revisiting Cézanne's landscape round Aix is unique.

The houses in which he worked and their atmosphere have changed a lot. The civilization in which he lived, as distinct from the civilization to which we can read his work as a signpost, has disintegrated. His studio is now in a suburb near a supermarket. The Jas de Bouffan with its large garden and avenue of chestnuts has become an island in a sea of autoroute works. The farm at Bellevue is inhabited but overgrown, broken down, by the side of a car dump. Students camp in the Château Noir at weekends.

The natural landscape is largely unchanged: the Mont Sainte-Victoire, the yellowy-red rocks, the characteristic pine trees are there as they are in the paintings. At first everything looks smaller than you expected. However close you get to one of Cézanne's subjects, it still looks further away than in the painting. But after a while, when you have got used to this, when you are no longer concentrating upon the appearance at any given moment of the mountain, or the trees, or the red roof, or the path through the wood, you begin to realize that what Cézanne painted, and what you are already familiar with because of his paintings, is the *genius loci* of each view.

One might suppose the houses where he painted to be haunted today by a social way of life gone for ever (fortunately). But the landscapes are haunted by their own essence. Or so it seems, because you cannot become innocent of the paintings you know. Mont Sainte-Victoire appears primordial, as does the plain beneath it. Wherever you look, you feel that you are face to face with the origin of what is in front of you. You rediscover the famous silence of Cézanne's paintings in the age of what you are looking at. I do not mean, however, the geological origin of the mountain; I mean the origin of the visibility of the landscape before you. Through this landscape – because Cézanne used it over and over again as his raw material – you come to see what seeing means.

Given this, it is not surprising that Cézanne's work had to wait about fifty years for a philosopher – and not an art historian or art critic – to define its general significance. (The particular significance of each work is of course indefinable beyond or outside its own self-definition as painting.) In 1945 the French philosopher Merleau-Ponty published an essay of seventeen pages entitled *Le Doute de Cézanne*.[1] These few concentrated pages have revealed more to me about Cézanne's painting than anything else I have ever read.

Merleau-Ponty quotes some of Cézanne's own remarks. Of the old masters Cézanne said: 'They created pictures: we are attempting a piece of nature.' Of nature he said: 'The artist must conform to this perfect work of art. Everything comes to us from nature; we exist through it; nothing else is worth remembering.' 'Are you speaking of our nature?' asked

---

1. Maurice Merleau-Ponty, *Sense and Non-Sense*, trans. Hubert L. Dreyfus, Northwestern University Press, 1964.

Bernard. 'It has to do with both,' said Cézanne. 'But aren't nature and art different?' 'I want to make them the same,' replied Cézanne.

At what moment can art and nature converge and become the same? Never by way of representation, for nature cannot by definition be represented; and the representational devices of art depend entirely on artistic convention. The more consistently imitative art is, the more artificial it is. Metaphoric arts are the most natural. But what is a purely visual metaphor? At what moment is green, in equal measure, a perceived concentration of colour and an attribute of grass? It is the same question as above, formulated differently.

The answer is: at the moment of perception; at the moment when the subject of perception can admit no discontinuity between himself and the objects and space before him; at the moment at which he is an irremovable part of the totality of which he is the consciousness. 'The landscape,' said Cézanne, 'thinks itself in me, and I am its consciousness.' 'Colour,' he also said, 'is the place where our brain and the universe meet.'

The Herculean task Cézanne set himself was to prolong this moment for as long as it took him to paint his picture. And paradoxically this is why he worked so slowly and required so many sittings: he never wanted to let the logic of the painting take precedence over the continuity of perception: after each brushstroke he had to re-establish his innocence as perceiver. And since such a task is never entirely possible, he was always dogged by a greater or lesser sense of his own failure.

What he could not realize was that in failing to paint the pictures he wanted, he heightened our awareness of the visible as it had never been heightened before. He bequeathed to us something far more valuable than masterpieces: a new consciousness of a faculty.

In his attempt to prolong this moment, to be faithful to his 'sensation', to treat nature as a work of art, he abandoned the systematic usages of painting – outlines, consistent perspective, local colour, the optical conventions of impressionism, classical composition, etc. – because he reckoned that these were only ways of constructing a substitute for nature *post facto*. The old masters, he said, 'replaced reality by imagination and by the abstraction which accompanies it'. Today we are so accustomed to thinking that the tradition of the old masters was challenged by increasing abstraction and finally by non-figurative art, that we fail to see that Cézanne was the most fundamentally icono-clastic of all modern artists.

Since Cézanne's death certain discoveries by psychologists have proved how true he was to his perceptual experience. For example: the perspective we live is neither geometrical nor photographic. When we see a circle in perspective we do not see a perfect ellipse but a form which oscillates round an ellipse without being one. There is something very poignant about Cézanne, shocked in moments of doubt by his own non-con-formity, fearing that his whole art was based on a personal deformity of vision, and it later being established that no painter had ever been as faithful to the actual processes by which we all see. But neither this poignancy nor the piecemeal confirma-tion by science of some of his innovations is central to the overall significance of his work.

Merleau-Ponty indicates wherein this significance lies:

> He did not want to separate the stable things which we see and the shifting way in which they appear; he wanted to depict matter as it takes on form, the birth of order through spontaneous organ-ization. He makes a basic distinction not between 'the senses' and 'the understanding' but rather between the spontaneous organization of the things we perceive and the human organization of ideas and sciences. We see things; we agree about them; we are anchored in them; and it is with 'nature' as our base that we construct our sciences. Cézanne wanted to paint this primordial world.... He wished, as he said, to confront the sciences with the nature 'from which they came'.[2]

This nature is not chaotic; it emerges into order because of 'the spontaneous organization of the things we perceive'. If you compare a drawing of a coat on a chair with many paintings of

---

2. Merleau-Ponty, op. cit.

Mont Sainte-Victoire from the side of the Château Noir made during the same period, you have an exaggerated demonstration of this principle. Not surprisingly the means of rendering the forms of both coat and mountain are similar, but, more importantly, the actual configuration of the coat resembles, to a remarkable degree, that of the mountain. It is an exaggerated, even aberrant case, because Cézanne was obsessed by that mountain; but we may presume that when drawing the coat he was as faithful as usual to his own perception.

At a different level of experience Gestalt psychology has established that in the act of seeing we organize. Nevertheless most psychologists tend to preserve the distinct categories, as applied to vision, of objectivity and subjectivity. In another essay called *Eye and Mind*, written fifteen years later in a village beneath Mont Sainte-Victoire, Merleau-Ponty attacks the conservative oversimplification of these categories:

> We must take literally what vision teaches us: namely, that through it we come in contact with the sun and the stars, that we are everywhere all at once, and that even our power to imagine ourselves elsewhere ... borrows from vision and employs means we owe to it. Vision alone makes us learn that beings that are different, 'exterior', foreign to one another, yet absolutely *together*, are 'simultaneity'; this is a mystery psychologists handle the way a child handles explosives.[3]

The space, the depth in Cézanne's later paintings refuses to close: it remains open to 'simultaneity': it is full of the promise of reciprocity. If you imagine taking up a position in the space of one of his pictures, the painting offers you the organizational guidelines of what you would see as you looked backwards or sideways to where you presume you are still standing. You look up at Mont Sainte-Victoire but within the terms of the painting, within its own elements, you are aware of the opportunity and the probable configuration presented by

---

3. Merleau-Ponty, *The Primacy of Perception*, ed. James M. Edie, trans. William Cogg *et al.*, Northwestern University Press, 1964.

what you would see looking down from the mountain.

Cézanne reasserted the value, complexity and unity of what we perceive (nature) as opposed to the counterfeit simplifications and singularity of European representational art. He testified that the visibility of things belongs to each one of us : not in so far as our minds interpret signals received by our eyes : but in so far as the visibility of things *is* our recognition of them : and to recognize is to relate and to order. It is apt that *blind* has come to mean not only unseeing but also directionless.

It seems to me that these conclusions are finally applicable to the Chinese monuments considered as things to be seen.

To honour individual living men by making them the subject matter of naturalistic art is to render them the creatures of another's vision instead of acknowledging them as masters of their own. And this is true whatever the cultural development of the people concerned. If comparable decisions were taken in other fields of social and cultural activity all revolutionary initiative and democracy would eventually disappear. Meanwhile the monuments may encourage production, the importance of which cannot be dismissed.

Art as a Standard of Perfection

Revolutionary Undoing

Some fight because they hate what confronts them; others because they have taken the measure of their lives and wish to give meaning to their existence. The latter are likely to struggle more persistently. Max Raphael was a very pure example of the second type.

He was born near the Polish–German border in 1889. He studied philosophy, political economy and the history of art in Berlin and Munich. His first work was published in 1913. He died in New York in 1952. In the intervening forty years he thought and wrote incessantly.

His life was austere. He held no official academic post. He was forced several times to emigrate. He earned very little money. He wrote and noted without cease. As he travelled, small groups of friends and unofficial students collected around him. By the cultural hierarchies he was dismissed as an unintelligible but dangerous Marxist: by the party communists as a Trotsky-ist. Unlike Spinoza he had no artisanal trade.

In his book, *The Demands of Art*,[1] Raphael quotes a remark of Cézanne's (in the context of a quite different analysis):

I paint my still lifes, these *natures mortes*, for my coachman who does not want them, I paint them so that children on the knees of their grandfathers may look at them while they eat their soup and

---

1. Max Raphael, *The Demands of Art*, trans. Norbert Guterman, Routledge & Kegan Paul, 1968.

chatter. I do not paint them for the pride of the Emperor of Germany or the vanity of the oil merchants of Chicago. I may get ten thousand francs for one of these dirty things, but I'd rather have the wall of a church, a hospital, or a municipal building.

Since 1848 every artist unready to be a mere paid entertainer has tried to resist the bourgeoisization of his finished work, the transformation of the spiritual value of his work into property value. This regardless of his political opinions as such. Cézanne's attempt, like that of all his contemporaries, was in vain. The resistance of later artists became more active and more violent – in that the resistance was built into their work. What constructivism, dadaism, surrealism, etc., all shared was their opposition to art-as-property and art-as-a-cultural-alibi-for-existing-society. We know the extremes to which they went: the sacrifices they were prepared to make as creators: and we see that their resistance was as ineffective as Cézanne's.

In the last decade the tactics of resistance have changed. Less frontal confrontation. Instead, infiltration. Irony and philosophic scepticism. The consequences in tachism, pop art, minimal art, neo-dada, etc. But such tactics have been no more successful than earlier ones. Art is still transformed into the property of the property-owning class. In the case of the visual arts the property involved is physical; in the case of the other arts it is moral property.

Art historians with a social or Marxist formation have interpreted the art of the past in terms of class ideology. They have shown that a class, or groups in a class, tended to support and patronize art which to some degree reflected or furthered their own class values and views. It now appears that in the later stages of capitalism this has ceased to be generally true. Art is treated as a commodity whose meaning lies *only* in its rarity value and in its functional value as a stimulant of sensation. It ceases to have implications beyond itself. Works of art become objects whose essential character is like that of diamonds or sun-tan lamps. The determining factor of this development – internationalism of monopoly, powers of mass-media communication, level of alienation in consumer societies – need not concern us here. But the consequence does. *Art can no longer oppose what is.* The faculty of proposing an alternative reality has been reduced to the faculty of designing – more or less well – an object.

Hence the imaginative doubt in all artists worthy of their category. Hence the fact that the militant young begin to use 'art' as a cover for more direct action.

One might argue that artists should continue, regardless of society's immediate treatment of their work: that they should address themselves to the future, as all imaginative artists after 1848 have had to do. But this is to ignore the world-historical moment at which we have arrived. Imperialism, European hegemony, the moralities of capitalist-Christianity and state-communism, the Cartesian dualism of white reasoning, the practice of constructing 'humanist' cultures on a basis of monstrous exploitation – this entire interlocking system is now being challenged: a world struggle is being mounted against it. Those who envisage a different future are obliged to define their position towards this struggle, obliged to choose. Such a choice tends to lead them either to impotent despair or to the conclusion that world liberation is the pre-condition for any new valid cultural achievement. (I simplify and somewhat exaggerate the positions for the sake of brevity.) Either way their doubts about the value of art are increased. An artist who now addresses the future does not necessarily have his faith in his vision confirmed.

In this present crisis, is it any longer possible to speak of the revolutionary meaning of art? This is the fundamental question. It is the question that Max Raphael begins to answer in *The Demands of Art.*

The book is based on some lectures that Raphael gave in the early 1930s to a modest adult education class in Switzerland under the title 'How should one approach a work of art?' He chose five works and devoted a chapter of extremely thorough and varied analysis to each. The works are: Cézanne's *Mont Sainte-Victoire* of 1904–6 (the one in the Philadelphia Museum), Degas's etching of *Madame X leaving her bath*, Giotto's *Dead Christ* (Padua) compared with his later *Death of Saint Francis*

(Florence), a drawing by Rembrandt of *Joseph interpreting Pharaoh's dreams*, and Picasso's *Guernica*. (The chapter on *Guernica* was of course written later.) These are followed by a general chapter on 'The struggle to understand art', and by an appendix of an unfinished but extremely important essay entitled 'Towards an empirical theory of art', written in 1941.

I shall not discuss Raphael's analysis of the five individual works. They are brilliant, long, highly particularized and dense. The most I can do is to attempt a crude outline of his general theory.

A question which Marx posed but could not answer. If art, in the last analysis, is a superstructure of the economic base, why does its power to move us endure long after the base has been transformed? Why, asked Marx, do we still look towards Greek art as an ideal? He began to answer by speaking about the 'charm' of 'young children' (the young Greek civilization) and then broke off the manuscript and was far too occupied ever to return to the question.

'A transitional epoch,' writes Raphael,

always implies uncertainty: Marx's struggle to understand his own epoch testifies to this. In such a period two attitudes are possible. One is to take advantage of the emergent forces of the new order with a view to undermining it, to affirm it in order to drive it beyond itself: this is the active, militant, revolutionary attitude. The other clings to the past, is retrospective and romantic, bewails or acknowledges the decline, asserts that the will to live is gone – in short, it is the passive attitude. Where economic, social, and political questions were at stake Marx took the first attitude; in questions of art he took neither.

He merely reflected his epoch.

Just as Marx's taste in art – the classical ideal excluding the extraordinary achievements of paleolithic, Mexican, African art – reflected the ignorance and prejudice of art appreciation in his period, so his failure to create (though he saw the need to do so) a theory of art larger than that of the superstructure theory was the consequence of the continual, overwhelming primacy of economic power in the society around him.

In view of this lacuna in Marxist theory, Raphael sets out to

develop a theory of art that I call empirical because it is based on a study of works from all periods and nations. I am convinced that mathematics, which has travelled a long way since Euclid, will some day provide us with the means of formulating the results of such a study in mathematical terms.

And he reminds the sceptical reader that before infinitesimal calculus was discovered even nature could not be studied mathematically.

'Art is an interplay, an equation of three factors – the artist, the world and the means of figuration.' Raphael's understanding of the third factor, the means or process of figuration, is crucial. For it is this process which permits him to consider the finished work of art as possessing a specific reality of its own.

Even though there is no such thing as a single, uniquely beautiful proportion of the human body or a single scientifically correct method of representing space, or one method only of artistic figuration, whatever form art may assume in the course of history, it is always a synthesis between nature (or history) and the mind, and as such it acquires a certain autonomy vis-à-vis both these elements. This independence seems to be created by man and hence to possess a psychic reality; but in point of fact the process of creation can become an existent only because it is embodied in some concrete material.

The artist chooses his material – stone, glass, pigment, or a mixture of several. He then chooses a way of working it – smoothly, roughly, in order to preserve its own character, in order to destroy or transcend it. These choices are to a large measure historically conditioned. By working his material so that it represents ideas or an object, or both, the artist transforms raw material into 'artistic' material. What is represented is materialized in the worked, raw material; whereas the worked raw material acquires an immaterial character through its representations and the *unnatural* unity which connects and binds these representations together. 'Artistic' material, so defined, a substance half physical and half spiritual, is an ingredient of the material of figuration.

A further ingredient derives from the means of representation. These are colour, line and light and shade. Perceived in nature these qualities are merely the stuff of sensation – undifferentiated from one another and arbitrarily mixed. The artist, in order to replace contingency by necessity, first separates the qualities and then combines them around a central idea or feeling which determines all their relations.

The two processes which produce the material of figuration (the process of transforming raw material into artistic material and the process of transforming the matter of sensation into means of representation) are continually interrelated. Together they constitute what might be called the matter of art.

Figuration begins with the separate long-drawn-out births of idea and motif and is complete when the two are born and indistinguishable from one another.

The characteristics of the individual idea are:

1. It is simultaneously an idea and a feeling.

2. It contains the contrasts between the particular and the general, the individual and the universal, the original and the banal.

3. It is a progression toward ever deeper meanings.

4. It is the nodal point from which secondary ideas and feelings develop.

'The motif is the sum total of line, colour and light by means of which the conception is realized.' The motif begins to be born apart from but at the same time as the idea because 'only in the act of creation does the content become fully conscious of itself'.

What is the relation between the pictorial (individual) idea and nature?

The pictorial idea separates usable from unusable elements of natural appearances and, conversely, study of natural appearances chooses from among all possible manifestations of the pictorial idea the one that is most adequate. The difficulty of the method comes down to 'proving what one believes' – 'proof' here consisting in this, that the opposed methodological starting points (experience and theory) are unified, brought together in a reality of a special kind, different from either, and that this reality owes its pictorial life to a motif adequate to the conception and developed compositionally.

What are the methods of figuration? 1. The structuring of space. 2. The rendering of forms within that space *effective*.

The structuring of space has nothing to do with perspective: its tasks are to dislocate space so that it ceases to be static (the simplest example is that of the forward-coming relaxed leg in standing Greek figures) and to divide space into quanta so that we become conscious of its divisibility and thus cease to be the creatures of *its* continuity (for example, the receding planes parallel to the picture surface in late Cézannes).

To create pictorial space is to penetrate not only into the depths of the picture but also into the depths of our intellectual system of coordinates (which matches that of the world). Depth of space is depth of essence or else it is nothing but appearance and illusion.

The distinction between actual form and effective form is as follows:

Actual form is descriptive; effective form is suggestive, i.e. through it the artist, instead of trying to convey the contents and feelings to the viewer by fully describing them, provides him only with as many clues as he needs to produce these contents and feelings within himself. To achieve this the artist must act not upon individual sense organs but upon the whole man, i.e. he must make the viewer live in the work's own mode of reality.

What does figuration, with its special material, achieve?

Intensity of figuration is not display of the artist's strength; not vitality, which animates the outer world with the personal energies of the creative artist; not logical or emotional consistency, with which a limited problem is thought through or felt through to its ultimate consequences. What it does denote is the degree to which the very essence of art has been realized: the undoing of the world of things, the construction of the world of values, and hence the constitution of a new world. The originality of this constitution provides us with a general criterion by which we can measure intensity of figuration. Originality of constitution is not the urge to be different from others, to produce something entirely new, it is (in the etymological sense) the grasping of the origin, the roots of both ourselves and things.

One must distinguish here between Raphael's 'world of values' and the idealist view of art as a depository of transcendental values. For Raphael the values lie *in the activity* revealed by the work. The function of the work of art is to lead us from the work to the process of creation which it contains. This process is determined by the material of figuration, and it is within this material, which Raphael discloses and analyses with genius, that mathematics may one day be able to discover precise principles. The process is directed towards creating within the work a synthesis of the subjective and objective, of the conditional and the absolute within a totality governed by its own laws of necessity. Thus the world of things is replaced within the work by a hierarchy of values created by the process it contains.

I can give no indication here of the detailed, specific and unabstract way in which Raphael applies his understanding to the five works he studies. I can only state that his eye and sensuous awareness were as developed as his mind. Reading him one has the impression, however difficult the thought, of a man of unusual and stable balance. One can feel the profile of an austere thinker who belonged to the twentieth century because he was a dialectical materialist inheriting the main tradition of European philosophy, but who at the same time was a man whose vital constitution made it impossible for him to ignore the unknown, the as yet tentative, the explosive human potential which will always render man indefinable within any categorical system.

Since we cannot know ourselves directly, but only through our actions, it remains more than doubtful whether our idea of ourselves accords with our real motives. But we must strive unremittingly to achieve this congruence. For only self-knowledge can lead to self-determination, and false self-determination would ruin our lives and be the most immoral action we could commit.

To return now to our original question: what is the revolutionary meaning of art? Raphael shows that the revolutionary meaning of a work of art has nothing to do with its subject matter in itself, or with the functional use to which the work is put, but is a meaning continually awaiting discovery and release.

However strong a given historical tendency may be, man can and has the duty to resist it when it runs counter to his creative powers. There is no fate which decrees that we must be victims of technology or that art must be shelved as an anachronism; the 'fate' is merely misuse of technology by the ruling class to suppress the people's power to make its own history. To a certain extent it is up to every individual, by his participation in social and political life, to decide whether art shall or shall not become obsolete. The understanding of art helps raise this decision to its highest level. As a vessel formed by the creative forces which it preserves, the work of art keeps alive and enhances every urge to come to terms with the world.

We have said that art leads us from the work to the process of creation. This reversion, outside the theory of art, will eventually generate universal doubt about the world as given, the natural as well as the social. Instead of accepting things as they are, of taking them for granted, we learn, thanks to art, to measure them by the standard of perfection. The greater the unavoidable gulf between the ideal and the real, the more inescapable is the question. Why is the existing world the way it is? How has the world come to be what it is? *De omnibus rebus dubitandum est! Quid certum?* 'We must doubt all things! What is certain?' (Descartes). It is the nature of the creative mind to dissolve seemingly solid things and to transform the world as it is into a world in process of becoming and creating. This is how we are liberated from the multiplicity of things and come to realize what it is that all conditional things ultimately possess in common. Thus, instead of being creatures we become part of the power that creates all things.

Raphael did not, could not, make our choices for us. Everyone must resolve for himself the conflicting demands of his historical situation. But even to those who conclude that the practice of art must be temporarily abandoned, Raphael will show as no other writer has ever done the revolutionary meaning of the works inherited from the past – and of the works that will be eventually created in the future. And this he shows without rhetoric, without exhortation, modestly and with reason. His was the greatest mind yet applied to the subject.

Past Seen from a
Possible Future

Has anyone ever tried to estimate how many framed oil paintings, dating from the fifteenth century to the nineteenth, there are in existence? During the last fifty years a large number must have been destroyed. How many were there in 1900? The figure itself is not important. But even to guess at it is to realize that what is normally counted as art, and on the evidence of which art historians and experts generalize about the European tradition, is a quantitatively insignificant fraction of what was actually produced.

From the walls of the long gallery, those who never had any reason to doubt their own significance look down in perpetual self-esteem, surrounded by gilded frames. I look down at the courtyard around which the galleries were built. In the centre, a fountain plays sluggishly: the water slowly but continuously overbrimming its bowl. There are weeping willows, benches and a few gesticulating statues. The courtyard is open to the public. In summer it is cooler than the city streets outside: in winter it is protected from the wind.

I have sat on a bench listening to the talk of those who come into the courtyard for a few minutes' break – mostly old people or women with children. I have watched the children playing. I have paced around the courtyard, when nobody was there, thinking about my own life. I have sat there, blind to everything around me, reading a newspaper. As I look down on the courtyard before turning back to the portraits of the nineteenth-century local dignitaries, I notice that the gallery attendant is standing at the next tall window and that he too is gazing down on the animated figures below.

And then suddenly I have a vision of him and me, each alone and stiff in his window, being seen from below. I am seen quite clearly but not in detail for it is forty feet up to the window and the sun is in such a position that it half dazzles the eyes of the seer. I see myself as seen. I experience a moment of familiar panic. Then I turn back to the framed images.

The banality of nineteenth-century official portraits is, of course, more complete than that of eighteenth-century landscapes or that of seventeenth-century religious pieces. But perhaps not to a degree that matters. European art is idealized by exaggerating the historical differences within its development and by never seeing it as a whole.

The art of any culture will show a wide differential of talent. But I doubt whether anywhere else the difference between the masterpieces and the average is as large as it is in the European tradition of the last five centuries. The difference is not only a question of skill and imagination, but also of morale. The average work – and increasingly after the sixteenth century – was produced cynically: that is to say its content, its message, the values it was nominally upholding, were less meaningful for the producer than the finishing of the commission. Hack work is not the result of clumsiness or provincialism: it is the result of the market making more insistent demands than the job.

Just as art history has concentrated upon a number of remarkable works and barely considered the largest part of the tradition, aesthetic theory has emphasized the disinterestedly spiritual experience to be gained from works of art and largely ignored their massive ideological function. We spiritualize art by calling it art.

The modern historians of Renaissance and post-Renaissance art – Burckhardt, Wölfflin, Riegl, Dvorak – began writing at the moment when the tradition was beginning to disintegrate. Undoubtedly the two facts were linked within a fantastically complicated matrix of other historical developments. Perhaps historians always require an end in order to begin. These historians, however, defined the various phases of the tradition (Renaissance, Mannerist, Baroque, Neo-Classic) so sharply and explained their evolution from one to the other with such skill that they encouraged the notion that the European tradition was one of change without end: the more it broke with or remade its own inheritance, the more it was itself. Tracing a certain continuity in the past they seemed to guarantee one for the future.

Concentration upon the exceptional works of a couple of hundred masters, an emphasis on the spirituality of art, a sense of belonging to a history without end – all these have discouraged us from ever seeing our pictorial tradition as a whole and have led us to imagine that our own experience of looking today at a few works from the past still offers an immediate clue to the function of the vast production of European art. We conclude that it was the destiny of Europe to make art. The formulation may be more sophisticated, but that is the essential assumption. Try now to see the tradition from the far distance.

'We can have no idea,' wrote Nietzsche, 'what sort of things are going to become history one day. Perhaps the past is still largely undiscovered; it still needs so many retroactive forces for its discovery.'

During the period we are considering, which can be roughly marked out as the period between Van Eyck and Ingres, the framed easel picture, the oil painting, was the primary art product. Wall painting, sculpture, the graphic arts, tapestry, scenic design, and even many aspects of architecture were visualized and judged according to a value system which found its purest expression in the easel picture. For the ruling and middle classes the easel picture became a microcosm of the whole world that was virtually assimilable: its pictorial tradition became the vehicle for all visual ideals.

To what uses did the easel picture pre-eminently lend itself?

It permitted a style of painting which was able to 'imitate' nature or reality more closely than any other. What are usually termed stylistic changes – from classical to mannerist to baroque and so on – never affected the basic 'imitative' faculty; each subsequent phase simply used it in a different manner.

I put inverted commas round 'imitative' because the word may confuse as much as it explains. To say that the European style imitated nature makes sense only when one accepts a particular view of nature: a view which eventually found its most substantial expression in the philosophy of Descartes.

Descartes drew an absolute distinction between mind and matter. The property of mind was self-consciousness. The property of matter was extension in space. The mind was infinitely subtle. The workings of nature, however complicated, were mechanically explicable and, relative to the mind, unmysterious. Nature was predestined for man's use and was *the ideal object of his observation*. And it was precisely this which Renaissance perspective, according to which everything converged on the eye of the beholder, demonstrated. Nature was that conical segment of the visible whose apex was the human eye. Thus imitating nature meant tracing on a two-dimensional surface what that eye saw or might see at a given moment.

European art – I use the term to refer only to the period we are discussing – is no less artificial, no less arbitrary, no closer to total reality than the figurative art of any other culture or period. All traditions of figurative art invoke different experiences to confirm their own principles of figuration. No figurative works of art produced within a tradition appear unrealistic to those brought up within the tradition. And so we must ask a subtler question. What aspect of experience does the European style invoke? Or more exactly, what kind of experience do its means of representation represent? (Ask, too, the same question about Japanese art, or West African.)

In his book on the Florentine painters Berenson writes:

It is only when we can take for granted the existence of the object painted that it can begin to give us pleasure that is genuinely artistic, as separated from the interest we feel in symbols.

He then goes on to explain that the tangibility, the 'tactile value' of the painted object, is what allows us to take its existence for granted. Nothing could be more explicit about the implications of the artistic pleasure to be derived from European art. That which we believe we can put our hands upon truly exists for us; if we cannot, it does not.

European means of representation refer to the experience of taking possession. Just as its perspective gathers all that is extended to render it to the individual eye, so its means of representation render all that is depicted into the hands of the individual owner-spectator. Painting becomes the metaphorical act of appropriation.

The social and economic modes of appropriation changed a great deal during the five centuries. In fifteenth-century painting the reference was often directly to what was depicted in the painting – marble floors, golden pillars, rich textiles, jewels, silverware. By the sixteenth century it was no longer assembled or hoarded riches which the painting rendered up to the spectator-owner but, thanks to the unity that chiaroscuro could give to the most dramatic actions, whole *scenes* complete with their events and protagonists. These scenes were 'ownable' to the degree that the spectator understood that wealth could produce and control action at a distance. In the eighteenth century the tradition divided into two streams. In one, simple middle-class properties were celebrated, in the other the aristocratic right to buy performances and to direct an unending theatre.

I am in front of a typical European nude. She is painted with extreme sensuous emphasis. Yet her sexuality is only superficially manifest in her actions or her own expression; in a comparable figure within other art traditions this would not be so. Why? Because for Europe ownership is primary. The painting's sexuality is manifest not in what it shows but in the owner-spectator's (mine in this case) right to see her naked. Her nakedness is not a function of her sexuality but of the sexuality of those who have access to the picture. In the majority of European nudes there is a close parallel with the passivity which is endemic to prostitution.

It has been said that the European painting is like a window open on to the world. Purely optically this may be the case. But is it not as much like a safe, let into the wall, in which the visible has been deposited?

So far I have considered the methods of painting, the means of representation. Now to consider what the paintings showed, their subject matter. There were special categories of subjects: portraits, landscapes, still life, genre pictures of 'low life'. Each category might well be studied separately within the same general perspective which I have suggested. (Think of the tens of thousands of still-life canvases depicting game shot or bagged: the numerous genre pictures about procuring or accosting: the innumerable uniformed portraits of office.) I want, however, to concentrate on the category which was always considered the noblest and the most central to the tradition – paintings of religious or mythological subjects.

Certain basic Christian subjects occurred in art long before the rise of the easel painting. Yet described in frescoes or sculpture or stained glass their function and their social, as distinct from purely iconographic, meaning was very different. A fresco presents its subject within a given context – say that of a chapel devoted to a particular saint. The subject *applies* to what is structurally around it and to what is likely to happen around it; the spectator, who is also a worshipper, becomes part of that context. The easel picture is without a precise physical or emotional context because it is transportable.

Instead of presenting its subject within a larger whole it offers its subject to whoever owns it. Thus its subject *applies* to the life of its owner. A primitive transitional example of this principle working are the crucifixions or nativities in which those who commissioned the painting, the donors, are actually painted in standing at the foot of the cross or kneeling around the crib. Later, they did not need to be painted in because physical ownership of the painting guaranteed their immanent presence within it.

Yet how did hundreds of somewhat esoteric subjects apply to the lives of those who owned paintings of them? The sources of the subjects were not real events or rituals but texts. To a unique degree European art was a visual art deriving from literature. Familiarity with these texts or at least with their personae was the prerogative of the privileged minority. The majority of such paintings would have been readable as representational images but unreadable as language because they were ignorant of what they signified. In this respect if in no other most of us today are a little like that majority. What exactly happened to St Ursula? we ask. Exactly why did Andromeda find herself chained to the rocks?

This specialized knowledge of the privileged minority supplied them with a system of references by which to express subtly and evocatively the values and ideals of the life lived by their class. (For the last vestiges of this tradition note the moral value still sometimes ascribed to the study of the classics.) Religious and mythological paintings were something more than mere illustration of their separate subjects; together they constituted a system which classified and idealized reality according to the cultural interest of the ruling classes. They supplied a visual etiquette – a series of examples showing how significant moments in life should be envisaged. One needs to remember that, before the photograph or the cinema, painting alone offered recorded evidence of what people or events looked like or should look like.

Paintings applied to the lives of their spectator-owners because they showed how these lives should ideally appear at their heightened moments of religious faith, heroic action, sensuous abandon, contrition, tenderness, anger, courageous death, the dignified exercise of power, etc. They were like garments held out for the spectator-owners to put their arms into and wear. Hence the great attention paid to the verisimilitude of the *texture* of the things portrayed.

The spectator-owners did not identify themselves with the subjects of the paintings. Empathy occurs at a simpler and more spontaneous level of appreciation. The subjects did not even confront the spectator-owners as an exterior force; they were already theirs. Instead, the spectator-owners identified themselves *in* the subject. They saw themselves or their imagined selves covered over by the subject's idealized appearances. They found in them the guise of what they believed to be their own humanity.

The typical religious or mythological painting from the sixteenth century to the nineteenth was extraordinarily vacuous. We only fail to see this because we are deceived by the cultural overlay that art history has given these pictures. In the typical painting the figures are only superficially related to their painted surroundings; they appear detachable from them : their faces are expressionless : their vast bodies are stereotyped and limp – limp even in action. This cannot be explained by the artist's clumsiness or lack of talent; primitive works, even of a low order of imagination, are infinitely more expressive. These paintings are vacuous because it was their function, as established by usage and tradition, to be empty. They needed to be empty. They were not meant to express or inspire; they were meant to clothe the systematic fantasies of their owners.

The easel picture lent itself by its means of representation to a metaphorical appropriation of the material world : by its iconography to the appropriation by a small privileged minority of all 'the human values' of Christianity and the classic world.

I see a rather undistinguished Dutch seventeenth-century self-portrait. Yet the look of the painter has a quality which is not uncommon in self-portraits. A look of probing amazement. A look which shows slight questioning of what it sees.

There have been paintings which have transcended the tradition to which they belong. These paintings pertain to a true humanity. They bear witness to their artists' intuitive awareness that life was larger than the available traditional means of representing it and that its dramas were more urgent than conventional iconography could now allow. The mistake is to confuse these exceptions with the norms of the tradition.

The tradition and its norms are worth studying, for in them we can find evidence such as exists nowhere else of the way that the European ruling classes saw the world and themselves.

We can discover the typology of their fantasies. We can see life rearranged to frame their own image. And occasionally we can glimpse even in works that are not exceptional – usually in landscapes because they relate to experiences of solitude in which the imagination is less confined by social usage – a tentative vision of another kind of freedom, a freedom other than the right to appropriate.

In one sense every culture appropriates or tries to make the actual and possible world its own. In a somewhat different sense all men acquire experience for themselves. What distinguishes post-Renaissance European practice from that of any other culture is its transformation of everything which is acquired into a commodity; consequently, everything becomes exchangeable. Nothing is appropriated for its own sake. Every object and every value is transmutable into another – even into its opposite. In *Capital*, Marx quotes Christopher Columbus writing in 1503: 'By means of gold one can even get souls into Paradise.' Nothing exists in itself. This is the essential spiritual violence of European capitalism.

Ideally the easel picture is framed. The frame emphasizes that within its four edges the picture has established an enclosed, coherent and absolutely rigorous system of its own. The frame marks the frontier of the realm of an autonomous order. The demands of composition and of the picture's illusory but all-pervasive three-dimensional space constitute the rigid laws of this order. Into this order are fitted representations of real figures and objects.

All the imitative skill of the tradition is concentrated upon making these representations look as tangibly real as possible. Yet each part submits to an abstract and artificial order of the whole. (Formalist analyses of paintings and all the classic demonstrations of compositional rules prove the degree of this submission.) The parts look real but in fact they are ciphers. They are ciphers within a comprehensive yet invisible and closed system which nevertheless pretends to be open and natural.

Such is the tyranny exercised by the easel painting, and

from it arises the fundamental criterion for judging between the typical and the exceptional within the European tradition. Does what is depicted insist upon the unique value of its original being or has it succumbed to the tyranny of the system?

Today visual images no longer serve as a source of private pleasure and confirmation for the European ruling classes; rather, they have become a vehicle for its power over others through the mass media and publicity. Yet it is false to draw a comparison between these recent commercial developments and the hallowed tradition of European art. Their references may be different: they may serve a different immediate purpose; but their determining principle is the same – a man is what he possesses.

Delacroix was, I think, the first painter to suspect some of what the tradition of the easel picture entailed. Later, other artists questioned the tradition and opposed it more violently. Cézanne quietly destroyed it from within. Significantly, the two most sustained and radical attempts to create an alternative tradition occurred in the 1920s in Russia and Mexico, countries where the European model had been arbitrarily imposed on their own indigenous art traditions.

To most young artists today it is axiomatic that the period of the easel picture is finished. In their works they try to establish new categories in terms of media, form and response. Yet the tradition dies hard and still exerts an enormous influence on our view of the past, our ideas about the role of the visual artist and our definition of civilization. Why has it taken so long to die?

Because the so-called Fine Arts, although they have found new materials and new means, have found no new social function to take the place of the easel picture's outdated one. It is beyond the power of artists alone to create a new social function for art. Such a new function will only be born of revolutionary social change. Then it may become possible for artists to work truly concretely and constructively with reality itself, to work with what men are really like rather than with a visual etiquette serving the interests of a privileged minority; then it may be that art will re-establish contact with what European art has always dismissed – with that which cannot be appropriated.

A World to Gain

Czechoslovakia Alone

1 : August 1968[1]   The clandestine radio stations are still broadcasting in Czechoslovakia as I write. Freedom of expression was crucial to the late Czechoslovak situation. Not because such freedom has an absolute value in all circumstances, as hypocritically claimed by bourgeois social democracy; but because this freedom during the last four months was the most direct means of reawakening the Czechoslovak people to a sense of their own political power.

In May 1963 a conference was held in Czechoslovakia on the subject of Kafka. Among the principal speakers were Ernst Fischer, Eduard Goldstücker who was elected President of the Czechoslovak Union of Writers in January of this year, and Roger Garaudy from France. The outcome of the conference could have been narrowly interpreted as merely a semi-official 'rehabilitation' of a great Czech writer. But its implications were far wider, for it was in the works of Kafka that one could find the vocabulary to define all the most negative aspects of the national experience of the preceding fifteen years: experience of a massive secret police repression and of the bureaucratization of thought, social life, national planning, politics and morals.

Today the club of ex-political prisoners who have been re-

---

1. This article, first published in *New Society*, 29 August 1968, was written three days after the invasion of Czechoslovakia.

habilitated or who claim rehabilitation includes about 80,000 members. To have some idea of the scale of the repression one should add to this figure tens of thousands who were either executed or who died. Yet the effects of such repression cannot finally be counted in terms of the number of victims. Because these victims included both real political opponents and the most loyal communists, all political categories came to seem arbitrary and meaningless. All political dialogue was reduced to a monologue of prosecution and defamation.

The extent of the bureaucratization was too complex and far-reaching to describe here. But two consequences of it are particularly significant. Compared with other socialist countries, the Czechoslovak wage and salary structure was egalitarian. The differential between skilled and unskilled workers or between workers and technologists and intellectuals was slight. But since this 'egalitarianism' had no political content and was contradicted by the lack of any possibility of democratic participation at any level, it became an authoritarian levelling process which destroyed all incentives and initiative. The bureaucracy thus transferred to the people a sense of being anonymous, passive members of a gigantic circular civil service.

The simultaneous power and futility of the bureaucracy was revealed most obviously in its theory and practice of economic planning. Czechoslovakia is, relative to its population, the third greatest producer of cement in the world, yet for years it has been impossible for a Czech to buy on the legal market one sack of cement to mend a roof or build a wall with. A large metal works producing sheet used to turn out material which was too thick to be usable and was immediately bought as scrap in order to be re-melted. A factory in Prague producing nails had to meet a per annum quota expressed in tons. The simplest way of meeting this quota was to produce massive six-inch nails. As a result, no smaller nails were available on the market. The stock of unsaleable products now accumulated in Czechoslovakia is worth 200 billion crowns.

Some Czechs argue that the reason they were the first to liberate themselves from a bureaucracy which, although it had a specific character in their own country, was general to all socialist states, was that they have a longstanding national democratic tradition. A workers' party, they point out, was legally established in Czechoslovakia ninety years ago: whereas in czarist Russia it was only ten years earlier that the serfs had been freed. I find this reasoning inadequate. What rouses a passion for freedom is not exclusively, or even principally, an experience of parliamentary democracy. (An extraordinary passion for freedom was born and developed in the early Russian Soviets.) Czechoslovakia was briefly, until last week, the first country truly to begin liberating itself from Stalinist bureaucracy because in Czechoslovakia the resulting contradictions were exceptionally acute.

Czechoslovakia is a small country (population 14,000,000) and was already industrially advanced in 1948. These two circumstances meant not only that the consequences of primitive, para-military, centralized planning were particularly disastrous, but also that these consequences were particularly evident to the mass of the people. Ten years ago Czechoslovakia still functioned for the outside world as the shop window of socialist Europe. But this was possible only because its initial productive advantages had not yet been entirely squandered. The first five-year plan of 1948 was prolonged to seven years; the second was unsuccessful; the third was abandoned in 1960 after two years and replaced by one-year plans which paralysed development of complex industries requiring a longer minimum planning perspective. At this point the planners' recognition of their own failure further increased the effects of that failure. Instead of reducing the field of their absolute authority, they chaotically reduced the duration of their plans. Ten years ago party opponents of such planning were already pointing to the evident economic decline of the country. The decline became more and more obvious.

The second major contradiction arose as the result of the national question between Czechs and Slovaks. This was not a matter of a suppressed minority but of two equal nations, one of which, despite nominal guarantees to the contrary, continually dominated the other. The bureaucracy, centralized in Prague (and not Bratislava), intensified the antagonism and became the butt of both nations. Slovaks saw the bureaucracy as the instrument of Czech domination; Czechs blamed the ineptness of the bureaucracy for the constant resentment of the Slovaks. Predictably, it was in Slovakia that the strongest opposition groups were first formed within the party.

Thirdly – and here the national democratic tradition *is* relevant – Novotný's Czechoslovakia was the last of the socialist countries to begin the reluctant and superficial process of 'destalinization'. Thus, when abuses of legality began to be admitted, there developed, in the light of the inadequacy of the admissions elsewhere, and in the knowledge that abuses could still continue even after so-called 'destalinization', a demand for far-reaching investigations, reforms and safeguards. This was an example of the last becoming the first.

What was the political character of those who were able to take advantage of the contradictions to oust Novotný and his supporters? Roughly they can be divided into two groups : those who worked within the party and in its central committee, and those (mostly writers, economists, philosophers, etc.) who worked outside it. The latter were at first able to be more sweeping in their criticisms and demands. But both groups were elites. The government was changed from above rather than from below.

In general, the attitude of the two groups to immediate popular participation (student demonstrations, workers' councils, etc.) was cautious. At the same time they realized that their whole justification and position depended upon initiating the widest possible democratization. Their preliminary role was already determined by the previous twenty years of repressive bureaucracy to which they were opposed : they had to form a conduit of power from the state apparatus towards the populace. Some would have proved themselves incapable of performing any further significant role, especially those whose political energy was concentrated solely on the issue of the liberalization of ideas. Others would have developed with the situation which they had helped to bring about. But all realized that their first role compelled them to leave solutions open :

We declare with full responsibility that our society has entered the difficult period when we can no longer rely on traditional schemes. We cannot squeeze life into patterns, no matter how well-intentioned ...[2]

To accuse the new leaders of pragmatism, scepticism or, as now in Moscow, of encouraging counter-revolution, is a solipsism. Twenty years of Stalinism had made it inevitable that any liberation from it would be accompanied by tendencies which could be interpreted as pragmatic, sceptical, etc. Let us note the elements of the inherited situation of January 1968.

1. The productive forces were in the hands of the state, which, whatever its abuses of power, did not represent a property-owning class. There was no economic basis for the existence of antagonistic classes. Furthermore, the old property-owning class had disintegrated and no longer existed as a potential power group.

2. As a result of primitive centralist planning, the national economy was in a state of profound crisis which it was difficult to analyse in detail because the planners had inserted their own unreal values into the structure of the economy itself. (No economist to whom I talked blamed the crisis primarily on unfavourable trade agreements with the U.S.S.R. It is misleading to speak of Soviet economic imperialism and to equate it with that of the West.)

3. A widespread demoralization of the population expressed itself in political cynicism and poor productivity (and an increasingly low birthrate). This demoralization was the result of the uninterrupted political monologue, repression and the mindlessness of the egalitarianism. The working day in Czechoslovakia begins at about 6.30 a.m. and ends at about 2.30 p.m. Many workers spent the late afternoon or evening working on the private market – usually using black-market material. The

---

2. Action Programme of the Czechoslovak C.P., April, 1968.

money they earned in this way exacerbated their desire for commodities which were unavailable. All fields of activities encouraged numerous rackets.

4. The bi-national state was unnecessarily divided against itself.

In such a situation the immediate necessity was to reactivate and repoliticize the people by offering them political responsibility. Hence the crucial role of liberty of expression in all sectors. Anything less would only have meant transforming a ruthless authoritarianism into a more benign one. It was necessary for the people to begin to take over what had been constructed in their name, to take possession of the content of the socialist forms which had been rigidly and distortedly formalized. There were of course risks in such a policy and these risks will appear magnified to those 'revolutionaries' who have become habitual defenders of the compromise achievements of revolution instead of advocates of new revolutionary achievement – those for whom a leap is always an unjustified risk. Yet the risks in Czechoslovakia were not foolhardy. The basis for a counter-revolution, for a return to capitalism, did not exist.

The major risk was that the people would not rise to the opportunity offered them but would remain trapped within those conflicting factional interests which had been developed, if not created, by twenty years of Stalinist rule.

Despite its unexpectedness, Moscow's intervention in Czechoslovakia is not an illogical development. If we failed to expect it in military form, it was because we did not appreciate how near its end was the Kremlin's claim to lead a world communist movement; we did not appreciate that this leadership was about to lose even the reality of its own self-interest. Russian intervention in some form, however, was inevitable because the present Russian leadership cannot afford to have its own neo-Stalinist model challenged.

At the same time, the more it is challenged the more it reverts to purely Stalinist policies and thus demonstrates the essential unreality of its half measures.

Given the inevitability of some form of Russian intervention, we must add to the four inherited elements of the Czechoslovak situation a fifth element which was about to be created : the national Czechoslovak reaction to Russian interference. It would be foolish to classify this as patriotism and to pursue the matter no further. It was this national reaction in response, first to East German slanders about the presence of Western troops in Czechslovakia and later to the threats of the Warsaw letter, which reduced the risk of fragmentation within the country and united both Czechs and Slovaks behind Dubček. More than that, it quickened a sense of political participation and immediately began to transform people's values.

Workers in many places spontaneously offered to work for nothing on Saturdays in order to contribute to the national fund. Those for whom, a few months before, the highest ideal had been a consumer society, offered money and gold to help save the national economy. (Economically a naïve gesture but ideologically a significant one.) I saw crowds of workers in the streets of Prague, their faces lit by an evident sense of opportunity and achievement. Such an atmosphere was bound to be temporary. But it was an unforgettable indication of the previously unused potential of a people : of the speed with which demoralization may be overcome.

Despite the personal tragedies involved, it is neither heartless nor unreasonable to hope that the military intervention will now further accelerate the historical processes involved. Within Czechoslovakia, its petty-bourgeoisie as always hesitant, the initiative for change has passed into the hands of factory committees, local parties and the workers' councils which had just begun to be formed. This means a far more radical politicization at the base than Dubček and his colleagues had thought possible.

Czechoslovak workers now face a more conscious and important choice than has been offered them for twenty years. In this choice, however harsh, many will recognize and rediscover their political power. Who can believe that they will wish to use this power to re-establish capitalism? It is doubtful whether even the Russian leadership believed this. Their true fear was elsewhere.

The Russian leaders feared the Czechoslovak party congress, scheduled for 9 September. Apart from discussing the new status of Slovakia and the economic reforms, the congress was to decide on new forms of inner party democracy. Whatever the exact form chosen, the intention was to legalize opposition groups and factions within the party, and to abandon the practice of 'democratic centralism' as institutionalized and made an article of religious faith by Stalin after the expulsion of Trotsky. This was to be the party political equivalent of the freedom of expression given to the press and public.

And this is what the Russian leadership feared, for it would have undermined their own dictatorial powers. The example would have spread to other parties both inside and outside the communist bloc. Yet in suppressing the Czech example, the Russian leadership shows that the principle of democratic centralism, first formulated by Lenin to meet the special circumstances of a small, illegal revolutionary party – and still useful in such circumstances – has now been extended and distorted.

What ultimately was at stake in Czechoslovakia was the continuity of the present form of leadership of the Russian model. Almost despite itself, the Czech party has been forced to challenge this continuity in order to put an end to Stalinism and rediscover its own revolutionary meaning.

2 : February   A conference on Czechoslovakia, organized by the
1969   Bertrand Russell Foundation, took place in Stock-
holm on 1 and 2 February 1969. Its final declaration announced a larger conference to be organized by the foundation in London in May and, at the same time, appealed

to communist parties and communists to refuse participation
in the forthcoming May conference of communist parties in
Moscow, unless Soviet troops were first withdrawn from Czechoslovakia.

Four Czechs tried to come to Stockholm from Prague. Two
were detained at Prague airport. Two arrived, Josef Pokstefl,
who was the convener of the clandestine fourteenth congress
of the Czech communist party (in August 1968 after the Soviet
invasion) and Lubomir Holecek, a student leader who was a
close friend of Jan Palach's. Palach asked for him to come and
talk to him before he died, and in the event Holecek was the
last person Palach spoke to. It was Holecek who gave the
funeral oration before a mourning crowd of 200,000 people.

I want to report Holecek's speech because in my opinion
it was the most significant one made at the conference.

All the preceding day he had taken notes on the other
speeches which were translated to him. He was a philosophy
student. Nothing distracted him from listening and composing
his reply – least of all the curiosity, interest or friendliness of
the rest of us sitting round the table. He was narrow-cheeked,
pale but wiry-looking. He wore dark glasses which he never
fingered. Occasionally during the speeches he leant across to
speak in Czech to Pokstefl.

As he addressed us, his way of speaking suggested an unusual
attitude to the words he was using. Crudely one might describe
it as follows : he had learned to speak as a child : later he had
seen whole vocabularies falsified and rendered meaningless : he
had come to mistrust all words : slowly and recently, active
individual choices had begun to recharge words with meaning
for him. It was as though he had learned to speak *for the second
time*. He spoke fluently and cautiously.

The report is not verbatim. He spoke in Czech and was halt-
ingly translated into French.

He said that he wanted to speak on behalf of his generation
of students in Czechoslovakia. There were considerable differences between his generation and their contemporaries in the
West. He had spoken to Rudi Dutschke before he was shot at,

and he had been struck by how deeply experience (not aims) separated them.

Ninety per cent of the students in Prague were fully conscious of their country's postwar experience and, as a result, were committed to action. But only a small minority were influenced by the situation in the West or the Third World.

The Western left's sense of solidarity with the Czechs had increased after the invasion. Yet the invasion had changed nothing in terms of principle. The struggle from January 1968 onwards – and its preparation had begun long before – was always of more than local national significance; it should have been placed in the context of the world-wide struggle for national independence.

The reforms of the 1968 Action Programme came too late; hence an explosive situation. But the dynamic of that situation was to establish, not refute, socialism.

Difficulties were inherited from the past. The Novotný regime had prevented all horizontal communication – for instance between students and workers. To begin with the workers did not speak. The first necessity had been to break the power of the secret police : the second, to break the power of the ruling oligarchy. We had to establish freedom of speech, news and assembly. We had to force the ruling caste to respect public opinion. We had to educate our politicians. Above all, we had to free people of fear.

Only somebody who appreciates the enormity of these tasks is in a position to appreciate the final breadth and spontaneity of the popular unity which was born, when in June the mass of the working class dispensed with its official paid representatives and began to speak and make known its demands with its own voice. This mass movement had displayed an extraordinary tolerance which had extended even to its previous oppressors. The old power apparatus was never really destroyed.

We of the younger generation were too naïve. We did not understand the true nature of Soviet policy. We believed in the formal guarantees concerning our rights of national independence. Like many of the New Left in the West, we lived in a dream. We believed in ideals and ignored reality.

Only after the threats contained in the Warsaw letter did we recognize the danger facing us. In July we began to argue and agitate for the need for preparing and organizing various means of defence. Our warnings were published. We had realized the extent of our earlier naïvety, but Dubček had not. We were unable to act effectively in the light of what we could foresee. Before you criticize us, you too must learn to be objective and to understand our situation as it was.

Some have said that our ideas tended to be elitist. After twenty years of Stalinist education, my generation suffered from an overwhelming sense of a minimal, fragmented reality which applied to all experience – social, cultural and political. Everything was at its smallest. A generation educated like that does not learn the necessary methods of political struggle, not even the legal ones. A generation educated like that does not know how to be happy. Its perspective is despair. Only in an academic sense were we an intellectual elite – and certainly never an economic one.

The difference between generations has acquired an historic significance in Czechoslovakia. Political leaders who are now in their fifties or early sixties – Dubček's generation – still believe in certain myths. I can ask them to change their views, but there is little chance of their being able to do so. Their spirit was formed by their personal experience of the Comintern, Nazi concentration camps and small communist partisan groups. After the war they took over the political apparatus. Their dream was of limitless power *in order to change everything.* In 1968 we asked them to accept pluralism. Their vision, however, was essentially monopolistic and their political sense oddly amateur. They had been unable to develop politically because for twenty years all questioning had been silenced and any popular political activity stifled.

The next generation – Comrade Pokstefl's generation – witnessed terrible events and inherited the catastrophic economic crisis of the 1960s. They had to propose reforms which took account of the reality they inherited.

My generation has certain reservations about the proposed reforms. We saw that the new model of socialism was, in a sense, born of the Novotný regime. Nevertheless we appreciated its realism. For example, we accepted Ota Šik's economic plan as a provisional one; he himself never claimed that it was a new model or an ideal solution; but it was an attempt to come to terms with, and solve, the specific economic crisis of Czechoslovakia.

What are the plans of my generation in 1969?

1. To pursue a current of political thought opposed to all forms of Stalinism and yet not indulging in dreams. For us it is a necessity to reject some of the dreams of the New Left in the West. With such dreams we would be buried.

2. To maintain our links with the working class and trade union organizations. We speak daily in factories to gatherings of up to a thousand workers. Last week there were 200,000 people at our public demonstration. We do not tell workers what they should do: we simply try to share our experience with them. The trade-union movement is now ready for a political struggle and can only, conceivably, be stopped if subject to extreme illegal repression.

Meanwhile the generation represented here by Comrade Pokstefl – and my own – will continue to work for, and prepare, an alternative model of socialism. It may take us one year, it may take us ten.

And what do we hope for from the West?

That the Western communist parties understand the significance of what is being done in their name by the present Soviet leadership. That the New Left understand and also criticize us, but that they distinguish between dreams and reality. That the anti-imperialist front develop a programme of struggle which does not ignore the question of the small nations of central Europe. Finally, that socialists in the West try to curb the capitalist and imperialist propaganda aimed at Czechoslovakia. Nothing can harm us more than 'the support' and appeals of various radio stations, materials and 'aid' sent to us from the West.

We, who work at and constitute the base of what was once the great bureaucratic pyramid, believe that we have certain possibilities and capabilities. Perhaps we even underestimate them. The few who wield power – both in the socialist world and in the capitalist – perhaps overestimate their power. And in this there may lie hope for us all ...

3 : April This month in Prague there took place an inter-
1969 national seminar on socialism and revolution, or-
ganized by the students' council of the faculty of nuclear physics of Prague University. About fifty participants – most of them under thirty – came from the West. During the discussion, between 100 and 150 Prague students were present. They included the most important leaders of the student movement and a certain number of foreign, mostly African, students studying in Prague.

On the first day the Czechs informed us that the seminar had been officially banned and we were asked whether we wished to continue with it. Since it was the Czechs who would suffer any repercussions there might be, we made it clear that they should make the decision. They decided that the seminar should continue. It continued for three days in a basement common-room at the university of Strahov. Whilst it continued, a coup d'état by certain pro-Russian Czech generals was being prepared. This coup was prevented (or postponed?), probably by the efforts of President Svoboda.

Each day began with a lecture by a professor who sympa-thized with the students' initiative. The first of these, a philo-sopher of about forty, was a leader of the Czech Maoist group which, since the evident failure of Dubček's government to offer effective resistance to the Russians, has apparently increased its influence, although this is still relatively small, among both students and workers. He argued that the Soviet policy of peace-ful coexistence meant a division of the world between the

United States and the Soviet Union in order to preserve the apex of a pyramid at the base of which five sixths of the world were being mercilessly exploited and were living at a far lower level of subsistence than 200 years ago. He saw the Russian invasion of Czechoslovakia last August as the first proof in Europe of this two-power agreement to divide the world.

He defined the present system in Russia as a form of state capitalism. The development began, he argued, in the thirties when, as a result of the industrialization programme, a technologically trained managerial group emerged to challenge the position of the old Bolshevik leadership. During the war this leadership was incapable of organizing the war effort without a closer collaboration with the managerial group, who thus increased their power and privileges. In 1948, changes in Soviet civil law legalized many forms of private property, and at the same time the educational system was changed to allow the privileged to perpetuate their privileges. At the nineteenth Party Congress in 1952 the bureaucrats and the managerial group combined and proceeded to safeguard their shared power by coopting their own (unelected) representatives on to the Central Committee and Politbureau. Formally the means of production still belonged to the people, but from the nineteenth Congress onwards, all powers of decision were firmly in the hands of a new privileged ruling class.

He did not believe that the developments in Czechoslovakia up to January 1968 had led to state capitalism; the system, although profoundly corrupt, had remained a purely bureaucratic one. The negative aspects of the reform programme of last spring suggested, however, that the party bureaucrats and the managerial technocracy might have soon merged, as earlier in Russia, to form the ruling class of a state capitalist system. It was not, of course, this which had frightened the Russians – but the danger of the working class and some groups of intellectuals exploiting the fluidity of the situation to establish a form of democratic socialism.

He went on to say that, in twenty years, the ruling classes of Europe – east and west – would understand nothing of what was happening in the world. Meanwhile it was necessary to create an integrated European revolutionary movement, and the vision of this movement might well be sustained by the Chinese example of permanent revolution. When cross-questioned later about the Chinese attitude to Stalin and the cult of Mao, his replies strikingly lacked the authority with which he had spoken about the political realities of eastern Europe.

I have tried to report this philosopher's speech at some length because it was the most interesting formal contribution to the seminar, but also because, despite the many truths it contained, it revealed in embryo a weakness which both tragically and farcically was eventually to wreck the whole conference. This is the weakness of not being able to see when a theory ceases to explain reality but on the contrary starts to hide it. Most situations are worse than political theories allow if one judges those situations by theoretical criteria. Thus theories console. But worse, they encourage the habit of continually believing in theoretical solutions.

After the philosopher's speech on the morning of the first day, a number of Western participants – following three ex-Provos from Holland – insisted that all future discussion should be as informal and open-ended as possible. Nobody should have the right to speak uninterrupted. Everybody had the right to ask a speaker or questioner to explain himself and to come out of his closed system of argument. Nobody should have the right to be boring.

This proposal was accepted by the Czech chairman and the proceedings of the next three days developed accordingly. (The speeches of the two other invited professors were uninterrupted but treated as outside, non-contributory events.) Complex expositions were precluded. Any reference to any established body of opinion was suspect. Prepared statements were dismissed as academic. Everything was arranged to encourage spontaneous, frank dialogues, the sharing of personal reactions and experiences.

The great advantage of such procedural freedom was that it

made the eventual truth brutally clear – no formulae hid it. It became absolutely obvious that no dialogue was possible between the Czech students and their visitors from the West. Goodwill, sympathy, occasional jokes, were inadequate in face of a fundamental formative difference of experience. Both sides, increasingly impatient to communicate as it became increasingly clear that they couldn't, spoke past their listeners to mirror images of themselves.

A Dutch student maintained that the revolution could only begin from within the individual, that his personal rejection of the neo-positivist values of industrial society was already a revolutionary act.

An Argentinian declared that she found the same confusion of ideas in London and Paris as she had found in Buenos Aires.

An American student said that he feared that the Czechoslovaks were unaware of the necessity of world revolution. What did they think of 'Che'? he asked. Were the Czechs not petty-bourgeois? He had been shocked to see in one of the student rooms a photograph of 'Che' pinned up next to a photograph of Jack Kennedy.

A British sociologist suggested that our attitude to reality should be less aggressive and should perhaps be more like the attitude of an artist to the material he uses.

The Czechs, with the listening plugs of their radios in their ears – there was simultaneous translation – stared into the middle distance. Every so often one would get to his feet to say : 'You do not understand us.' What divided them from their visitors was what had nominally brought them together – the Russian tanks : their different understanding of what political power actually means.

A woman from the *Sozialistische Deutsche Studenten* in Germany suggested that students who had decided on the same future profession should syndicalize themselves whilst still students.

An eloquent revolutionary agitator from New York urged the Czech students to resist, to mobilize the people. Let them consider the example of Cuba and how a small group of guerrillas had finally triumphed. And he added that the Czechs were not alone, that their comrades in the West would continually agitate on their behalf.

The Czechs accepted his sincerity but doubted his reality. A Dutchman explained how the Provos had appealed to the public to reject their consumer society, to refuse to buy more commodities than they strictly needed.

A political activist from London described the daily struggle in British factories to resist anti-trade-unionist legislation and his group's long-term aim of creating workers' councils to act as soviets. Could some of the lessons they had learned apply to the Czech situation? His was the longest and most passionate speech, which remained uninterrupted. After it a Czech student remarked: 'Do you know what most of us would reply to all that you have just said? We'd ask you whether you had read Dostoyevsky's *The Possessed*.' The activist, who had held the floor with such force, shook his head – not to answer 'No': he had surely read it – but as though to free his face from a mesh of cobwebs into which he had mysteriously and inadvertently walked.

A Czech replied to the American question of the previous day. All over our country, he said, there is a shortage of accommodation. In many schools and universities four or five students share the same room. They do not always share the same opinions. Doubtless one student had pinned up the photo of 'Che', another the photo of Kennedy.

The most authoritative of the Czech student leaders spoke slowly into the microphone in his hand. When you speak to a Czech student, he said, you speak to somebody who has been educated to be politically obedient. Any of us who dissented were accused of taking up an *apolitical* standpoint. Some of us who were 'apolitical' in this way, became political. But what formed us was not our interest in western Europe, nor in Marx, nor in Heidegger; it was our own experience of being manipulated. What you are teaching me, we said to our teachers, is not what I know about life.

We had no programme in those days of the mid sixties, we

had only a kind of honour. You know what happened in 1967 and 1968 and what our part was in it. Today we cannot afford your luxury of dreaming. We must reckon with the foreseeable consequences of every step we take. The recent phantasmagoric statements of the Czech Praesidium are worse than the official statements of Novotný – for they are being made today not only to hide the truth from the Czechoslovak people but also to satisfy the invader. The power apparatus today is exactly the same as it was before January 1968. Slovakia has a different status. Ministers have come and gone. But nothing has now to be *undone* in order to return to the past. The right wing of the party will justify the Russian occupation; everything we hoped for last spring will be said to have been the result of Western propaganda.

Our special situation, he continued, is how to get out of our situation. We have to accept it and oppose it. We shall lose our struggle to organize mass opposition. We go to speak at factories every day. We can still get in. Yet sufficient revolutionary elements do not exist. We must continue the struggle knowing that we must lose it. If we did not continue, we would degenerate. Our tragedy is not that our lives are in danger; it is our impotence which is dangerous.

As soon as he had finished, another speaker from the West began as though he had heard nothing. I think he referred to Marcuse. I was looking round the crowded, smoky basement. There were about 150 people in it, standing, sitting, making signs that they wanted the microphone. It was a unique moment. But most of us, with our eyes on the future which allowed us such different expectations, had already discarded it.

A second Czech student made the same point as the first more aggressively. Every step we take will have its repercussions here, he said. It is this which forces us to be honest about our actions. What would be the consequences of your ways of thinking if they were ever put into action? You adapt facts to your theories – you violate reality. And so you cannot even guess at the consequences.

The Czechs were now sitting together in a row and speaking one after the other.

Can none of you understand our situation? Did you come here for nothing?

Here is one of our problems. How much are we going to have to collaborate, and how much should we refuse to do so?

You must resist, shouted somebody, you are not alone.

If we do not collaborate at all, we will influence nothing.

An Indian woman took the microphone. What I have to say, she said, is to the Czechs. I come from the Third World and the situation you are now in is familiar to us. You *are* alone. It is futile to expect anything else. You are alone with your own experience as the Algerians were, as the Vietnamese are, as the El Fatah in Palestine is. From your recognition of this fact arises the first possibility of your creating, after centuries of accepting one form of conquest after another, your own identity. This intervention virtually closed the seminar. It was a way of formulating the conclusion to which the Czechs had been slowly driven since the first day.

And other conclusions contained within this one? They seem to me to be far-reaching and they will require considerable time and space to work out. On 29 August 1968, on my return from Czechoslovakia, I wrote in *New Society* about the current situation there. My analysis of what had happened between January and August 1968 still seems to me to stand up. But this analysis led to a prophecy which has turned out to be false. I wrote that the Russian invasion was likely to intensify the struggle of the Czechoslovak working class for a new and more democratic model of socialism.

Today at every street corner in Prague one can see the numerals 4:3 ... 2:0 chalked or painted on walls, doors and windows. They refer to the victories of the Czechoslovak ice hockey team over the Russians. There is not a single political slogan to be seen.

I underestimated the effect of twenty years of Stalinism, and the lack of effective opposition leaders. I underestimated the extent to which the Communist Party had become a political fiction. Most seriously of all, I underestimated the effect on Czechoslovakia of the Russian use of force. The Russians have been able to create by force a reality to confirm their lies. They claimed that Czechoslovakia in August was politically demoralized, anti-Russian, anti-socialist. It was not true. Now, under the impact of force and the hopelessness created by this force, it is to a considerable degree true. This is why, for Czech students, political theory has receded into unreality.

Since I was in Czechoslovakia Husak has replaced Dubček. Dubček, however impotent he became, represented the last vestige of the Czechoslovaks' hope that they could create their own form of socialist democracy : Husak, whatever his own record of opposition to Novotný, has now taken over as the manager of a political solution dictated by Moscow. This development dramatically confirms the ever-diminishing range of political choice open to the Czechs. The problem for the Czech students at this moment is the one they foresaw three weeks ago and it is a problem of ethics not politics : of how to behave honourably in an intolerable situation.

The Nature of
Mass Demonstrations

Seventy-three years ago (on 6 May 1898) there was a massive demonstration of workers, men and women, in the centre of Milan. The events which led up to it involve too long a history to treat with here. The demonstration was attacked and broken up by the army under the command of General Beccaris. At noon the cavalry charged the crowd : the unarmed workers tried to make barricades : martial law was declared and for three days the army fought against the unarmed.

The official casualty figures were 100 workers killed and 450 wounded. One policeman was killed accidentally by a soldier. There were no army casualties. (Two years later Umberto I was assassinated because after the massacre he publicly congratulated General Beccaris, the 'butcher of Milan'.)

I have been trying to understand certain aspects of the demonstration in the Corso Venezia on 6 May because of a story I am writing. In the process I came to a few conclusions about demonstrations which may perhaps be more widely applicable.

Mass demonstrations should be distinguished from riots or revolutionary uprisings although, under certain (now rare) circumstances, they may develop into either of the latter. The aims of a riot are usually immediate (the immediacy matching the desperation they express) : the seizing of food, the release of prisoners, the destruction of property. The aims of a revolutionary uprising are long-term and comprehensive : they culminate in the taking over of state power. The aims of a demonstration, however, are symbolic: it *demonstrates* a force that is scarcely used.

A large number of people assemble together in an obvious and already announced public place. They are more or less unarmed. (On 6 May 1898, entirely unarmed.) They present themselves as a target to the forces of repression serving the state authority against whose policies they are protesting.

Theoretically demonstrations are meant to reveal the strength of popular opinion or feeling: theoretically they are an appeal to the democratic conscience of the state. But this presupposes a conscience which is very unlikely to exist.

If the state authority is open to democratic influence, the demonstration will hardly be necessary; if it is not, it is unlikely to be influenced by an empty show of force containing no real threat. (A demonstration in support of an already established *alternative* state authority – as when Garibaldi entered Naples in 1860 – is a special case and may be immediately effective.)

Demonstrations took place before the principle of democracy was even nominally admitted. The massive early Chartist demonstrations were part of the struggle to obtain such an admission. The crowds who gathered to present their petition to the Czar in St Petersburg in 1905 were appealing – and presenting themselves as a target – to the ruthless power of an absolute monarchy. In the event – as on so many hundreds of other occasions all over Europe – they were shot down.

It would seem that the true function of demonstrations is not to convince the existing state authority to any significant degree. Such an aim is only a convenient rationalization.

The truth is that mass demonstrations are rehearsals for revolution: not strategic or even tactical ones, but rehearsals of revolutionary awareness. The delays between the rehearsals and the real performance may be very long: their quality – the intensity of rehearsed awareness – may, on different occasions, vary considerably: but any demonstration which lacks this element of rehearsal is better described as an officially encouraged public spectacle.

246

A demonstration, however much spontaneity it may contain, is a *created* event which arbitrarily separates itself from ordinary life. Its value is the result of its artificiality, for therein lie its prophetic, rehearsing possibilities.

A mass demonstration distinguishes itself from other mass crowds because it congregates in public *to create its function*, instead of forming in response to one : in this it differs from any assembly of workers within their place of work – even when strike action is involved – or from any crowd of spectators. It is an assembly which challenges what is given by the mere fact of its coming together.

State authorities usually lie about the number of demonstrators involved. The lie, however, makes little difference. (It would only make a significant difference if demonstrations really were an appeal to the democratic conscience of the state.) The importance of the numbers involved is to be found in the direct experience of those taking part in or sympathetically witnessing the demonstration. For them the numbers cease to be numbers and become the evidence of their senses, the conclusions of their imagination. The larger the demonstration, the more powerful and immediate (visible, audible, tangible) a metaphor it becomes for their total collective strength.

I say metaphor because the strength thus grasped transcends the potential strength of those present, and certainly their actual strength as deployed in a demonstration. The more people are there, the more forcibly they represent to each other and to themselves those who are absent. In this way a mass demonstration simultaneously *extends* and *gives body* to an abstraction. Those who take part become more positively aware of how they belong to a class. Belonging to that class ceases to imply a common fate, and implies a common opportunity. They begin to recognize that the function of their class need no longer be limited; that it, too, like the demonstration itself, can create its own function.

Revolutionary awareness is rehearsed in another way by the choice and effect of location. Demonstrations are essentially urban in character, and they are usually planned to take place as near as possible to some symbolic centre, either civic or national. Their 'targets' are seldom the strategic ones – railway stations, barracks, radio stations, airports. A mass demonstration can be interpreted as the symbolic capturing of a city or capital. Again, the symbolism or metaphor is for the benefit of the participants.

The demonstration, an irregular event created by the demonstrators, nevertheless takes place near the city centre, intended for very different uses. The demonstrators interrupt the regular life of the streets they march through or of the open spaces they fill. They 'cut off' these areas, and, not yet having the power to occupy them permanently, they transform them into a temporary stage on which they dramatize the power they still lack.

The demonstrators' view of the city surrounding their stage also changes. By demonstrating, they manifest a greater freedom and independence – greater creativity, even although the product is only symbolic – than they can ever achieve individually or collectively when pursuing their regular lives. In their regular pursuits they only modify circumstances; by demonstrating they symbolically oppose their very existence to circumstances.

This creativity may be desperate in origin, and the price to be paid for it high, but it temporarily changes their outlook. They become corporately aware that it is they or those whom they represent who have built the city and who maintain it. They see it through different eyes. They see it as their product, confirming their potential instead of reducing it.

Finally, there is another way in which revolutionary awareness is rehearsed. The demonstrators present themselves as a target to the so-called forces of law and order. Yet the larger the target they present, the stronger they feel. This cannot be explained by the banal principle of 'strength in numbers', any more than by vulgar theories of crowd psychology. The contradiction between their actual vulnerability and their sense of invincibility corresponds to the dilemma which they force upon the state authority.

248

Either authority must abdicate and allow the crowd to do as it wishes: in which case the symbolic suddenly becomes real, and, even if the crowd's lack of organization and preparedness prevents it from consolidating its victory, the event demonstrates the weakness of authority. Or else authority must constrain and disperse the crowd with violence: in which case the undemocratic character of such authority is publicly displayed. The imposed dilemma is between displayed weakness and displayed authoritarianism. (The officially approved and controlled demonstration does not impose the same dilemma: its symbolism is censored: which is why I term it a mere public spectacle.)

Almost invariably, authority chooses to use force. The extent of its violence depends upon many factors, but scarcely ever upon the scale of the physical threat offered by the demonstrators. This threat is essentially symbolic. But by attacking the demonstration authority ensures that the symbolic event becomes an historical one: an event to be remembered, to be learnt from, to be avenged.

It is in the nature of a demonstration to provoke violence upon itself. Its provocation may also be violent. But in the end it is bound to suffer more than it inflicts. This is a tactical truth and an historical one. The historical role of demonstrations is to show the injustice, cruelty, irrationality of the existing state authority. Demonstrations are protests of innocence.

But the innocence is of two kinds, which can only be treated as though they were one at a symbolic level. For the purposes of political analysis and the planning of revolutionary action, they must be separated. There is an innocence to be defended and an innocence which must finally be lost: an innocence which derives from justice, and an innocence which is the consequence of a lack of experience.

Demonstrations express political ambitions before the political means necessary to realize them have been created. Demonstrations predict the realization of their own ambitions and thus may contribute to that realization, but they cannot themselves achieve them.

The question which revolutionaries must decide in any given historical situation is whether or not further symbolic rehearsals are necessary. The next stage is training in tactics and strategy for the performance itself.